C000051280

CHAPTER ONE

Death's Shadow

1

The pain was like a stake piercing a vampire's heart when the news of Aaron Smith, a beloved classmate at Thomas Hill High, being missing got around at the beginning of the summer holidays, back on July 1st, the day of Eli's birthday.

It was as if the seed had already been planted when, just a couple of months prior, Castlehead had been struck with the suicide of another (and at the time, former) Thomas Hill student, Isabella Rose-Eccleby. Between then and finding out about Aaron, a joke began to spread around town that these occurrences were starting to feel like traditions that none of the townsfolk wanted. And it was after the news about Aaron that the seed of a corrupt Castlehead truly began to grow.

Or maybe it had already grown, and these events were just spreading roots.

Previous Castlehead events such as the mysterious killing of Sharron Rose back in 2009 – which hadn't been solved until a month after Isabella's death, for the father himself had openly admitted what he had done and was more than willing to pay the price – and the Mayoral Election assassination of 1977 became more like mythical legends than true town history. The eyes of the town had opened, though, when the

Castlehead Criminal Investigation Department had issued a statement that this was no laughing matter; Aaron had been beloved and popular with even those of rival schools, and his death hurt a lot of people – especially those close to him, like Jason, Anna, Eli, Kelsey, Brandon, and Elizabeth (or 'Z', if you'd rather be her friend).

2

Summer was meant to be fun, not a time in which the majority of the students wished to attend school again. Those beginning Year 9 at Thomas Hill High were about to enter a difficult part of their school lives; not because of what would eventually happen, but because this was the year they would choose their GCSEs. Also, on the first day of term, in September, Thomas Hill was about to welcome a new student to the family.

Jason woke to the sound of the alarm on his phone at 6:30am, wishing for an extra six hours in bed. However, as he had been personally asked by Principal Keeper, in the middle of August, to show this new kid around the school, there was no way he could back out. Jason was loyal like that, always putting others in front of himself – still with a desire to learn the ways of the writer, all in the hope of one day publishing at least one book. There was no time to write, his mother would say, only time to care about and excel at his upcoming GCSEs.

He sat up, yawning, vision fuzzy until he rummaged around on the window sill for his glasses. Swooping his feet off the bed, Jason rubbed his eyes and then finally turned the ongoing alarm off.

Jason wasn't the tallest, despite being one of the oldest in the year, at 5ft 4in; a twig of a boy, with short, brown hair. Jason knew he was liked by the same number of students who disliked him. Having the same routine every day (wake up, cup

To Denise,

Enjoy the read with your favourite bottle of red wine.

For Mam and Grandma — my Biggest Supporters.

All the best

THE CORRUPT
A Castlehead Novel

Joshua Meeking

Grosvenor House
Publishing Limited

All rights reserved
Copyright © Joshua Meeking, 2022

The right of Joshua Meeking to be identified as the author of this
work has been asserted in accordance with Section 78
of the Copyright, Designs and Patents Act 1988

The book cover is copyright to Joshua Meeking

This book is published by
Grosvenor House Publishing Ltd
Link House
140 The Broadway, Tolworth, Surrey, KT6 7HT.
www.grosvenorhousepublishing.co.uk

This book is sold subject to the conditions that it shall not, by way of
trade or otherwise, be lent, resold, hired out or otherwise circulated
without the author's or publisher's prior consent in any form of binding or
cover other than that in which it is published and
without a similar condition including this condition being imposed
on the subsequent purchaser.

This book is a work of fiction. Any resemblance to
people or events, past or present, is purely coincidental.

A CIP record for this book
is available from the British Library

ISBN 978-1-83975-943-7

of tea, dress, go to school, linger about at break and lunch, come home, have dinner, write, then sleep) didn't actually bother him. As a matter of fact, he liked the privacy. On the other hand, though, there was that bit of him that longed for something more than just that same old routine. Maybe there was a place where those like Jason felt welcome; a place that would understand him.

Simply, he was *that* kid at Thomas Hill High.

In the meantime, he had to focus on getting to school an hour prior to the first bell – not on some fantasy that wasn't going to come true.

Not wanting to disturb his mother, Gemma, Jason tried his best to get changed as quietly as possible. He sneaked past her bedroom and crept down the stairs, which creaked louder with every step. Passing the utility room, Jason then headed into the kitchen to pack himself a small lunch. Nothing special, just a sandwich, a packet of crisps, and an apple.

By 7:30am, Jason had wrapped his coat around himself and left the house for the bus. He had locked the door behind him, leaving his mother, who didn't have work that day, to sleep.

The water-proof coat didn't stop him shivering in the cold September wind. Autumn was clearly on the horizon as leaves began to turn red and fall from the previously lively trees. What had once been seen as a six-week holiday cherished by many, with the sun beaming down, with a slight breeze, had ended and turned into a dull time, not only because it was autumn, but because of the gaping hole left by Aaron's death.

Fifteen minutes after he reached the bus stop, the bus arrived, which would then stop directly outside his school after fifteen more minutes. The bus was empty, and Jason tried his best to block out the powerful engine so that he could have an extra ten-minute sleep.

3

Jason pressed the bell and the bus screeched to a halt right outside Thomas Hill High.

"Thank you," Jason said deeply.

The driver didn't respond, and, by the grunt, Jason knew all the driver wanted to do was get the shift over and done with.

The double doors closed one after the other, and Jason watched the bus slowly pull away before turning his full attention to the large black gates; beyond those gates was the school.

"A children's prison," students who cared more for being popular would say.

Although Jason wasn't fond of his current educational institute, he never acted like he didn't want to learn. Walking through those gates and into reception wasn't exactly paradise, but it was somewhere to go that wasn't home.

He knocked twice on the main entrance doors to the school, which opened with a buzzing noise as the receptionist pressed a button underneath her desk.

"You're here for the tour?" she asked, eyes on her computer, still typing away.

All Jason could see was a black, bee-hive hairdo. He nodded.

"They'll be done in a minute; they're just finalising a couple of things."

Jason didn't need the receptionist to tell him to take a seat on one of the comfortable grey chairs. He whipped his bag off his shoulders and placed it in between his legs as he sat patiently, beginning to hum to himself, and brainstorm. As he hummed, mostly in a world of his own already, Jason turned his head and saw the second set of glass doors, which would take him into the main hall. In the distance, two small specks began to grow as they walked closer; one was markedly smaller than the other.

The taller of the two – who was in a shirt, tie, trousers pulled up too high, and polished shoes – pushed and held the door open for the boy, whom Jason assumed was the new kid.

"Sir," said Jason politely, with the new kid rolling his eyes at the greeting.

"Jason," replied the teacher. "This is Josh, our new student."

Jason and Josh nodded silently at one another.

"I just want you to show him around, tell him what to do and what NOT to do. Understand?"

Jason rose, swung his bag back onto his shoulders, and said, "Yes, Mr Keeper."

Principal Keeper smiled brightly, glancing back and forth at his two students.

"Okay then, I'll leave you two to it."

He led Jason and Josh into the main hall, the largest section of the entire school, Jason would explain, where all the students had lunch – packed or cooked.

Before reaching the four expanded lunch tables that stretched down to a door that took you onto the yard, Jason and Josh passed narrow hallways leading to the offices of the headteacher and deputy. In the far corner of the main hall stood a packed crowd of smaller tables. As they walked side by side, the two boys kept eye contact to a minimum, but Jason noticed that this kid was roughly the same height, perhaps even skinnier than he was (which he didn't know was even possible) but had short, messy, black hair.

Passing the tables where the food would be served, they heard the dinner ladies behind the shutters preparing the meals for the day, and then the wind hit them suddenly as they walked out onto the yard. They headed towards an ancient, mouldy brick building and a tall, all-glass, modern one, that somehow contrasted beautifully with one another.

"These buildings are the English and Sci—"

"Who's this Aaron kid that Mr Keeper mentioned?" Josh said out of the blue.

Jason froze and Josh instantly saw the wide eyes of his tour guide.

"An old student?" he guessed.

Jason sighed, and flatly explained, "Aaron was a student. Great kid, had a bright future ahead of him. I was quite close to him actually. A lot of us were."

"*Were?*"

"At the start of the summer holidays, reports of him being dead came in and… well… It was a massive loss."

They began to walk slowly across the yard, closer to the Science department.

"No one knows how he died," Jason went on. "They're still trying to figure it out."

"Well, they must've found something after two months?"

"The Castlehead Criminal Investigation Department — let's just say — don't have the greatest track record. You heard about the death of Isabella?"

Josh shook his head, invested in this town more than Jason had expected.

Jason explained, "*The Curse of the Rose-Eccleby Family*, they called it. Ten years ago, this woman named Sharron Rose mysteriously died in her house, Wardle Gardens. It wasn't until spring that it was revealed that her husband, Anthony, killed her. But that was after Isabella killed herself, and Anthony admitted what he'd done. The C.C.I.D didn't actually figure it out."

What have I got myself into? Josh thought, looking around the yard, half surprised and half excited.

"Mr Keeper said the school is holding an assembly at the end of the week for him," informed Josh.

"And so, they should," said Jason proudly. They walked into the Science department and began to ascend to the upper floors. "Ah, well." Jason shrugged jokily. "Welcome to Castlehead, mate."

3

As the main hall began to fill up, it was in Jason and Josh's best interest to head to their form class, where their tutor would give the daily announcements. Most of the students at Thomas Hill hung around in the main hall; either seated at the long tables or the small section of squared tables in the far corners, or remained standing. Everyone knew where they had to be.

Those sitting in the corners, at the small square tables, were known as the popular kids; the long tables were reserved for the try-hards and nerds; and those who stood weren't well-known in the school. Some would decide to find a spare seat in a different department building — the social pariahs.

Jason led the new kid through a pair of double doors leading to the Musical Theatre department, but not before being bombarded by a group of lads in tracksuit bottoms and oversized jackets, all with the same beans-on-toast haircut, led by a boy strutting confidently and a girl who would normally have done the same, but looked strained. The 'leader' shoulder-barged Josh, who didn't react, but Jason turned and sneered at him as the group continued walking.

"What happened to him?" Jason asked himself through gritted teeth.

He shook his head, and they carried on to the Musical Theatre department, turning left at the end of the hall and stopping at a single wooden door that stood out from the purple and grey surroundings. In the door handle's place was a keypad that resembled a miniature calculator. Jason typed in a code and the door slowly swung open.

Josh jumped at the sharp turn they had to take after walking through the door. Turning right, they walked up a stairwell which took them to the upper floor of what looked like a completely different building. Downstairs was the Maths department, and up was the Language department. It was like a maze.

This hallway was narrower than any Josh had seen before. He had to walk behind Jason as he looked at all the hand-drawn country flags stapled to both walls.

Like the bus Jason had arrived on, they skidded to a halt in front of the very last classroom at the end of the hallway.

Jason tapped on the door, with Josh peeking as best he could through the window, which was mostly covered by past students' work — inspiration. A short, white-haired teacher sitting at the front desk waved them in, and they entered, smiling.

"Welcome back, Jason," greeted the teacher, with a smile on her face like an air hostess — fake and forced.

"Thank you, Miss."

She snapped her head towards Josh.

"And you must be our new student?" she guessed.

"Yep," said Josh.

"Well, class doesn't start for another five minutes so, if you want, you can take a seat. I'll be handing out timetables. Don't worry. You'll be fine," one of the five Year 9 form teachers said reassuringly to Josh.

The five minutes went by like a snap of the fingers, then, in single file, the other students entered and took their seats. The last two were the lad and lass that Josh and Jason had bumped into. Josh tried not to look at them, but Jason clearly flared his nostrils at them both, mockingly winking at the girl without the lad noticing.

8

She looked like she was about to collapse into a heap on the ground.

"She doesn't look too good," whispered Josh to Jason. They sat on the front row, alongside a girl with bushy blonde hair and great moon glasses, and a scrawny boy with a pointy nose, trying to keep himself small and his head down. "Is she okay?"

"No, it is Kelsey, after all," scoffed Jason, and then, noticing the look on Josh's face, added, "Oh, you mean why's she holding her stomach?" He scoffed again. "She'll get what she deserves."

"Why?"

"Bitch, she is. Always tries to make herself look good, thinks she's better than everyone else. *Daddy's little girl*," he mocked, causing Josh to snigger.

While they spoke with a whisper, the rest of the class continued to ramble on like a flock of attacking seagulls.

The teacher rose and stood at the front of the class, clapping her hands.

"All right, settle down," she said in a put-on formal tone. The class didn't respond. "OI!"

The class fell silent.

Jason snapped his head around to the back of the class where he saw the lad with a comforting arm around Kelsey's shoulder. She had her head tucked down and was squirming. As the lad glanced back at Jason, Jason's eyes narrowed and he sighed, turning back around to face the whiteboard.

I don't know why I bother, he thought. *Shit happens, people move on. Friends move on.*

4

Half an hour had passed and the student schedules had been handed out. Jason and Josh weren't in many of the same classes, so, to ensure he didn't get lost, Jason introduced Josh to the girl next to them, Anna.

"You won't get lost with Anna," said Jason.

All Josh and Anna did was look at each other, both of them turning shades of red.

In the middle of the two, Jason leaned back and had a feeling Josh had in fact got *lost*.

"Never mind then," Jason added, neither Josh nor Anna taking notice.

Suddenly, one of the tables at the back screeched forward.

Everyone turned and saw Kelsey push her chair back, rise, and as if for her life, run out of the classroom with her hand over her mouth; her cheeks growing by three sizes and her face turning ghost white. The boy Josh assumed was her boyfriend got up suddenly, desperate to catch up, ignoring the teacher's orders to remain seated.

Kelsey rushed down the hall, hoping to get to the toilet in time. They were in the Musical Theatre department. She was like a cat trying to keep in a hairball. Ignoring the passing students looking concerned or letting out chuckles at her contorted face, Kelsey finally made it into the girls' toilets. At first, she thought she had taken the hinges off the cubicle door as it dented the wall. With her free hand, she lifted the toilet seat up and let out — what felt like — constant vomit. Her head was almost completely in the toilet and it reeked as though several people had used it before her.

"You okay?" a faint voice said from behind her.

Kelsey didn't respond, coughing the last of the sick up. Regaining her breath, dreary-eyed, she flushed the chain and stood upright, turning to see a figure all in black, their face hidden by a hood.

"Are you okay?" the figure repeated, her lips barely moving.

The significant height difference between them was clear to Kelsey, even as tears filled her eyes. But Kelsey knew this girl to be in the same Year as her, and that she only appeared randomly.

"I'm fine! Get out of my way!" barked Kelsey, shoulder-barging the figure as she left the toilets, her nerves shocked, a worried look on her face.

She didn't care if lessons had begun; Kelsey needed to be alone and compose herself before she got worked up.

"Kelsey!" shouted a guy, his voice echoing as he chased Kelsey into the main hall. "Wait, what's wrong?"

"Please, Eli, not now!" Kelsey cried, stopping to allow Eli to catch up, her head pounding. It was unclear whether she was hanging her head in shame or so that she didn't have to make eye contact with her boyfriend, whom she had been seeing since Year 8. "I've got to go."

"Why? Just tell me what's up," he said, sounding more irritated than sincere. "Kelsey, ju—"

"Please!" she cried again, tears now flowing down her face, her wrists caught in Eli's clutches. "I'll talk to you later."

Clearly in distress, Kelsey shoving her boyfriend wasn't meant to come across as violent, but the added guilt when she stormed out of the school didn't help her situation.

All Eli did was watch Kelsey run away.

Behind him, the figure in all black looked on, too.

Eli turned and shrugged at the figure. She didn't budge, but shivered when her phone buzzed in her pocket. She glanced at it, and a moment later, the figure looked up and stormed out of the school, too.

Eli rubbed his forehead and began to walk back to class, trying to comprehend what had just happened.

Dating for just over a year must count for something, right? Surely, they were at a stage in their relationship where if something was wrong, they could at least work things out? Kelsey was always so confident, that's what Eli loved about her, so this was a side of her he had never seen before. Something was wrong, and, admittedly, he was worried. Only a rare few knew when Eli was on edge; this first day back was now one of those days, and the person who noticed something was wrong wasn't a member of his friendship group – *anymore*.

5

Despite the Castlehead Criminal Investigation Department being untrustworthy for as long as the town as a whole could remember, that didn't mean Chief Pattison and Deputy Ton didn't feel for those they weren't able to help. A darkness had spread over the C.C.I.D offices that day — and it wasn't because of the overcast weather.

The offices of the chief and deputy were separate to those who answered calls or waited patiently on standby. For the most part, it was quiet in the offices, above the interrogation rooms and prison.

All was silent in the chief's office. Pattison sat at his desk, head down, pen scribbling away on some forms. On the desk, alongside the forms, was a telephone and two pots of pencils and highlighters. Under the desk were drawers containing files, his laptop, and papers that hadn't been looked at in about a year.

Pattison glanced up and looked through his office window and saw the rows of empty chairs, a few officers who did in fact work there scattered around, typing away. Deputy Ton was out on patrol with a trainee.

Suddenly, the telephone rang.

"Yeah?" he said, picking up the phone. "Okay…" He sighed, and then added, "Send them up," before putting the phone down again. Sighing louder, Pattison scratched his prickly grey beard, knowing a scene was about to be made…

"ARE YOU SERIOUS!?" roared a middle-aged man in a smart jacket and jeans. He slammed his hands onto the desk, leaning over it, almost nose to nose with Chief Pattison. There was a fire in this man's eyes, and rage boiled up inside him, about to burst. "HOW DARE YOU!"

"Okay, okay," said the chief calmly, trying to explain.

"HE ISN'T DEAD!"

"Clarke, listen," said the chief firmly. "Your son has been missing for months now. We couldn't find him. Our only option was to announce—"

"ANNOUNCE THAT HE IS DEAD!? NO! YOU DON'T GET TO DECIDE. AARON HAS BEEN MISSING FOR MONTHS, YOU HAVEN'T DONE A DAMN THING, AND NOW YOU'RE CLOSING THE CASE? WHAT KIND OF SHIP ARE YOU RUNNING?"

"A very tight ship, Clarke!" Chief Pattison snapped. "I understand what you're going through, but do not, AND I MEAN, DO NOT come in here and tell me how to run my crew," he added, all while Clarke stood with his arms folded, shaking his head.

"You don't know what I've been through," argued Clarke, lowering his voice but still enraged. "These past two years have been hell. We were meant to move, you know that. But no. The hell had begun, and now someone above thinks I don't deserve happiness anymore. I've lost my family, dammit."

Beginning to choke up, Clarke shook his head again with distaste and didn't know what he would do if Chief Pattison said the wrong thing.

"I'm sorry," said Pattison plainly, scratching his grey head of hair. "There's nothing else I can do." Clarke's fists clenched.

The chief began to add, "Madam Mayor and the council—"

"Madam Mayor and the council what?"

"The council doesn't want any more bad publicity for the town. It's not in my power to do anything about it. First the Rose-Eccleby family, and now your son. Clarke—"

"So that's why the hunt's been called off?" Clarke began pacing, his fists pressed against his mouth. He was trying to restrain himself. "Screw you. And the council."

Walking towards the door, Clarke slowly turned the knob and opened it slightly.

"Clarke," said the chief, rising. Clarke was halfway through the door before he turned, holding the door ajar. "I really am sorry."

All Clarke did was scoff, shake his head a final time, and leave the office with the door thudding shut. It didn't matter if no one believed him, Clarke was certain that he didn't deserve this suffering; he didn't deserve losing Aaron, the one constant that put a smile on his face — even in the toughest of times.

Chief Pattison collapsed back into his office chair, sighed, and sat there for a moment, wondering what the C.C.I.D could have actually done to help Clarke... Or if they could've done more. The image of that first night would never be erased from the chief's head: the pouring rain, flashlights on, the sound of thunder rumbling the ground like an earthquake, and the yelling voices of Castlehead's pedestrians on the search for one Aaron Smith.

"*Sir?*" A cracking voice knocked Pattison back into reality like an alarm clock taking away dreams — or nightmares. He looked around and noticed it was coming from the radio hooked onto his chief uniform.

"*Sir, are you there?*"

Unclipping the radio, Chief Pattison placed it near his mouth so that he could respond.

"Yes, I'm here, Deputy. What is there to report?" he asked powerfully.

"You're going to have to come down to Newgate ASAP."

Pattison jumped out of his seat and rushed out of his office while Deputy Ton continued to inform him that there had been a fire. *"It's spreading rapidly!"*

"I'm on my way."

6

The IT girl was known for dressing in leggings and skirts, with tops that revealed her belly, and for having straight, chocolate brown hair, smooth and melted like a Dairy Milk waterfall, and sparkling blue eyes. She liked the attention. Loved it, actually. However, never in her wildest dreams would Kelsey — full name Kelsey Evans — think she would be slacking off school to walk up to a till and handing the cashier a white rectangular box.

The cashier glanced at the clearly uncomfortable girl and then back at the box, his eyebrows raised by her purchase. He pressed a few beeping buttons on the till before handing the box back. She paid with cash, not card, so that her father would not find out.

"Take care," said the cashier, who had a nametag with the name *William* on it clipped to his ironed white shirt.

She left without a thank you or farewell, but accidentally bumped into an entering customer with a black hood on that covered their eyes, looking as uncomfortable as she did, upon her exit. The only thing on Kelsey's mind was to find a secluded area so nobody would find her red-handed.

At the end of the road, two fire engines and a bunch of police cars passed in a hurry, their sirens alerting those on the road to let them through.

Kelsey tried her best to hide her face from the sun attempting to break through the clouds, and was desperate to find even the smallest of shops that had a toilet. But for a Monday morning, all the shops were surprisingly heaving with people. She couldn't risk it. She reached the end of the road, where traffic lights stood, without any luck; even turning onto the next road wasn't going to help her.

Gulping and starting to tremble once again, Kelsey had a feeling it was going to come down to the last resort: going home and facing the consequences head on.

7

The remainder of the week was close to normal for the students of Thomas Hill High, but the assembly in honour of fellow — now lost — Year 9 student Aaron Smith was drawing nearer and nearer. It was in all of their heads, though many kept their feelings to themselves.

Josh seemed to enjoy his first week, predominantly spending lunches with Anna and Brandon (the name of the boy, Josh found out quickly, that sat on their table in form class). Jason sat in empty classrooms at these times, trying to get a synopsis down for a story he wanted to write. As for Eli and Kelsey… they hadn't been seen since the first day back.

On the Tuesday before the assembly, Kelsey sat in her bathroom, awaiting an answer. She had to work her way up to finally taking the test. Tapping her feet, the waiting gave her a funny feeling. Her eyes started to fill with tears.

"Ten… Nine… Eight…" she counted in a whisper. She shut her eyes tight as if anticipating a surprise. "Five… Four… Three… Two… One." Opening her eyes, staring straight at the test in her hand, she began to tremble again. "No!" she cried.

Two lines. How am I going to tell him? thought Kelsey, finally finding the strength to rise from the toilet. *They will be devastated.*

She wasn't glowing yet, but her crimson face could give away her secret.

As she rose, Kelsey heard the front door slam shut. *Shit.* She stuffed the test at the bottom of the full bin beside the bath and tried not to make a sound as she walked down the carpeted — yet still creaky — staircase, walking through the passage into the living room where she saw her father, Donovan, tossing bags of shopping on the couch.

"Hey, sweetie," he said deeply, picking up the remote control to turn on the TV. He then picked up a smaller control that worked the fireplace on the wall opposite the window, which let in the light and the sight of the small driveway and patch of grass. "Why aren't you in school?"

"I've been sick. Sorry, Daddy," she explained innocently.

As her father began to walk towards her, Kelsey felt a stinging pain all over her body, as if she were being poked by a thousand knives. She began weeping helplessly again.

"Hey, it's okay. Don't worry, I'm not mad." Donovan hugged his daughter. He was about double the size of her, her head up against his stomach when they embraced lovingly. "Why don't you go to bed and I'll fix you a drink?"

Kelsey nodded, releasing the embrace and trying her best to smile honestly. As he walked back to the bags of shopping to haul them into the kitchen, Kelsey's attempt at a smile faded.

"Daddy…" she said, her voice trembling and her tone soft and innocent still.

"Yeah?" said Donovan from the kitchen, his attention mostly on packing the bags of shopping away. "What's—"

"I'm pregnant," Kelsey revealed quickly. It had slipped out, and Donovan shuddered at this sudden revelation, dropping the last bag of shopping. It was like his whole body had gone numb.

"It's true, Daddy."

Without warning, he ran to her, grabbed her by the arms like a clamp, kneeled down to her height and turned as purple as a plum.

"I—"

"How is this possible?" he asked rhetorically. Although still at a low tone, there was a shakiness in Donovan's voice and he tightened his grip, easily bruising his daughter like a tomato. "Get out of my sight. NOW!"

Donovan shoved her away and remained kneeling, head hanging as Kelsey started upstairs to her room, where she cried in the corner until she couldn't cry anymore.

His 14-year-old daughter... pregnant? How could this happen to his little girl?

From above, Kelsey could hear bangs and crashes; Donovan was in a fit of rage.

But, this time, it wasn't because he came home intoxicated.

8

Friday had finally arrived. There was no doubt that all of the Year 9s were dreading the upcoming assembly. Mr Keeper personally, along with fellow staff members, had prepared the sports hall for the occasion. And the breaking news that Madam Mayor would be hosting and making a speech added an entirely new level of importance to this day.

The sports hall was commonly used for football, netball, or basketball practice; today, P.E lessons had been moved outdoors, as the hall had been filled with chairs set in 10 rows of 20, facing a podium where a large, framed photo of Aaron on a stand would be next to those who would remember him with kind, honest words.

Mr Keeper entered through the green side doors with a fire exit sign above, wanting to take in this day by himself for a moment. Never in his two-decade teaching career had he been required to honour a student in this way.

Mr Keeper walked up to the podium and looked out at the sea of empty seats, then around at the elevated basketball hoops on either side of the hall. The sound of the same side door opening caused him to turn his head, and, for the first time that day, he smiled.

"Madam Mayor!" he said with delight.

"Ryan," she replied, nodding and accepting the extended hand when he walked up to her. Her dress was as black as her hair, like the midnight sky, and as smooth as her chocolate skin. Tall and thin, Madam Mayor always wore heels that made her taller than she already was. "Glad to be here."

"Thank you for doing this," said Keeper.

"My pleasure. I always liked Aaron. Kind, clever young man. A real shame."

They walked back up to the podium together.

"But," began Keeper hesitantly, "is it true?"

"What?"

The sudden question appeared to take the mayor by surprise.

"Is he really... you know?"

"Dead?" she assumed.

Keeper nodded and waited for a response. "Look, I don't like doing it, but as mayor it is my responsibility to assume these things. And whether or not we find the body is still up in the air. In all honesty, this town can't afford any more bad publicity. The curse of Castlehead has cost us millions, and driven us to a point where we are on our own. Those in Valeland are the only ones willing to help."

Something told Keeper that Madam Mayor wasn't talking about Valeland helping to find Aaron. "Anyways," she added swiftly, "that's not why we're here. We're here to honour Aaron."

Luckily for the mayor, teachers entering the hall broke up this conversation and took their places at the sides of the chairs, awaiting the Year 9s. The current audience of teachers all looked at the door that the students would enter through, taking deep breaths.

It was almost time.

The main school caretaker, Mr Roan, placed the stand to Mr Keeper's right, who resumed his place at the podium. Mr Roan whistled suddenly, sending a shockwave through most of the teachers, who hadn't expected it, and ushered in two fellow caretakers in the same black overalls. One took the top of the large frame as the other took the bottom. They heaved it in and steadily planted it onto the stand. All the teachers began to beam with emotion, as if it was a sudden realisation that their student was not returning. Sad happiness, for although he was gone, it was right Aaron was getting a nice send-off.

Nevertheless, when the students finally started to enter in an orderly fashion, all in their own clothing, which made them stand out as individuals, some students muttered that the photo of Aaron Smith felt like he was looking back and was there in person.

They started to fill the rows of seats from the back. Keeper watched on and heard intimidated whispers coming from his students, because the news that Madam Mayor would be hosting hadn't got around the school yet. He was expecting a full house, but seeing that single empty chair at the end of the front row concerned him.

Gesturing for a teacher to come to him, he whispered, "Where's Kelsey?"

"No idea. She hasn't been seen all week," the plump, bald-headed teacher said. "Neither has—" The small teacher, who resembled a ball with arms and legs, looked up at the seated students, and spotted Eli a few rows from the front, making conversation with his group and a bunch of girls in the row in front, like he had just found Wally. "Never mind."

"Okay," said Keeper, still trying not to show how anxious he really was. "Let's get started." He straightened up at the podium, looked out at his students and bravely welcomed them to this unfortunate event. And from that point, there was no dry eye in the audience. "... And now, I'm sure most of you noticed, I'm not going to take up the entire time up here, and I would like to welcome Madam Mayor of Castlehead."

Madam Mayor replaced Keeper at the podium. Most would have prepared for an occasion like this, but there were no small pieces of paper to read from in sight.

"I've not prepared for this, at all. It's heart-breaking, knowing that such a tragedy has struck our town again. And, more specifically, this school. Now, I know that most — or probably all — of you knew Aaron to a certain degree and I can't imagine the pain his inner circle is currently feeling."

At that point, Eli looked to the back row to get a glimpse of Jason, feeling hurt. Or was it guilt? Jason, however, kept his eyes on the mayor.

"I believe Aaron was the heart and soul of this school, and whatever happened to him, he didn't deserve. He wasn't a sinner. He was a generous, loving young man who had a bright future ahead of him." It appeared now that Madam Mayor had started to choke up, but knew she had to remain strong for her people. "Everyone needs a friend like Aaron in their life, and he will never know how much he will be missed." She looked up, as if past the roof of the sports hall and into the heavens. "Fly high, Aaron, and watch over us with your kind eye."

Then, her last motion before leaving the podium, Madam Mayor blew a kiss upwards, concluding with a warm, "Thank you".

She would claim that everything she said up on that podium was from the heart and that she had meant every single word. But Castlehead, and knowing the town's current state, was still firmly planted at the front of her mind.

Madam Mayor had said that she hadn't prepared her speech, but it sure seemed like it.

9

The sun was beginning to set on a day that would never be forgotten, and all the students at Thomas Hill High were relieved to be released from the children's prison for the weekend. Some would stay in and chill, make the most of their Xboxes or PlayStations, or their limited time with their families; others would sneak out at night, get fake IDs and head into main Castlehead to proudly explore the nightlife. A rare couple, however, would be inadvertently reuniting after almost two years of not having had a complete conversation.

"Would you like a refill, Jay?"

"Cheers, Carl," said Jason, glancing up for a second to see Carl nod, smile, and walk away to get him another free refill of his favourite latte.

Carl's Cafe was an original establishment built in Castlehead only a decade after the town was founded by Peter Michael sometime in the late 19th century. It had been passed down from one generation to the next, ending up in the custody of Carl Craig, an honest businessman who branched his business off across all areas of Castlehead by the 90s; bakeries, bars, exclusive restaurants; everything he did was legit, and he showed his passion through his welcoming smile and chit-chat, making every single one of his customers feel like they deserved to be in one of his establishments. On this Friday night, he worked at the cafe that was so close to his heart that there would be a cold void, like the upcoming autumn chill, in his soul should anything bad happen.

Jason typed away on his laptop, happy and in a world of his own. His eyes were fixed on the document on the screen and his fingers automatically punched away at the keys. The words came out freely, yet with a purpose: to tell a story. He wasn't satisfied with his work being satisfactory.

After a couple of minutes, Carl gently planted the cup and saucer on the round table, and Jason nodded his thanks. The coffee was frothy at the very top, decorated with a leaf made from said froth; it tasted as good as it looked, and the beverage made Jason feel warm inside — just like his writing did — on this damp day.

At odd points, Jason would look out of the window from his favourite table at the cafe, watching the sky turn from a golden orange to a navy blue. Night had fallen, and Jason had lost track of time. But it proved that Jason had made the most of it. He felt a kind of pleasure — sense of achievement — from the amount of time he had spent writing what he hoped would be his *magnum opus* — or, if not his magnum opus, something that would kick-start his career.

Jason, along with Carl, had thought the cafe had seen the last of its customers for the night. When the bell above the opening door rang, Carl returned to the counter from cleaning the empty tables.

"How can I help?" greeted Carl with that welcoming smile, despite it being 9:45pm.

Jason remained in his seat, typing away and not wanting to stop.

"Just a tea to take away, mate," said a familiar voice.

Jason lost focus, looked up, and huffed, hoping Eli didn't notice.

Eli tapped on the counter to the beat of a song on the television, which stood on a high shelf in the corner of the café. He looked both ways before double glancing at Jason. The eagerness to walk over and say "Hello" could be seen on Eli's face, but he was debating in his head whether or not he should. Frequently glancing back and forth from the screen to his old friend, Jason could see that something was troubling the boy.

"There you go, son," said Carl.

The sight of the cup gave Jason hope that Eli would just leave him be, but watching him out of the corner of his eye as he silently walked across to the table, Jason knew he wasn't going to hold back on what he had to say.

"Can I sit?" asked Eli quietly, already placing the tea on the table.

"If you must," said Jason with a sneer, the fake smile fading away instantly.

Eli sat opposite Jason. The table was almost overcrowded with empty cups and a now closed laptop. The silence was awkward, neither of them knew what to say, and they barely looked at one another directly.

"Been a while," began Eli. "I me—"

"Stop small-talking me. What're you doin' here, Eli?" said Jason firmly.

"Was just here to get a cup of tea, but obviously you're here, so I thought—"

"You thought what? That you'd waltz in here and talk to me as if we've been best mates for the past two years?"

"Jay, I came over to say hello... And that I need some advice—"

"So, I go from your best mate since nursery to your *royal adviser*?" said Jason ignorantly.

"I'm worried about Kelsey. She's been *off* lately," Eli explained.

Despite the remark he had just made, Jason could tell by Eli's face that he was sincerely concerned about his girlfriend.

"Yeah, she did seem weird on Monday," he began, a bit more subtle and honest. "Haven't seen her, or you, in fact, in school all week." *Screw it*, he thought. "So, okay then, what's going on?"

"She's just been acting weird," said Eli after a sip of his tea. "She even said she was coming in for the assembly, but—"

"No sign of her. Yeah, I noticed," finished Jason before taking a sip of his coffee.

"That your latte?" guessed Eli. "You still get your gingerbread one at Christmas?" Jason nodded. "What're you working on? Another story?" he guessed again.

"A short story for this contest. If I win, it goes to a publisher and might get released as a book."

"Is it about that Isabella girl?" Eli chuckled and waited for an answer.

Jason was always one to give credit where credit was due; with an impressed look on his face, Jason looked at Eli, surprised that he recalled these things, knowing that he would write something worthy of being published such as the story revolving around the death of Isabella.

"It is, actually," chuckled Jason.

There was silence again, and together, they slurped their respective drinks to break it. But when the television showed the 10 o'clock news, it caught both of their attention.

"This just in…"

The remaining three civilians in the cafe turned their heads to the television, and Jason gestured at Carl to turn the volume up a touch. He did so, and the broadcast showed the scene from the past week and the raging fire that occurred.

"You heard about the fires?" asked Eli, turning his head back to Jason for a reply.

"Yeah," answered Jason.

"The C.C.I.D still haven't found the causes!" yelled Carl from the counter, watching intently with the customers.

"We go live to the scene of the incident at Smith's Pharmacy."

The television screen cut to a live shot of the location of the fire. Something seemed familiar about the name of the pharmacy; Eli and Jason clicked at the same time.

"Isn't that—" started Eli.

"Aaron's dad's work," said Jason and Eli in unison, fascinated and sorrowful at what Clarke had been through this past year; first Aaron, now his thriving business. What next?

They looked back at the 80s-style television, which showed a shot of the building burnt to a crisp; its windows were shattered, and police tape blocked the entrance in an 'X' formation. It looked like the door had been kicked off its hinges; nails could be seen hazardously poking out of the doorway.

"We'll get back to you as soon as we've received updates," informed the posh voice-over, who spoke with received pronunciation.

10

What the cameras didn't catch, however, was that police cars were parked askew along the street of the scene, with Clarke standing, waiting anxiously at the entrance of his work. After only filming a snippet of live footage, the authorities forced the news team to shut the cameras off, for the chief and deputy knew that false confirmations would just sizzle the pot of rumours even more.

"So…?" said Clarke, twiddling his thumbs.

Chief Pattison and Deputy Ton made their way under the police tape and out of the store one after the other with looks of sorrowful pity.

"We may have found the cause of the fire," said Pattison, unveiling from his back trouser pocket a detached plug. He handed it to Clarke, who examined it. "After close examination, Clarke," the chief added, "there was nothing else that could've potentially started it."

"That's impossible. Just last week the health—"

"I'm sorry."

Clarke sighed, and thought it would be best not to brew up an argument with the law.

"Is that it, then?" asked Clarke, looking up at the officers with irritation in his eyes.

"Not quite," answered Deputy Ton. "It wasn't just that plug. It was an extension cord in the back, and one of the sockets was almost torn off the wall."

Clarke expressed a sudden look of bewilderment, recalling the last time the pharmacy had had a health inspection.

"That's impossible." Clarke shook his head. "It must have been contaminated or something," he suggested, his pitch higher and his words quickening. "Everything was fine this morning, according to William, the man working in the shop—"

Pattison cut him off, saying in a reassuring tone, "You're lucky the fire didn't spread, or we would've had a disaster on our hands. I'll get in touch with William and ask him a few questions. Until then, get home and try to rest."

11

The television in the Evans household was also on the news channel. But only to break the silence. Kelsey's father had been giving the pregnant teen the silent treatment ever since she had told him the news, but they still sat on the couch together for meals and TV. Their empty plates sat on their laps.

Kelsey was scared to look across the far side of the couch where her dad sat, but bravely did so anyway. She saw him notice her out of the corner of his eye, sigh and rub his head; it was an action he always performed when he wasn't happy with her.

"Daddy?" she whispered.

"Just make sure to tell Eli sooner rather than later," said Donovan.

He placed the empty plate on the floor and reached over the side of the couch where a small cabinet sat trapped in the corner between the couch and fireplace. Kelsey heard the thud of the cabinet door and saw her dad holding a white tub with writing on a label too small to read. Twisting the top off, Donovan saw that Kelsey looked curious.

"What're those tablets for?" she asked.

"My pains," he said, groaning while taking two small pills out of the tub. He didn't need water to help swallow them but they caught the back of his throat as they went down to do their magic: relieve the pain. "I just don't take them in front of you, because I don't want you to worry."

After putting the top back on the tub, Donovan groaned again as he reached out and placed the medication on the mantelpiece.

Kelsey rose and, without being asked, took their plates into the kitchen. But what Donovan didn't suspect was that she only did it to get a glimpse of what the small print read.

A single bit of the labelling, at the bottom of the tub, in bold letters, caught her attention: **DO NOT TAKE WHEN PREGNANT.**

Donovan still didn't suspect a thing that night when he went up to bed; Kelsey offered to clean up downstairs, to make up for her actions, she said. She did, in fact, clean up, but her heart wasn't set on making the house spotless; her heart was set on that medication.

In the kitchen, with the medication on the counter like it was staring at her, Kelsey leaned over the sink and filled it up with silent tears.

Donovan was in a deep sleep while Kelsey fought to take control of her breathing as her weeping became something like hysterical laughter. She knew what she was doing was a horrible thing, but she had to think about herself, Eli, and her dad, and the impact that this new baby would have on their lives if she decided to keep it. How would the baby cope in a town like Castlehead, under the circumstances in which it would be born?

The clock struck midnight, and Kelsey turned all the lights off and headed upstairs as quietly as possible, still sniffling. She came to a halt when reaching the landing, torn between the doors that stood ajar in front of her. It was like Kelsey had suddenly blacked out; creeping into her father's bedroom, trying to make no sound to wake him, she felt, was an act done by instinct, not choice. She then lay on the empty side of her dad's bed, whispering his name to see if he would budge; all she received in response was his snoring. She poked him, but didn't want to startle him when doing so; he groaned as a way to ask what she wanted.

Looking up at the ceiling, she inhaled deeply. For a moment, she had second thoughts. What Kelsey was about to do could result in her and Donovan's relationship being even more strained than it already was.

A common phrase that was thrown around Castlehead was that you would pay for your sins sooner or later.

"I've got something to tell you, Daddy." Kelsey continued to look up at the ceiling as she spoke. She took another deep breath, and added earnestly, "No one will know of *our* mistake."

CHAPTER TWO

Closed Casket

1

The news had been dropped and the rumours appeared to be true; not only did Donovan find out in the first week of September that his daughter had killed her baby and still hadn't put the pieces back together by the second half of the autumn month, but, on top of that, students at Thomas Hill High spread the rumour that Aaron Smith's body had been found, only for a laugh or to get attention. But the public wouldn't know until later on if the body found near Sunvalley Park and Michael Manor was a match for Aaron.

Only those who were there in person knew.

2

They say don't always judge a book by its cover, and the girl known as the White Shadow is a perfect example. People who saw this girl would commonly spot her all in black, with a hood over her head, and the paleness of her ghostly face. It was a gamble when she would be seen in Thomas Hill High, for she left whenever she desired.

She was one to keep herself to herself, but when a situation arose, she would ask what the problem was. Just like when she had asked Kelsey what was wrong when she heard her being sick in the girls' bathroom.

Every time she headed home, whether that was throughout the school day or at the final bell, like the rest of the students — as she should — the route was always the same: walk up into the hills that surrounded Castlehead and not to be heard from until she felt like it.

Those hills, like security guards, protected the outside world from the horrors within the north-eastern town. But what Elizabeth — commonly known as Z — would stumble upon when walking up into those hills one day was like stepping into a nightmare.

The stars twinkled above the town like a thousand eyes, but when Z entered the army of trees in the hills, that vision was obstructed. Owls hooted, the bushes rustled, and Z walked warily when she cut off the main road that led up to Michael Manor onto a dirt track that was only visible in the day. Only the brave went up into the hills; stories circulated for decades about the haunting events that happened. Z, however, didn't go up there because she was brave. She went up because she had to.

As she ascended deeper into the trees, reaching a flat surface, she began to hear crunching from beneath her feet; not the snapping of twigs. The track had changed to gravel, becoming more visible, making it easier for Z to see where it led. A bit further up, the gravel began to expand into a large, round patch surrounded by trees. Like the hills did for the rest of the world, those trees protected this patch of sacred land. It wasn't sacred for being home to riches such as silver or gold. It was sacred to those who inhabited the patch. This patch was Sunvalley Park.

Scattered around were run-down trailers, their windows mostly boarded up and their locks broken. Z watched, hiding in the trees still, smiling at a group of fellow inhabitants gathering around a burning campfire with bottles of beer and a guitar. Sunvalley Park was the only place that made Z feel even the slightest bit of warmth. Those who lived there were her family; it didn't matter if they weren't blood. Those at Sunvalley Park looked out for one another, because it wasn't like Madam Mayor and the council were going to.

Z slipped down a slope, fully entering Sunvalley Park, to be greeted by jovial cheers and the raising of bottles. Only those who lived here saw the girl smile, and, like every time, no matter how many times a day she returned, Z received the same greeting, and it made her grin.

"Hi, Z!" said those who sat around the fire, in unison. "Want to join us?"

"I wish I could, but—" She jerked her head towards the trailer on the edge of the park.

"Oh, okay. We understand," a man with a football-shaped head said, the moon reflecting off his bald scalp. "Hope everything's okay, Z."

"Thank you."

She nodded unconvincingly, looking back at the trees for a second, gulped, and darted for the trailer.

The group around the fire watched indirectly, hoping she wouldn't notice that they kept their eyes on her. She opened the trailer door then slammed it shut behind her. The coast was clear, and they could finally give their honest opinions about Elizabeth's situation.

"What's going to happen to her?" the bald man said.

"We'll look after her. We always have and will," said the grey-headed woman next to him.

3

BANG! BANG! BANG!

"Okay! Okay! I'm coming."

Eli jumped awake at the sound of rapid banging on the front door. Running down the stairs, Eli had no idea who could be knocking at this time of night. *Probably some tramp*, he thought, making himself chuckle as he entered the long, narrow kitchen attached to the small utility. The key was already in the door; he twisted it and heard the click. Opening the back door, he was ready to give this tramp a piece of his mind.

"Who is it!?" roared Lisa, Eli's mother, from her cosy bed, still in a sleepy state.

Her son didn't reply, eyes wide on Kelsey standing there, her own eyes flooded with tears. Nothing needed to be said; acting on instinct, he pulled her into a hug, which she looked in desperate need of. He had to shush her to calm her hysterical breathing.

"What's wrong?" he kept asking, remaining in the hug. "Come on, tell me."

But she couldn't — even if she wanted.

Releasing the embrace, Eli, his arm still wrapped around Kelsey's shoulders, brought her into the sitting room and placed her on the couch. It wasn't until she had sat down that Eli saw she was shaking, as if she had walked through a river of ice. But despite the autumn wind increasing by the second half of September, this was a fearful tremble.

Unaware her boyfriend had left her side, Kelsey snapped back into reality for a moment when she saw Eli return from the kitchen holding a glass of water. Kelsey cupped the glass when handed to her, but didn't take any sips. They sat in silence, and that was perhaps enough for Kelsey to feel even the slightest bit better.

Suddenly, there was thumping from the stairs. Entering the spacious living room in a grey nightgown was Lisa. She was a small woman with long, curly hair the colour of a raven. She froze in the doorway at the sight of the couple.

"Kelsey? What're you…? What's wrong, hun?" she said soothingly as she darted to the couch, sitting on the other side of the girl whom she already treated like a daughter-in-law. She wrapped her arm around Kelsey's shoulders and looked across at Eli, who had the same curious look on his face. "It'll be okay. Tell us, please, what happened."

4

The Night Kelsey Told Donovan

Looking up at the ceiling, she inhaled deeply. For a moment, she had second thoughts. What Kelsey was about to do could result in her and Donovan's relationship being even more strained than it already was.

A common phrase that was thrown around Castlehead was that you would pay for your sins sooner or later.

"I've got something to tell you, Daddy." She continued to look up at the ceiling as she spoke. She took another deep breath, and added earnestly, "No one will know of *our* mistake."

The bed creaked, but Kelsey continued to stare upwards. She said nothing more, but turned her head slightly and saw that Donovan had flipped over and was looking at her with silent rage.

"What?" he whispered. "Please tell me this is some kind of sick prank."

When Kelsey didn't respond and continued to stare at her dad, Donovan sat up, swooped his legs off the bed, back turned to Kelsey, stood up, and made his way around the bed with Kelsey's eyes following his every move. "This…" He now stood, towering over his daughter who sat up slightly. "It's not true." He snatched her wrist and tightened his grip as she tried to escape; Kelsey tried leaping off the bed and heading for the door, but nothing could loosen Donovan's vice grip. He then pulled her in close with little-to-no power, grabbed her shoulders and threw her against the side wall, causing a thud. "This is because of everything I've done, isn't it? You've planned this with Eli—"

"Eli and I have always been careful," snarled Kelsey, showing no pain or terror; she was confident, despite the force she had been struck with. "You wouldn't want this news to get around, would you?"

BANG!

Donovan punched the wall an inch from his daughter's face. He had turned beetroot red and shook with disdain. Kelsey began to gather that she may have crossed the line by threatening to blackmail him, for she started to squirm in his grasp, still pressed against the wall. He then tossed her back onto the bed as easily as throwing a ball.

Kelsey watched as he towered over her once more.

"You thought I hurt you before? You're not going to tell anyone, because I'm going to make sure you stay my little girl."

Kelsey kicked and screamed as Donovan pounced forward and tried to grab her legs. The bed continued to creak, feeling like it was going to give. Kelsey, still kicking rapidly, aiming for her dad's face, scooched back as far as she could go but forgot that the bed wasn't everlasting.

She tumbled off. Her hand slipping off the edge felt like she was at the edge of a cliff, below her a bottomless pit.

Kelsey leapt to her feet and made a break for the door on the other side of the room. Donovan realised what she had in mind, jumping for her as she ran, as if he was trying to rugby tackle her. The door was wide open, the hall leading to freedom just inches away.

Donovan missed the tackle, causing another thud as his body hit the ground. He reached out for his daughter's ankle, desperate.

The hallway was so close. Kelsey reached out to it as she wriggled her ankle to escape the clutches of her fallen father; his grip was too tight. There was only one way to escape...

"GET OFF ME!" she cried, turning, using her free foot to kick Donovan in the face.

He released his grip and cried out in pain as Kelsey made a run for it; Donovan's vision was blurred by the impact, his hands over his face to stop the bleeding from his nose, which now resembled splattered red paint on mush.

Donovan, with the help of the bed, managed to rise. But, as he attempted to walk straight, his vision was still blurred, one hand still covering his nose and the other reaching out for a wall, or handle, or basically anything that would support him. Before he knew it, however, just as he reached the top of the stairs, he heard the front door slam shut.

Where to go? Kelsey thought as she walked out of the garden and onto the street lit only by street lamps. She swore she heard a shout come from her house after she slammed the door shut.

"YOU'RE NOTHING, Kelsey! LOVE ME! LOVE ME!" was what Donovan roared after she left.

But the question still remained: Where was she going to go?

5

Present Day

"Why didn't you come straight here, though?" asked Eli after Kelsey had finished telling them what happened. Eli and Lisa's arms were still wrapped around Kelsey's shoulders as she sniffed. Her tears had stopped. "Where have you been staying for the past couple of weeks? It's nearly October."

"At a friend's. My grandma's, too. He followed me there, though, so that's when I came here," she explained.

"So," Lisa sighed, "I know you said you had a massive argument, but what was it actually about?"

Kelsey's eyes began to flood with tears again.

"He... he was drunk," she said as she tried to catch her breath. "I couldn't stay there anymore."

That's the only thing you've told us, thought Eli, wanting to speak up. Both Lisa and Eli wanted to believe her, but she had blatantly lied, though her tone was convincing. There was something that Kelsey wasn't telling them. Eli knew it but felt as though things would get worse if he bombarded her with more and more questions.

Lisa advised, "We need to get social services involved."

"NO!" Kelsey cried. "Anything but that."

"Kelsey, you are more than welcome to stay here," offered Lisa.

"Yes," agreed Eli. "For as long as you need."

"But," started Lisa, "something has to be done."

6

It was far from the norm for Kelsey to wake up to no shouting father ordering her to tend to him as if her only purpose in life was to serve him. The feeling of waking up next to a boy who actually loved her, in his single bed, was more than pleasurable.

The alarm clock rang, and the sound pulsated through the couple, waking them immediately. They sat up at the same time, looked at each other and dreaded the thought of having to go into school. With the bed pressed alongside the window wall, Kelsey leaped over Eli with a grunt and exited the room for the bathroom across the landing. The house felt a lot like the layout of Donovan's, only without the bitter atmosphere, and where every move made by Kelsey could mean another merciless assault.

As he heard the trickling of the sink faucet, Eli rubbed his eyes and got out of bed himself. He headed across to the wardrobe in the far corner of his room and took out clothes that resembled the dark outfit he had worn on the first day of term. Kelsey returned as Eli had just finished changing, and changed too. Lucky she already had a selection of clothes waiting for her after the many, many nights spent at her boyfriend's. Their eyes ended up locking onto one another, with thoughts of what could be achieved in the ten minutes before they had to leave.

"Youse probably want to see this!" shouted Lisa from the bottom of the stairs.

Their eyes rolled as their lips almost touched.

"I think it's about that Aaron boy."

Eli looked at Kelsey, then to the open door with a curious look on his face; Kelsey not so much.

Eli grabbed the black backpack that always sat on the floor leaning against the foot of his bed, and headed out the door, across the carpeted landing and down the stairs. Halfway down, he heard more footsteps coming from behind, and knew that Kelsey was following him. But perhaps she wasn't coming down for the same reason as Eli.

They entered the sitting room one after the other and there they saw Lisa on the edge of the couch, glaring intently at the television.

Eli walked across and sat next to his mother while Kelsey headed into the kitchen.

It was the news channel. A well-dressed man stood, with a microphone in his hand, in front of a winding road leading up into a forest of trees on a hill. He stared into the camera intently, ignoring the harsh winds that attempted to push him out of frame.

"Our team at CN Studios have just received word," the reporter said formally, *"that the police are currently up in these hills investigating a ditch that an anonymous caller, supposedly a hiker, came across late last night."* He ushered the camera to follow him closer to the hills as he held his hand up to his ear, hoping for more announcements.

"You think it could be him?" asked Eli, eyes still locked on the television, not noticing Kelsey standing in the doorway to the kitchen, watching them impatiently.

The man came to a halt, his hand slowly lowering from his ear, and then looked back at the camera. Did he lose signal? No sound came from the TV, but it looked like the reporter's mouth was moving... but not as if he were talking. It was contorted.

"Oh, what's happened?" Lisa asked rhetorically, beginning to rise.

But then there was a sound — a gulp — that came from the scene, making Lisa freeze in an awkward, distressing position, like she couldn't decide whether to remain seated or stand up.

"We will keep you updated as soon as we hear more details on the matter," the reporter said hurriedly before the camera cut to a woman in the studio standing in front of large screens.

"In other news..." began the reporter.

Lisa turned the volume down, and the mother and son looked up at Kelsey, who had her arms folded. *"Could finding the truth behind unsolved mysteries be as easy as putting on a pair of glasses? Find out after the break,"* they had heard before Kelsey caught their full attention.

"Are you ready to go?" she said crudely, like it wasn't a question at all. To Eli, it sounded like a command.

"Yeah."

Eli rose, and followed Kelsey into the kitchen and out the back door, all while Lisa watched.

"See you later, Mam," she heard.

Before she could say "Goodbye" too, the door had slammed shut.

7

The school stood tall beyond those gates, and Kelsey sighed, knowing the repeated six-hour torture they would have to endure. Turning to her boyfriend for a reaction, she sensed that Eli wasn't himself.

As they walked to the main entrance, he continued to scan the grounds for something... or someone. They saw, when entering reception, that the main hall was packed with students — just like any other day — but Eli squinted, still searching for that particular something he was looking for.

Eli pressed his face up against the glass doors that led to the main hall, continuing to scan the area, as students noticed and laughed hysterically.

Kelsey hid her face from the crowd, turning away and raising her hand as a barricade. As she turned her face towards the reception desk, she saw the receptionist attending to two familiar students, and one she hadn't seen before. She turned back to Eli and lightly tapped him on the shoulder, making him stop his scanning.

"Aren't those his friends?" she asked.

Eli glanced up in the direction of the desk and nodded when he noticed Anna, Brandon, and the new kid, Josh.

Kelsey quickly glanced back at the main hall where the students still laughed and muttered, knowing that they would be the topic of conversation for the next week.

"I'll catch you later." She pecked him on the cheek and speed-walked through the main hall and directly to class, where she hoped no one would bombard her with questions that were made to insult her, her face turning red.

Eli slowly walked over to the reception desk, tilting his head, trying to get a glimpse of Anna and Brandon's faces.

"You don't know where he is, then?" Eli heard Anna ask the receptionist.

The receptionist looked up once again from her computer, groaning, her eyes rolling to the back of her head.

"No, for the third time. We'll ring his parents if we don't see him by lunchtime. Remember, it is only five minutes until lessons," replied the receptionist, turning her attention back to the computer and typing away once again.

"Is this about Jason?" Eli butted in. "Have you heard from him?"

Brandon, Anna and Josh stepped back from the desk and turned their heads to Eli, partly surprised at him talking to *kids like them*. It was common for Eli to pass Brandon and Anna in the hallways, but never for them to have a conversation that lasted longer than ten seconds; the largest exchange they had was when Eli and his friends would cuss them out for playing terribly in P.E.

"I heard from him last night, about homework," said Brandon, his voice deep, "but that's it."

"New kid, what about you?" snapped Eli, which, by the look on his face, Josh didn't appreciate much.

"No. Haven't spoken to him in a few days, actually."

"Why do you care, anyway?" said Anna. "Thought you weren't friends anymore."

The school bell rang at that moment.

"Eli!" a loud voice shouted from behind him. Eli turned and saw a group of lads and lasses with curious looks on their faces, all of whom had almost identical clothes on.

"What're you doin', mate?" the loud-mouthed kid asked, his hair spiked up as if he had just been swirled in a toilet. Eli's face suddenly turned red with humiliation, his mouth moving, trying to form an excuse, but no words came out. "Come on!"

Walking towards his group, Eli rubbed the back of his neck.

Brandon, Anna and Josh watched the group enter the main hall and break off to go to their separate lessons.

Anna then asked, "So, you'll definitely let us—"

"YES!" barked the receptionist.

And on that note, Josh, Anna and Brandon left the receptionist to get on with her work. They were unaware that her eyes followed them out, not blinking.

Break time had come around after two slow hours, and there was still no sign of Jason; Brandon considered heading to the computers where he would often see him work on stories he never let anyone read, but even there he wasn't found. Heading back through the doors into the main hall, he stood for a moment and found Anna and Josh sitting at a small square table in a corner which, if he hadn't taken a second glance at, he wouldn't have noticed.

"Not there?" guessed Anna as she saw Brandon walk over. As he sat with them, Brandon shook his head. "He might just be ill?" Anna suggested, lifting her pink bag from the floor and placing it on her lap.

"No. He was fine yesterday," said Brandon.

BANG!

All the students in the main hall snapped their heads towards the bang; the double doors that led to the Musical Theatre department crashed against the walls from the force of the girl in all black as she opened them. She raced up towards reception, glancing back with a worried look at the students who were watching her like hawks, then burst through the doors leading outside.

"She's always leaving," complained Anna. "Why haven't they suspended her yet?"

Nobody answered her question.

"That was so weird," said Brandon.

"Why'd you think she did that?" said Josh.

"Did what?" asked Anna, rummaging through her bag, looking for a revision book.

"She kept glancing back as she left," said Brandon.

Again, there was silence; the three of them scouted their brains for a possible reason behind her strange actions. The school knew her to leave quite often, especially — it was rumoured — when she couldn't be bothered with school. This year, however, she was disappearing more and more frequently… noticeably since Aaron's death. It was odd enough to see her all in black on the rare occasions they caught her in lessons; yet the knowledge of her keeping her cards close to her chest brought up the idea that there might just be a dark streak within, desperate to be unleashed.

8

The White Shadow walked towards the hills as the wind made the cars parked on the faint double yellow lines rock. Despite the harsh weather conditions, Z didn't stumble on her way up towards Sunvalley Park, nor was she going to allow it; what she would stumble upon, however, was something like a nightmare.

More branches ended up on the dirt tracks every few minutes as the force of the wind snapped them off the almost leafless trees. Beneath her feet, she felt the crunch of the leaves, in their stunning autumn colours, and the sky was more visible now than it would be in the summer or spring. She found herself back on the dirt track that cut off the main road leading up to the mysterious, daunting, Michael Manor, and continued along, with one thing on her mind…

To get home in time.

Birds sang soothingly, bushes rustled, and the crunching continued; above all that, however, was a peculiar sound that didn't belong in a wilderness atmosphere.

It was the faint, ear-aching sound of police sirens.

The sound took Z off course.

She cut off from the dirt track and zigzagged her way through trees with no tracks to lead her. As she walked deeper into the trees and headed further up the hill, the sound grew louder. Eventually, reaching another section of flat surface. In the near distance, Z made out flashing blue lights.

It was when two police cars came into view that Z noticed yellow police tape stretching out and around the trees that surrounded the scene. She hid stealthily behind a tree close to the scene to keep a watchful eye, admittedly with a desire to overhear essential information that hadn't been revealed to even Madam Mayor herself.

Poking her head out from behind the tree, Z caught sight of two C.C.I.D officers on their hands and knees, giving the impression that — from her vantage point — they were digging. But she thought differently when she heard the sound of groaning, and saw them struggling to yank something out of the ground.

No progress was made, and Z had perhaps gone a little over her head with this desire. The thought of heading back down to Sunvalley Park came to mind. She took a couple of steps, and then stopped. Looking back at the scene, she noticed, in the far corner, a wide dirt track, and another set of sirens was drawing nearer and nearer.

Z set herself back behind the tree, poking her head out again to capture what would happen next.

Okay, just a few more minutes, she thought.

Notwithstanding this order to continue heading back to Sunvalley Park for the original reason she had left Thomas Hill in the first place, Z, deep down, had an urge to see if the Castlehead Criminal Investigation Department would actually solve a case for once.

Another police car made its way down the bumpy track, its siren now off, and parked next to the others, which surrounded the two officers on their hands and knees. The car door opened.

"Chief Pattison," whispered Z to herself.

Chief Pattison scanned the area as he slowly walked over to the officers.

"Anything since this morning?" he asked the officers, crouching down on one knee, his hands planted firmly on the ground to keep himself steady.

The officers looked up for a moment, their momentum lost for a second.

"We've almost got this thing out," said one of them, pulling again.

"What if it's... you know?" whispered the other, matching his partner's strength.

Pattison rose to his feet, watching them pull. He looked around again. When in the direction of Z, she hid completely behind the tree, remaining calm. After a second, she poked her head out again and saw that Chief Pattison was still watching the officers.

"Well," he breathed, "we've got to prepare for the worst, haven't we?"

The officers' groans grew louder and louder. They raised themselves into squatting positions, their hands deep in the hole.

From his viewpoint, a few steps away, Pattison got a glimpse of plastic. A bag.

Z gasped at the sight; whatever was in that hole began to be pulled smoothly out, and the strain was relieved as the officers rose to their feet, teeth gritted, hands firmly clasped on what they didn't realise were corners of a body bag.

"On three," one of the officers suggested. The other nodded, their teeth still gritted. "One. Two. Three!" They pushed down for a boost and used all their strength to pull out the thing that had been buried in that hole.

"WOAH!"

They used all their strength and ended up tumbling to the floor, but they had succeeded.

Chief Pattison moved an inch closer in awe, jaw dropping and eyes wide. He was so struck by what had been dug up that he didn't help his officers up from the ground. The officers joined him in standing positions, replicating their chief's gawking expression.

"Is it him?"

Although tempted to enter the scene like a lost traveller, Z — in her right mind — remained behind the tree. It was like something out of a television drama; she was hooked, and had to watch how the C.C.I.D reacted to finally finding the body of Aaron Smith. If it was him, that is.

"It's him," confirmed Pattison. "Send an ambulance out here. We can get the body to the main road. I'll alert the mayor once the area has been cleared. Let's just hope there were no witnesses."

Z despised imagining the corpse in the bag; the boy's eyes open wide, like he was surprised. His look, however, wasn't one of surprise. Vacant, his expression must've been. Aaron's face was white as a sheet, with the added accessories of scarred wrists, a busted nose, and missing teeth.

As the two officers carried the bag up the wide dirt track to the main road where the ambulance would eventually meet them, Z wanted to intervene. The unbearable thoughts just lured her in more.

And Z had witnessed every moment of it.

She left with a troubled look on her face, gulping every few minutes, hurting her throat, and biting her nails. With her nerves shot — which was extremely rare for Z — she couldn't help but wonder at the notion that Clarke was not going to take this well… and whether the C.C.I.D was going to find the truth to all this.

There was no campfire alight when Z found Sunvalley Park. In fact, no one was out. It looked abandoned.

She made her way into the park and across to the trailer she called home. The door was nearly off its hinges, and the two steps leading up had been caved in. As she swung the door open, she saw floating dust particles in the air, the couch covered in clothes, and the television not even plugged in. Nobody was using it, so what was the point?

She turned right into the joining kitchen; cupboard doors were wide open, dishes overflowed the sink and the drainer, and, for weeks, there had been a stench coming from the fridge, like rotten cheese. Z ignored it, telling herself that she would sort it out later.

Later never came for Z.

Passing the kitchen, she walked through a doorway with no door attached, into a small, narrow, carpeted corridor with doors on either side. To her right were the bathroom and toilet; the left took her into her bedroom where she spent some nights, a spare bedroom that was never in use, and the bedroom she needed to enter.

Hesitantly pushing the door to this bedroom open, she poked her head into the room, like she had done when hiding behind the tree. Through the thin, paper-like walls, the sound of a siren could be heard passing outside.

The ambulance, she supposed.

In this room, there was nothing more than a sofa bed, and a wardrobe in the far corner. That was all; a lot like a room in a care home.

The bed creaked, and Z glanced down. She entered the room. The bed creaked one more time, and the figure occupying it struggled to open their eyes.

"*Nieta*, you came," breathed the elderly woman. Her wild grey hair was like a mad scientist's, the gown she wore was like one from a hospital, and there was barely any pigment in her skin. "I'm so happy." It hurt for her to smile; the slightest of movements weakened her. "I thought you weren't coming."

"Of course I came, *Abuela*," said Z, kneeling down next to her grandmother's rough, wrinkly hands. "You called. Do you want your tablets?" It hurt Z's grandmother to even nod. "Okay."

Z gave a faint smile to her innocent grandmother, patting her cold hand. She rose, walking around the bed to the wardrobe, where the piles of medication had been stashed.

It wasn't for clothes. The wardrobe had been installed with many shelves for mainly paperwork. There was a gap between the bottom shelf and the bottom of the wardrobe itself; that space was used to store the medication. She crouched and examined the many small plastic bottles, which she kept picking up and tossing to one side in an attempt to find the right one. The tub she had rummaged around for sat at the very bottom of the pile.

That was it with Z's grandmother; whenever she rang, it was a gamble at what the problem was, and what the solution would be.

Z picked up the medication and squinted at the label. *Instant Pain Relief*, it said, in black letters.

Z rose again and walked back around to the side of the bed. She crouched again, clutching her abuela's hand whilst opening the bottle with her teeth.

"You don't come home at night," said the grandmother, looking up at the ceiling. "You are going to school, aren't you?" she asked.

The bottle popped open.

"Here, *Abuela*." Z tipped a single white pill onto her palm, stretched her arm out and forced the pill through her grandmother's closed lips. "Swallow."

The uncomfortable gulp made by Z's grandmother when she swallowed the pill, as it touched the back of her throat, made Z herself shiver a little. But it eventually went down.

"You didn't answer me," replied Willow, rather firmly, although still in a pained whisper.

"Rest, Grandmama."

Abuela Willow turned her head to face the opposite wall. She didn't say much, but Z knew that she wasn't keen on not knowing where her granddaughter was at all times. This had been the case even before she had fallen ill with this untreatable illness. The medication only relieved the pain slightly; it used to do more, but the medication was pretty much useless at this stage. It was inevitable that this was going to end in an unkindly way for Willow. It was just a matter of when it was going to happen. And grandmother and granddaughter had been having this conversation for the past four years.

Every day had been the same for Z's grandmother since the diagnosis. And she had been in Z's hands ever since. A girl of ten years shouldn't have had that kind of responsibility, but it was a responsibility Z had to take, for her parents were nowhere to be found, after the divorce a year prior.

Willow had been stable for a while, but then it had hit her. She had fallen down the stairs, her mind gone blank, vision blurred, a roaring headache, legs like jelly. And it was on a day when Z had felt lost, unable to handle the pressure of taking care of a woman seven times her age, when they were put in the hands of the residents at Sunvalley Park, who had taken them in like a family.

"That boy," Willow began to say slowly. "That boy was a gem in this town."

"Aaron?"

Z was surprised that Willow remembered talking about Aaron Smith's disappearance. She couldn't stare at her grandmother talking about this particular topic; she was intrigued by the scene further up the hill, but when anyone talked about it, she was guilt-ridden.

"Yes. This world is cruel, snatching a young soul's life, just like that." Willow continued to look up at the ceiling with a vacant expression as she spoke. "Clarke must be heartbroken."

"Yeah," agreed Z, nodding solemnly.

"First his wife, then his son, then his workplace."

Z turned her head, her eyebrows suddenly rising at what her abuela had casually said, like it was nothing.

"Wife?"

9

Repairs on Clarke's workplace had begun. Clarke would explain to whoever asked him about his work that the construction workers would just come and go as they pleased. It irritated him wholly, but he couldn't do anything about it. Like the C.C.I.D had said on the night of the fire, the said-to-be culprits of the fire were an extension cord and a plug socket almost torn completely off the wall.

Nevertheless, Jason had a different theory after meeting Eli in the cafe that night. It may have been a stretch but it was a possibility nonetheless. What if there was more to the fire than just unsafe electrical equipment? Jason lied to his mother that he was on his way to school.

It was just a matter of not getting caught.

The entrance had been barricaded by a moveable steel guardrail that was only planted at the entrance to stop people trespassing, and the windows had been boarded up by planks of wood.

Jason looked at the destruction that had been caused; he couldn't imagine what it would look like on the inside.

The ice-cold steel sent a tingle up Jason's arms and through his entire body. It screeched against the pavement as he tried to move it away from the entrance. Inside, it was like the building had been abandoned for many, many years, wearing away more and more every day. Jason took it all in, unsure where to start. Wires stuck out of the walls where sockets would have been, the long ceiling lights had been removed, just like all the shelves, and Jason was certain he heard the scurrying of rats in the back room.

He was careful with his footing, cautious of any secret alarms that may have been placed or could be triggered with one wrong step. Then it had occurred to him: *They would've been removed or burnt.* He walked down the store to where the counter and cash register would've been, the floorboards creaking with every step, and looked for anything that proved his theory right.

The floorboards continued to creak as Jason decided to tiptoe over to the back room that only staff were allowed in. Like the store itself, the back room had been cleared out; the shelves on all of the walls had been emptied, the window in the back wall that revealed a deserted car park had also been boarded up, and there was still no clear evidence as to why the shop would just explode into flames the way it had.

Jason suddenly twitched. All of a sudden, his toes began to curl up inside his school shoes, and that tingle he had felt when moving the barricade returned. Screeching came from the entrance, and the sound made him hide behind the wall. The screeching stopped, and, for a moment, Jason thought he had been busted. But the command to reveal himself from his hiding place never came.

Slowly poking his head out to see who, or what, was now in the shop, Jason raised his eyebrows in surprise to see a figure covered in darkness — helped by the minimal light coming through — crouching, appearing to be examining the premises, too. That was when Jason decided to reveal himself.

As the floorboards croaked once more, the figure jumped in surprise, rising and freezing, wondering who Jason was as he stood in the doorway. Slowly walking back into the main store with a raised eyebrow, Jason still couldn't make out who this figure was, as they were still blanketed in darkness.

"What are you doing here?" said the figure in a high pitched, nervous voice.

"I could ask the same thing," replied Jason, getting closer to the figure with every word.

"I'm writing an article about Mr Clarke Smith. I'm sure you've heard of him." The nerves had gone, and the figure began speaking in a more formal tone. "Ever since the interview he did the day after the fire, a new layer has been added to this mystery."

I knew it, thought Jason proudly. When repeating the statement in his head however, a word caught him off guard.

"Interview? There was no interview," argued Jason, flicking through his brain for anything about Clarke being interviewed. "Clarke wouldn't—"

"Oh, he did," the figure said confidently. "I'm guessing you've never heard of the A.P?" Jason looked blankly back at the figure. "Anonymous Podcaster?" Jason shook his head, his mind blank. The figure sighed in arrogant disappointment. "Ah, you amateur journalists. Always trying to figure out stuff yourself. Do your research next time."

Jason's blank expression transformed into an insulted one. There was no need for crude insults.

"Hang on a minute," he said, his voice raised a touch, but not enough to draw the attention of passing pedestrians, "what's with the insults? I'm not a journalist, nor an amateur in what I do."

"Then why are you here?"

"I'm… *looking* for material for my book. I write. Even had stuff printed in the local paper." Jason, although not really stretching the truth, didn't want to admit he was out there doing what a journalist would commonly do. "Who are you, anyways?"

Jason took another step forward as the figure took a step back into the light that shot through the entrance way, revealing a slim, short-haired brunette with glowing, emerald eyes and villainous red lips that drew him in for a kiss — that he had to hold back from, of course. She wore a smart shirt with slim-fit jeans, and was holding a clipboard and a pen.

Jason's natural skin tone turned to a rose pink, his cheeks popping, at first glimpse of the fine specimen standing before him. Beginning to drool like a dog desperate for a treat, it was like Jason was in a trance.

The girl edged back a bit, looking uncomfortable.

Snap out of it, Jason!

"I'm…" She was hesitant to say her name. "Maria." She began to circle the strange teen who wasn't blinking at her, trying to act as if she was searching for something to take notes on. "And… what about your name?"

Jason had snapped out of it, tracking her steady-paced movement around him.

"Oh, sorry. I'm Jason Rayne."

The sound of his name forced Maria to freeze on the spot. She circled him once more until she stood back in front of him, eyes wide with shock.

"Jason Rayne?" she repeated slowly. Jason nodded. "The Jason Rayne who's planning on entering the writing contest in hopes of a publisher recognising the talent he possesses?"

"Wait, how did you know?"

Maria grinned, explaining, "We've had our eye on you for a while."

"*We*?" Jason needed an explanation as to how this random Maria girl, whom he embarrassingly fancied, knew so much about him, despite them never meeting. "What are you on about?"

"Do you know of Desmond School for Creative Arts?"

Jason smirked, responding with, "Do you know the sun gives us light?"

Maria couldn't help but let out a chuckle.

"Well, we have in fact read your pieces in the paper, and we're sure you'll win the contest… because the school created it. And, well, if you don't tell anyone about this meeting… and I'm sure you don't want to get caught skipping school… I might be able to give you an offer you can't refuse."

Jason had no response. All that came out of his mouth were gasps and awkward noises. He was never one to get his hopes up, but to receive an offer from a school so exclusive that only those with a pure passion for the creative arts knew of it, and only the elite received offers and got accepted, would be life changing.

"Wow. I don't know—"

"Don't say anything."

Maria turned for the exit and began to leave, but stopped when Jason asked, "How will I know you've told the school about me?"

She slowly turned her head, looking back at Jason with a confident smirk.

"You'll see me again."

Maria turned back around and left without another word, leaving Jason in the middle of the run-down shop, with so many unanswered questions.

What had Clarke said in the interview?

10

Knowing that his grandparents were out, looking for some extra crafting desks for the utility where his grandad worked on his projects, and that his mother, Gemma, was working, Jason was proud of himself for successfully skipping school and being in the clear.

Jason carefully opened the door of his house on the corner of Chess Street, and entered the passageway. He haphazardly chucked his shoes off, chucked his bag under the coat hooks and strode into the dining room, the kitchen in view.

"Good day at school, son?"

He wasn't in the clear.

On one of the dining room chairs, with her arms folded, stern-faced, and breathing heavily like she couldn't contain her fury, was Gemma, not taking her eyes off her son, who had a perfect school attendance record. Until today.

Gemma rose and gestured at him to come forward. There was no jury in this courthouse, only a judge, and Jason knew by the look on Gemma's face that this judge's decision had already been made.

"Look, Mam—"

"Why weren't you in school?" she said, not wanting to hear excuses, just the truth. "You know... getting a call in the middle of your shift from your son's school and being informed that he hasn't turned up is one of the scariest things a parent hears, right?"

"Mam, I—"

"Don't bullshit me, son. Please just tell me."

"I wasn't feeling well."

His attempt at the oldest excuse in the book clearly hadn't worked.

"Son," she warned.

"Okay. Okay." Why did he even bother? He never learned, did he? Gemma saw right through him, reminding her son on numerous occasions that she knew when he was lying, as he would either stutter, or his lips would start trembling. Jason denied it, however, saying he couldn't feel his lips trembling. But he thought better than to tell another lie. *Just tell her*, he told himself. "I only said I was going to school, because... because I wanted to have a look at—"

"No! No! No!" Gemma sighed again. She tried her best to not raise her voice, as much as she wanted to. She knew immediately where he had been and what he had been doing instead of getting a good education. "Don't tangle yourself up in everything."

"I can't help it. I'm a writer, it's—"

"YOU'RE NOT A WRITER!" She had reached boiling point, and there was no way of cooling Gemma down. "Stop living out this fantasy that you're going to be this successful author. I mean, your stories are in a local paper in the hope of a publisher noticing, and that hasn't happened. It never will!"

"It's not a fantasy!" Jason had the guts to talk back to his mother.

"Son, you're going to be really disappointed when your dream doesn't come true. Think realistically for a change." Gemma could tell by the lack of eye contact that Jason didn't want to hear any of this. He planted himself on a dining room chair, arms folded and head down. "Writing isn't going to get you to university, son." Her voice had lowered to a more reasonable tone. She had let off steam, but maybe it was because she didn't know how much the writing truly meant to her son. All he wanted to do was make her proud, and, to do that, he thought, he should just do as she said — despite being adamant not to give up.

Gemma sat back down at the dining table, trying to get a look at her son's face. "Aaron's body has been found," she announced. Jason looked up, bewildered. "In the hills near Sunvalley Park."

"Oh, right," he said quietly, trying to seem unconcerned.

"There'll be a funeral, Clarke said, in which only inner circle are invited. He doesn't want to make a big fuss over it."

Inside, all of Aaron's close friends were relieved that they could say one final farewell to a true friend. It was going to be a day of remembrance. Although heart-breaking for many, some said, during the lead-up to the day at the end of September, that they were glad his body had been found, and that he could have an actual send-off. Others, on the other hand, said they would've much rather heard that he was found alive than dead.

11

All the guests had arrived at Central Church by 11:30am, September 30th, to witness the funeral of a boy lost by Castlehead too soon. The men and boys wore black suits and ties, the women and girls, appropriately, were in black dresses with large matching hats and veils.

Upon arrival, Clarke thanked everyone for attending, informing them that the service would begin at midday. The wake would take place at his good friends' bar, Gill & Susan'z.

Everyone waited outside the main entrance to the church, huddled in small groups, whispering about Aaron, how the day would proceed, and — everyone's main worry — how Clarke would cope.

Jason, Eli, and the others stood far from the rest of the guests, plodding around the graves, wanting to make conversation but simply not being able to. Many thoughts raced through their heads that day, but all circled back to the reason behind why it had to be Aaron. So innocent, so welcoming, yet ultimately dead in a closed casket.

Midday arrived, and everybody lined up at the entrance in an orderly fashion, awaiting the heavy, brown church doors to open. The church bell rang in the bell tower, and tears already began streaming down everyone's faces — all apart from Clarke's. He tried to retain a strong, straight face. The doors had been pulled slowly open by two men from the inside, making it look like they had opened of their own accord.

One by one, with Clarke leading the way, everyone entered and was mesmerised by the ancient beauty of it all; the architecture, the flooring, the altar, everything seemed so authentic and true. Rows of seats stared at the altar, where candles were lit, brightening the room, specifically the catafalque, on which the coffin lay. Despite Clarke stating that he didn't want a big fuss made, there was no empty seat in Central Church.

Next to the coffin, on a stand, was a photo of a smiling Aaron, and it reminded them all of the outlook he had on life, how optimistic he was, and that Aaron was genuine to the point of being brutally honest.

Father Avner walked up to the altar and stepped onto a small podium to the right of the coffin. He raised his arms in the air. The room turned silent.

"Bless everyone in this room," Father Avner said in a relaxing voice. He looked around at all the faces watching him, tissues wiping away the continuous tears. "Today, we say farewell to a boy who, like the Lord Almighty, brought light with him wherever he went. Today we say—"

Everyone turned their heads to the entrance doors as they slowly opened, and, for a moment, forgot that they were attending a funeral. The priest remained silent at the podium… that was, until gasps and whispers could be heard as a girl, like the others, in a slick, black dress, walked down the aisle that cut through the rows of seats. Unlike the other females, however, this girl had blood red lips and skin as white as a ghost.

"I thought she wasn't going to come," whispered Eli, leaning uncomfortably nearer to Jason's ear than he intended.

"I don't think anyone expected her to show," replied Jason, just as intrigued as everyone else, his eyes following the girl as she slowly stepped up to the coffin in which Aaron lay.

Z placed her hand gently on the lid, looked across at the photo, and gave a faint smile that nobody saw.

"*No tenía que suceder así,*" the priest heard her whisper.

She turned around and looked out at the sea of awed faces.

Z nodded once at the crowd, notably to Clarke, who sat in the front row, as an apology for interrupting, stepped down and joined Jason, Eli, Kelsey, Brandon, and Anna in the third row. Their parents, excluding Donovan, were in the row behind.

Not a word was said.

With the clearing of the priest's throat, it was time to continue the service.

"As I was saying," he said, "today we say goodbye to a boy who, like the Lord Almighty, brought light with him wherever he went. Today, we say farewell to Aaron Smith. By nature, Aaron was said to be a caretaker. I didn't know him personally, but I know from what I've heard that he was able to brighten anyone's day. Let's look at that word, *caretaker*. What exactly does that mean? It means you will do anything to make those around you happy, putting the desires of others before your own, just like when he found his friend Jason writing alone, and was the only one to go up to him. Or when he helped his friend Brandon revise for an exam, despite having a project due the next day."

Brandon turned awkwardly to look at his mother; she looked at him, not blinking, and he could tell there were things she wanted to say. Clearly, there were some things the straight-A student wasn't telling his mother, who took her profession in teaching university students very seriously.

Brandon turned his head again, back to the altar, gulping, wanting to solely focus on remembering his close friend, not admitting he needed help with a piece of schoolwork.

"You okay?" whispered Anna.

"I think it'll be me in a coffin next," he stated.

"Now, I would like to ask Aaron's father, Clarke, to come up," said the priest suddenly, stepping down.

Clarke took a deep breath before standing. He took another deep breath before taking his place at the podium.

He cleared his throat and started with, "I j-just wanted to say…" He cleared his throat again, hiding his cough, and eventually continued, "th-thank you all f-for coming. Aaron was blessed with such c-caring family and fr-friends."

The guests thought Clarke appeared unwell that day. Everyone knew this was going to be a difficult day, having to say goodbye to his son. But he looked physically sick; his face had lost its colour, he was stammering, and the podium shook rapidly as he clutched onto it with force. "This is the hard-hardest thing any person will have to do." Tears finally began to sting the corners of his eyes, and finally let them rip. "But when it's your boy, nothing can match the pain." Clarke sighed, looking up for strength, forcing himself not to cry. But then, his mouth opened and words didn't form. This was when he told himself to stop. "I'm sorry, son." He waved his hand in front of his face, shaking his head, and removed himself from the podium. "I can't do this. I just wanted us to all be in line."

Once Clarke had returned to his seat, madly sobbing, the priest stepped back onto the podium. For a moment, he didn't know what to say.

"Now, let's all bow our heads in silence," he suggested.

Everyone did, apart from Clarke, whose face was in his hands.

"And let's all reminisce silently about the boy that was Aaron Smith."

Silence quickly spread across the room, apart from a few sniffs here and there.

The priest ushered four pallbearers from the sides of the church up to the altar. Two of them took one end of the coffin while the other two mirrored them on the other end. They heaved the coffin onto their shoulders; and it was on that cue that everyone rose to watch the pallbearers escort Aaron and the coffin in which he lay out of Central Church and into the graveyard, Central Cemetery.

Clarke led the guests out of the church once the pallbearers had made it out onto the grounds. The glare of the sun disrupted the guests' vision, making them put their hands over their eyes and unintentionally bow their heads again.

Following the pallbearers past a bench commemorated to another beloved Castlehead citizen, a newly dug grave became visible; the last grave pedestrians would see when exiting the grounds onto St Christopher Road.

Like many of the graves on the church grounds before it, the newly-dug hole in which Aaron's coffin would be descending into would be neatly covered with artificial turf.

Placed delicately on the automatic lowering device, the coffin was ready to descend. Beside the gravestone, which was as smooth as marble, stood a pile of earth which would fill the grave after the service. One staff member gave a nod to another, who then pulled a small lever, activating the device.

The guests stood honourably, with Clarke at the foot of the grave, dropping a small flower in with the coffin, which had reached the bottom of the seven-foot-deep hole.

Crows began to squawk, and the guests made their way back to their cars to head to Gill & Susan'z, leaving Clarke to take in the moment.

"Come on, Clarke!" said a guest at the door of his car.

The grieving father turned his head to the exit, replying, "Okay, okay."

The convoy of cars followed one another up to the secluded hill on which the local bar stood. The bar itself was a popular social meeting point, hosting wakes, birthdays, and parties for occasions like Halloween and Christmas. As the name suggested, the pub was co-founded by sisters Gill and Susan Stanley.

The cars parked in an orderly fashion by the side entrance. Clarke entered first, with the group of teens following. The entrance led to a narrow hallway which split off in two directions; left took you to a set of stairs which led you up to rooms for guests to stay in, and right took you down a set of stairs into the main bar. They headed down into the bar. Under the red carpet, the stairs creaked.

A large portion of the pub had been taken up by scattered tables and chairs, with the bar counter the first thing to the guests' left when entering. On the opposite side were four booths, one of which was immediately taken up by Jason, Eli, Kelsey, Anna, Brandon, and — shockingly — Z.

She hadn't been expected to attend the funeral, never mind the wake.

Both Gill — a glasses-wearing lady with short blonde hair — and Susan — a short, tanned lady with jet black, shoulder-length hair — had decided to work on this day. They greeted the guests from behind the bar, mentioning to Clarke that they wished they could have attended the service, but they could bet it was beautiful.

"Well, if you need anything, just give us a shout," said Gill, handing Clarke a pint as he leaned on the bar.

"Thank you," he said, taking the pint and beginning to walk around.

He put on a thankful smile as everyone bombarded him with apologies for his loss and how beautiful the service was. Inside, however, he felt like it was just adding insult to injury. It was a breath of fresh air when he managed to get through thanking everyone for their heartfelt apologies, and the suffering was over.

Planting himself in a lonely seat in the corner of the bar, he watched everyone reminisce about his son. Often, people would join him to make little conversation. Nobody lasted longer than five minutes, and the guests understood why.

There wasn't much conversation coming from the booth of teens, either.

Z and Kelsey avoided contact with one another, sitting at opposite ends of the booth; Anna was on her phone texting Josh, who didn't come as he hadn't known Aaron; Brandon and Eli made awkward conversation, wishing they were anywhere else; Jason kept looking over at Clarke, waiting for the right moment.

"What's up, Jason?" asked Eli, startling Jason a touch, noticing his constant staring at the mourning father.

"Nothing," said Jason. *Go on, he's alone.* "I'll be back in a minute."

Jason removed himself from the booth and began to walk to the far corner where Clarke was sitting, drowning his grief with alcohol.

"Where you goin'?" yelled Eli from the booth, but Jason ignored him. He turned to Kelsey. "Wanna drink?"

Kelsey nodded, then asked, "Can we go soon?"

Jason scooted over to the lonely corner, watching Clarke, hoping he hadn't noticed his desire for a conversation that may not be best suited to a funeral environment.

"H-hi," began Jason nervously, about to pull a chair out for himself. "I'm sorry for your loss. Aaron was a good friend." Clarke nodded, downing the pint as if to escape the horrors he had experienced. "Err... can I sit down?"

Clarke gestured to the seat Jason was about to pull out. Jason assumed that was a yes.

"Thank you for coming. I know how close you were to my son."

"How are you feeling?" Jason knew it was a stupid question, but it was common practice. "I mean after your work and all that," he explained. *Should I?* Jason asked himself, his face showing concern. "I was hoping to ask you a question."

Clarke sighed, clearly rolling his eyes. He aggressively planted the empty pint glass on the table, then gestured to Gill, who stood behind the bar, for another, before responding with "Go ahead" in an unconvincing tone.

"What is the A.P?"

That single question changed the atmosphere. When Susan came over with the pint for Clarke, she realised that she shouldn't stick around.

The question came as a surprise to Clarke; his eyes were wide, initially expecting frequent questions about Aaron and what great things he did as a kid.

He thought nobody would find out.

Clarke hushed the curious teen, ushering Jason to lean forward across the table, but not enough to make it obvious that they were talking about something that Clarke didn't want revealed.

"How do you know?" growled Clarke.

Jason didn't want to say that he had found out from a girl he had never met before, so decided to shrug as a way of response.

Clarke sighed again. "The A.P stands for *Anonymous Podcaster*. It's a new segment on the radio that began not too long after Aaron went missing. It's not popular, but they asked me to come on and talk about Aaron and everything that the town was saying at the time. I thought I'd just go on, because I had nothing to lose, and the reason behind the podcast itself was to give advice. I went on, and the interviewer's voice had been altered to sound very deep, but also automated, like a robot. We talked for an hour, and I ended up mentioning that my workplace had caught alight. And that's when I told them—"

"Told them what?" asked Jason, intrigued, as if he were binge-watching a show.

"I told them that the C.C.I.D never listened, and that they jumped to conclusions about the cause being the faulty electrical wires or whatever. What you didn't see on the live news on the night of the fire was that after the cameras cut off, I tried to tell them, but Chief Pattison wasn't having it, interrupting me just before I wanted to say that the cause of the fire couldn't have been the electrics, as the week prior, the store had received 100% on the annual health inspection."

"You haven't tried to tell the C.C.I.D since?"

"Every time I ring, they just say that they're busy and they'll call back. But they never do," Clarke further explained.

How could Jason respond to that? He remained seated and speechless, arms crossed on the cold table. Resisting the urge to blurt this new found information out was difficult to do. His only two thoughts were: *Go on, tell Eli*, and *How could the wiring be sabotaged?*

However, now, with the information that Jason held close, it wasn't a matter of how anymore; it was who.

Jason was stuck on whether it was time to leave, or stay with Clarke, to process what he had just been told. If he stayed, Clarke could tell him more, but if he left, he could try to find out who had done it sooner, and get the word around the group.

In the end, Jason thanked Clarke for his time and returned to the booth, startling Eli by yanking him into the hallway that led to the side exit.

"What's up, like?" asked Eli.

"I've just spoken to Clarke. The fire wasn't caused by faulty wiring."

"But it was confirmed by—"

"They're just covering it up. Someone entered the store, somehow sneakily sabotaging the electrics when nobody was watching."

"So, you think—"

"It wasn't an accident."

Jason held back the full story as, at that moment, Kelsey walked up to the pair, coat around her shoulders.

Both boys fell silent.

Kelsey raised an eyebrow.

"We going, then?" she said, nudging Eli.

Behind her back, Jason nodded at Eli to agree, but followed up by shaking his head too, wanting him to remain silent until it was the right time to tell everyone else about the situation.

Kelsey snapped her head to Jason, having suspicions he was perhaps mocking her. If he were to do so, he would do it to her face.

"Yeah," said Eli.

From the back of the bar, Lisa joined them in the halls, also raising an eyebrow at the awkward silence, ready to go, too. "See you later, Jason."

Eli led the three of them to the exit, with Jason waving goodbye to them all, snarling at Kelsey, who stuck her tongue out at him.

12

The only sound during the drive back to Eli and his mother's house came from the radio. No one said a word. There was a slight urge from Eli to tell his girlfriend what Jason had told him, but he thought better of it, considering her attitude during the service; looking like she didn't care. He thought that she probably wouldn't care about the case, if she didn't even care about Aaron's death.

Lisa pulled up outside their house, exiting the car and pulling the front seat of her light green two-door car forward. Eli and Kelsey struggled to squeeze out, both expressing sounds of relief once on the pavement. They allowed Lisa to lead the way into the small front garden, which was barricaded from the street by a waist-height wooden fence, which made it easy for one to hurdle over.

Lisa stopped at the green back door, which, in the darkness, seemed black. She rummaged through her leather coat pockets for her keys.

As Eli's mother struggled to find the lock, Kelsey turned to her boyfriend, noticing his puzzled look.

"Are you okay?" she whispered in his ear.

"What? Oh. Yeah, I'm fine," he tried to say positively. "Long day."

The door opened of its own accord once unlocked. Lisa entered first, followed by Kelsey. Eli seemed distracted.

"All right, son?" asked his mother, looking back and seeing him in the doorway.

He was looking back at the gate. He froze, squinting at it. Eli could have sworn he saw a black silhouette illuminated in the moonlight. The figure wasn't upright, appearing to be slumped over, leaning on the fence. It was as if they were trying to get through the gate without noticing it was shut.

Eli shook his head and finally entered, forcing himself to believe it had just been a figment of his imagination.

Just as he shut the door, Lisa switched on the kitchen light.

Kelsey had entered the sitting room, collapsing onto the couch, grateful for the day finally coming to a close.

BANG! BANG! BANG!

The three knocks were more like shotguns firing.

Kelsey jumped up from the couch like a cat while Eli and Lisa edged back as far as they could.

Kelsey tiptoed to the doorway between the lounge and kitchen, poking her head through to see what the commotion was. Suddenly there were another three consecutive bangs, and then...

CRASH!

The door had been forced open.

Lisa let out a blood-curdling scream, searching for the best possible defensive weapon, while Eli froze, with no idea what to do. It was no figment of his imagination; a black silhouette was standing there, live and in person, stumbling in. Who it was was unclear, until they revealed themselves in the kitchen light.

Kelsey entered the kitchen, gasping and, to Eli and Lisa's confusion, shaking her head in disgust.

"Dad!"

Donovan was now clearly visible, his shirt ripped and untucked. He squeezed an empty can of beer and tossed it on the floor, as if this were his own home. Even from the back of the kitchen, the smell of alcohol flew into their faces like a huge gust of wind. He looked around, leaning on the sink, and that's when he noticed Kelsey in the doorway.

"YOU!" blurted Donovan, pointing at his daughter. "YOU ARE COMING WITH ME!"

He suddenly leapt forward, reaching out for his daughter. Kelsey dodged his sledgehammer-like hands. She couldn't bear to have that vice-like grip on her arms again.

"She's going nowhere," said Lisa firmly. "Leave now, and I won't call the police."

Donovan slowly turned his head to Lisa and Eli, bursting into laughter.

"Really?" he said, swaying from side to side. "You won't do anything. I've done nothing wrong. It's our children who have done wrong."

"Dad, don't you dare!" shouted Kelsey from the sitting room.

"Hon, what's he talking about?" asked Lisa, wary of Donovan inching closer to herself and Eli. Her phone was in hand. "Kelsey?"

And that's when Donovan clicked. A smirk suddenly appeared on his face as he looked back and forth. The smirk was accompanied by an arrogant chuckle.

"Oh! She hasn't told you, Lisa?"

Eli looked as confused as Lisa.

With Kelsey having moved closer, now was the time for Donovan to stir the pot of drama.

"My daughter is pregnant." He moved closer to Eli, nose-to-nose. "And you're the father."

Kelsey and Eli's eyes met. Before anything could be explained, however...

"GET OUT! GET OUT! GET OUT!" cried Lisa, shoving the drunk out on instinct. She slammed the door shut and turned to Kelsey and Eli. "I WANT YOU BOTH OUT BY TOMORROW NIGHT!" Eli and Kelsey tried to talk, but Lisa didn't want to hear their excuses. "NOW GET UP THOSE STAIRS!"

Kelsey knew that they shouldn't attempt to explain, especially on this night, and so she pulled a distraught Eli away up the stairs, not to be seen by Lisa for the foreseeable future.

13

Lisa wasn't the only one having to react to distressing news about their offspring that night. By this time, Clarke was the only one remaining downstairs at Gill & Susan'z; everyone else had either gone home, or to their rooms upstairs. From the bar, Gill and Susan watched closely as Clarke, surrounded by pint glasses on the table and on the floor, scrolled through his phone at photos of his departed son.

No emotion showed on his face, but the owners of the bar knew he was hurting. The memories came flooding back, just like the tears that began to stream down his face. Then he stopped scrolling, stopping on a photo of himself, with Aaron as a ten-year-old, and his wife.

"All I wanted was for you two to stay in line."

Perhaps they were listening, from wherever souls go after one passes away. But that's up to interpretation, isn't it? You believe whatever you want to believe. Whether that is you go to heaven if you've always seen the light, or hell if you've sinned – which many Castlehead residents had, even if they didn't intend to – or you believe you simply stop existing.

CHAPTER THREE

Sins and Rewards

1

"Bless me, Father, for I have sinned," pleaded Clarke in the confessional in Central Church, his hands clasped together and his head bowed slightly.

A transgression against divine law, those with religious beliefs see sinning as a hurtful act against God; nobody wishes to sin. But when you do, you hope to erase that sin from your memory; hope it won't come back to haunt you. And what did Clarke have to admit, and desire forgiveness for? Sins that couldn't be erased from his mind.

In that dark confessional box, which had been tinted with a touch of wine red, Clarke and Father Avner were unable to see the rays of the orange setting sun glaring through the church's stained-glass windows.

Clarke sat patiently, awaiting an answer, hands still clasped together.

"Continue, my child," said Avner, hidden from view.

"My last confession was over a year ago. Many things have changed since then, things that have caused me to curse and abuse my power—" (he didn't just abuse his power) "and so I apologise for all these sins, and for all that I cannot remember."

Clarke remained seated in the booth, awaiting an answer again. Deep down, there was more he wanted to confess, but even to the Lord Almighty himself, he couldn't bring himself to admit everything he had done wrong. All he had wanted to do was keep his family in line. Not this — not the suffering that he had endured up to this point. He didn't deserve it, he thought.

Everything I did, I did for us, he always said in his head before bed.

"The Lord asks you for an act of contrition, child."

Clarke took a deep breath and said, "O my God, as you are good to us all, I apologise that I have sinned against you. And with the help of your grace, I will not sin again."

Clarke didn't know whether this was true. There was something about his tone that made Avner believe Clarke was being true to God and — more importantly — himself. He could sense it. However, it tickled Clarke's mind that Avner wasn't being true. He was normally known for his wholesome words of wisdom and advice that had sent many down the right path. Tonight, his voice didn't seem as relaxed. Clarke could hear in the priest's voice the disturbance he may have felt. The voice almost seemed put on.

Father Avner would then go on to speak the words of absolution:

God, Father of mercies, through the death and resurrection of his Son, has reconciled the world to himself and has sent the Holy Spirit among us for the forgiveness of sins; through the ministry of the Church, may God give you pardon and peace, and I absolve you from your sins in the name of the Father, Son, and the Holy Spirit. Amen.

2

It was after the sun had set, and after the lights shone on the field of Thomas Hill High, when the school football team and their opponents were in the final five minutes of the match. If Valeland Robins attempted to shoot — with the score still being 0–0; a constant back and forth game — and if Eli didn't save the ball from hitting the back of the net, then it was game over for the Hill Magpies.

The battlelines had been drawn eighty-five minutes prior, on the first whistle. Both teams excelled in the annual football tournament. If there were seats, the crowd would have been sitting on the edges of them, the pitch also being brightened by the flashlights of parents' phones. Half of them couldn't wait to see that winning goal, while the other half couldn't wait for that winning save.

Eli stood in goal, his eyes following the ball wherever it had been kicked. He bent his knees slightly and spread his arms, ready. In practice, this is what he had been training for. But in reality, it was evident that his nerves had got the better of him. Usually, Lisa would give him a strong pep talk before the game, calming and motivating, but that wasn't the case tonight.

Whenever Eli saw that the ball wasn't coming closer, he took odd glances at the roaring crowd, standing in their warm jackets. Lisa was not where she would normally be; in her place, supporting him, was Kelsey Evans. Her brown hair blew in the increasingly strong winds. As much as he loved Kelsey being by his side, an event like this just didn't feel right without his mother there to witness. He refocused on the game and retained his stance as the clock began to count down from three minutes.

Eli rubbed his hands together for warmth. The cold had got to him, like it had the rest of the players. The sky had been cast with a wave of black clouds, blocking the shining moon.

But Eli was certain he wasn't letting the cold distract him now, for it was his time to shine.

The striker for the Valeland Robins made his way through the defensive line-up swiftly, leaping over attempted tackles while keeping the ball steady, until it was only the goalkeeper remaining.

"COME ON! SHOOT!"

"SAVE IT!"

Miss it in practice, it's okay. You can just try again. But miss it in the big game—

"And the entire school will hate you," Eli said aloud.

That single piece of brutally honest advice had not bothered Eli since the day Aaron had said it during the final practice, before the only other time the Hill Magpies had made it to the final. Eli had been in goal that day, too. But he had just shrugged at the advice.

It had been during practice, back when Aaron was still around, that the team had been split into two and played against each other. Eli always stuck with being goalie, for it was the only position he didn't get substituted. The last time they reached the final, Eli had a bad case of the flu. But Aaron was star striker almost every game. Eli never forgot how he would shoot for the goal. He would run up, inhale, and once the boot hit the ball...

"Eli!" shouted Kelsey suddenly, above all the cheering.

He didn't see the ball coming.

At one moment, the Robins' striker had been running up, and Eli was ready to catch the ball and be the saviour of Thomas Hill High's plummeting P.E department. But in the next moment, his mind went blank. He wasn't there; the atmosphere felt tingly, and in the striker's place was Aaron.

And, as if it never happened, the final whistle went, and Eli lay flat, looking up at the passing black clouds, not knowing what had just hit him.

The ball, that's what had hit him.

His fellow teammates and Kelsey came into a fuzzy view. Seeing more than ten heads towering over him at once didn't help Eli's state. They didn't appear happy. Kelsey was the only one helping him up.

"What happened, you idiot?" snapped Daz rhetorically, frustrated, his usually spiked hair now messy from the October weather.

"Did we win?" asked Eli drearily, only staying up through Kelsey clutching onto his arm.

"No. We did NOT win," said another teammate. "Knew you would ruin this for us," he added under his breath.

All of the team continued to glare at Eli, who still wasn't able to communicate properly. His eyes looked in different directions, unclear which way was straight ahead, and his legs melted every time Kelsey assumed he was stable.

"Thanks a lot," added the player sarcastically.

"*Yeah.* Thanks a lot, mate," spat Daz.

Nothing more was said about the game that night, to Eli's knowledge.

Daz and the other team members marched to the changing rooms, leaving Kelsey and Eli on the pitch. Eli's first thought was that of wondering if his fellow teammates were proud of his performance. Kelsey still had to keep her hurt boyfriend steady, although he was beginning to regain a stable mentality; he knew a bag of ice would help with the bump on his head.

"Okay?" asked Kelsey.

"Think so," Eli said, firmly planting his feet on the ground to regain his stability. It was then that he knew which direction was straight ahead, second glancing at the Magpies coach shaking hands with their opponents' coach. He then looked Kelsey in the eyes, a thought popping into his mind. Should he tell?

"Kelsey…"

"Yes?"

"I—"

"Eli!" shouted the coach as he jogged over to the couple. "What happened, son?" The coach resembled a gorilla, his hands the size of those oversized foam fingers fans used to get when attending a sporting event.

Eli shrugged.

"You've been like this for ages. What's up?"

Eli felt pressured to tell both his girlfriend — who knew vaguely what had been happening — and the coach — who knew absolutely nothing — the truth revolving around Clarke, Aaron, and the fire. All he could do was look away into the distance, at the school buildings.

"Look, I think it's best you take some time off," advised the coach.

"I think so, too," agreed Kelsey. Kelsey knew Eli wanted to talk, and that something was going on — and it wasn't because of the ball being shot into his head. "I'll take care of him."

The coach nodded, and Eli, as much as he wanted a say in the decision making, knew it was the right thing to do.

Whether he had suffered a head injury or not was unanswered, for Eli promised he was fine with ice and paracetamol before bed that night. But what *had* been answered, after the game, was that Eli would end up being the most hated guy in Thomas Hill High, as if he had slaughtered an animal, and wouldn't be welcome at the square tables any more.

3

The flashing blue lights of the fire engines didn't distract Josh and Anna from studying on Anna's bed that night.

Everything about Anna's room was pink. The lamp cast the pair's shadows on the only white wall in the room, and helped them see the books they had spread across the bed. They sat with their legs crossed, trying to hide their constant staring at one another in an attempt to actually focus on revision. But they couldn't.

Yes, perhaps the room had a bit too much pink, but that didn't bother Josh. What did bother him, was whether he should make his move or not. His decision would define the feelings each of them had experienced when in the presence of one another since Josh's first day at Thomas Hill High…

Passion and lust.

Their eyes met again.

They repositioned themselves onto their knees, thinking the same thing. Both of them desired the fireworks that would go off when their lips met for the very first time.

Josh had tried numerous times prior to get Anna alone — sometimes in school, sometimes at the bus stop, or even in the park — but none of those times seemed to be the *right* time. Maybe now was that time.

They scooched closer to one another, Anna pulling her bushy hair out of her face, Josh preparing by beginning to shut his eyes.

Anna's eyes began to shut, too. Their lips almost met.

This was it.

Yet, one mistake was made in that moment; Anna opened an eye.

She yelped, leaping backwards.

"What's wrong?" asked Josh, shaken by her action.

She wasn't dreaming this, was she? Josh was the one on the bed, not Aaron. Aaron was dead. Dead… right? Not there, lips ready to meet hers. There had been many times, back in Year 7, when that had happened, but that was the past. That didn't matter, anymore.

Memories suddenly returning to stun her, Anna had to take a set of deep breaths.

Josh didn't know what to do. He looked around the room, split between staying and leaving. It was then that he began to hear stomping up the stairs.

"You need to leave!" Anna ordered hysterically, clutching her chest.

"But—"

"JUST GO!" Anna pointed at the bedroom door, which had been swung open by her mother — whom Anna had clearly inherited her bushy hair from — and Josh didn't argue, clearly confused as to what he had done wrong. "Please."

Anna's mother let him squeeze past, hoping that nothing unimaginable had occurred between them. She continued to look at her daughter, who continued to take deep breaths.

She didn't attend to her, but reminded her, "That's what happens with boys. I thought you learned after that Smith boy. They distract you. I've had it for twenty years with your dad." They heard the front door slam shut, shaking the house. "I'll get you some water."

She left, leaving the door ajar.

Anna had begun to regain a steady breathing pattern, her head stinging as she tried to comprehend what had just happened. If it was just her mind playing tricks, then it wasn't funny. What happened years ago, when they would sneak off behind bushes and school sheds, were memories that couldn't be forgotten.

I know we didn't end on good terms, she thought. *But why me? Why now?*

She, like most of the town, still mourned Aaron's loss, as it was early days since the funeral. Even though it had been two years since they had split, Anna had been mourning the death more than she expressed to her friends.

4

Darkness covered Jason's room; his laptop screen was blank. He sat there, shouting "yes" every time Gemma had asked if he were okay as she heard pure silence from his room. Nothing was on the screen, but Jason still felt he was looking at something.

The laptop sat on his knee as he leaned against the headboard of his bed. Pressing a button, the laptop shot a white screen into Jason's eyes. It stunned him for a second; he had to blink back his sight. Pushing his glasses up his nose with a single finger, he began to type, as if it were natural. Unknowingly. There was no plot, no characters, no narrative; he just typed.

For Jason Rayne, inspiration came from many places, but mostly films and real-life experiences. After what he and his peers had been through in the past two months, he thought he'd take a break from the story for the competition and write something new and true — not forced and unreadable.

5

I felt like I was home, even though I wasn't. The sight of the school computer staring back at me that night, after all the students had left for home, was like being in a room of fresh air. I could write, and I was free from reality.

That morning, Mr Burnen secretly promised me the space after school hours, for he knew my desires. School was tolerable, but Mr Burnen always covered for me when I intended on getting some actual work done.

"Got him for detention," he would explain to the passing teachers.

"Again, Jason? That's nearly every week," teachers would say.

Although every teacher who said this exact thing said it with suspicion, especially when it started to become a tradition, but they never second-guessed my true intentions on one day getting noticed for my talent.

The hours of writing way after the gates should've closed turned into spending nearly every lunch and break seated at the very exact laptop in the open classroom of Mr Burnen.

"Look at him," students mocked, along with sniggers.

I would tend to just block out the noise, but it raised a fear within me. Rather open about what I wanted to do, nobody believed it; seeing me write in school was just a way for those non-believers to mock me for the dream I apparently was never going to achieve.

But this day was different. It seemed quiet, perhaps too quiet. That was until I heard...

"OI!" The voice sounded like it came out of a megaphone. "What're you doing, Jason?"

Here we go, I thought, rolling my eyes, preparing for the mocking to resume.

"Nothing," I replied reluctantly.

"Doesn't look like nothing. Tell me."

The tone had been turned down, more sincere than any other person who bombarded me with rhetorical questions that I knew I shouldn't answer.

"Writing," I admitted.

"Oh right. That's cool." I looked up from the screen and glanced upwards. To my surprise, it was a kid who I'd only known up until that point from my French class. This kid was Aaron Smith. Apart from that odd girl who appears whenever she wants, Aaron was the year's tallest student. Even when he leaned over my chair, the significant height difference was still as clear as day. "What's it about?"

Glaring up at him, I saw he had a similar pointed nose like that Brandon kid who I also didn't know too well at the time.

His ears were like an elf's, pointed and perked as if listening to everything that happened around town.

"Don't know yet."

And it was from that one meeting when an unlik—

6

The phone buzzed suddenly on the window sill, disturbing Jason's inner peace. He had been in the moment, in the zone. Rolling his eyes, he expected the caller to be unknown, but his eyebrows raised and he had to clean his glasses to make sure he was reading the phone correctly.

"Brandon? What's up?"

It was like Jason didn't know how to begin a conversation, for it was rare he would get a call from anyone that wasn't his mother.

"Yes…"

Brandon sounded breathless, as if he were in the middle of a sprint.

"Slow down…"

With the phone in between his shoulder and ear, Jason shut his laptop and gently placed it on the floor as he swooped off the bed.

"What?" His eyes widened. "Where?"

Switching the lamp on, Jason continued to listen.

"Okay. I'll be there."

The call ended, and Jason stuffed his phone in his jean pocket. He chucked his coat and shoes on, causing rattling thuds as he ran down the stairs, before leaping off the third step.

"Jason? What are you doing?" called Gemma from upstairs. Running through the kitchen, the dining room, and into the porch to the front door, he didn't respond. "JASON!"

As the door slammed shut, Jason heard his mother's growing irritation at his lack of response. But he knew that if he mentioned anything about meeting Brandon, Eli, Anna, and Kelsey, she wouldn't allow it, despite risking her punishing him with a curfew time.

"Jason!"

Gemma ran down the stairs, searching the entirety of the ground floor. Jason was nowhere to be found. He had left her perplexed.

Jason, not wanting to fuss around with buses, ran the entire way to their rendezvous point.

He had his suspicions, but he never dreamed that they could be true.

7

10 Minutes Earlier at Central Church

"Is there anything else, Father?" asked Clarke, triple-checking that he had cleared himself from the committed sins.

The touch of wine red was not visible by this point, as the setting sun had vanished beyond the horizon, and only candle light lit Central Church.

On the other side of the confessional, where the priest could not be seen, he uncharacteristically rolled his eyes. Father Avner typically kept his anger within him, not expressing it, even in the booth, where he was hidden from view.

"Well… there is just one thing," he said.

"Yes. Yes, anything, Father. What do I have to do?"

There was silence once more. Clarke anticipated an answer — perhaps to believe as hard as he could, or maybe pray a couple of times a night.

The priest's side of the confessional creaked.

Clarke began to pant and sweat. But it wasn't through anticipation.

"Pray," whispered the priest.

When Clarke heard no more, he began to rise from his seat, pulling the curtain away from the confessional.

"Wait!"

Clarke sat back down immediately.

"Pray. Pray God have mercy on your soul," added the priest deeply.

"What?"

And with the sweat running down his face, panting like a dog, he heard footsteps leaving the confessional, raising confusion. There was also the added smell of smoke shooting up his nose...

8

As if in an exam, Chief Pattison sat in silence as he scribbled on forms sent by Madam Mayor; forms he couldn't avoid. The rest of the floor, he noticed, when glancing up from the forms, was empty — all the employees who would sit at their respective desks had left for the night — apart from the receptionist, and Deputy Ton.

"SIR!"

Chief Pattison heard the call from his office; it had come from the door which opened onto the stairwell. That door swung open, and the deputy ran past all the office desks and computers without a second glance. He knocked rapidly on the glass of the chief's private office.

"Sir, it's urgent."

The chief rolled his eyes, slammed his pen on the desk as he rose, and held the door open for his deputy.

"Sir—"

"What is it? I'm busy here."

"You need to come with me."

The deputy gestured for his boss to follow him, but Ton didn't budge from his position at the door. "It's Central Church."

Don't tell me, thought Pattison.

He didn't need Deputy Ton to finish his statement to know what had happened to Central Church. The reports had come in across all Castlehead services; police had to barricade the intrigued — and horrified — crowds from the scene as the fire department battled the flames and had to find a way to stop the bell tower from collapsing onto the roads — and possibly some pedestrians.

Not only were they over the limit, speeding through traffic and red lights, but the police cruiser had reached the maximum on the speedometer. At least, that's how it felt.

When they pulled up at the scene, it was like Lucifer had broken loose from the depths, unleashing a terror unlike any other. As Central Church blazed, crying could be heard from the bystanders. People were passing judgement about the cause, and *those* kids were there.

Chief Pattison had jumped out of the car as it was screeching to a halt, with the deputy parking diagonally in the middle of the road. The chief ran towards the steel barricades and to the C.C.I.D officers who had arrived in an attempt to restrain the audience from getting close.

"Is everyone safe?" he yelled to a rookie officer holding a woman back, blocking out the aching sound of sirens.

"As far as I—"

A short, plump woman screamed, pointing at the main entrance. All in attendance turned their attention, and a series of screams and cries followed. The heavy doors had collapsed off their hinges onto the cemetery grounds, where the crowd stood.

Pattison squinted, for he was sure what the crowd cried at was a smoky silhouette of a figure in the church.

Clarke had taken in a lot of smoke. Avner was nowhere to be seen.

Clarke's vision was disrupted by the smoke and flames. The stained-glass windows had shattered onto the ground, and crumbs of ancient stone began to fall; soon becoming rocks, and then boulders. He was on his knees, searching for a way out.

Looking around, he had thought on instinct and saw a possible exit. He crawled to the glowing light; from the same direction, cries could be heard. For him, they were cries of hope. But to those watching Central Church burn, they were cries of grief for one of the town's oldest buildings.

As the ground shook every time a boulder dropped, Clarke failed to rise to his feet. The constant hacking had made him feel faint, and he felt like he was melting.

"SOMEONE GRAB HIM!" he had heard, having no strength left in his body. Clarke was only feet away from the exit to safety.

"NOW! BEFORE HE DOESN'T MAKE IT!"

Pattison saw Clarke collapse, face down, and he ran forwards as forceful cries of "No!" and "Don't do it!" were chanted on the grounds.

As he entered the church, aiding the fallen Clarke, Pattison was relieved to feel his pulse. He struggled to wrap Clarke's burnt arm around his shoulder, as he too began to take in many puffs of smoke, filling his lungs. The chief groaned as, unable to pick the citizen up, he dragged him outside.

Clarke didn't know he had been gently placed onto the grass. He could hear faint cries for help from Pattison.

"Get an ambulance!" coughed Pattison, giving desperate chest compressions to the lucky survivor. "Come on, stay with us, Clarke."

Amidst the carnage were Jason, Anna and Brandon, poking their heads out from behind three separate graves to catch what was happening right in front of them. The fire gave all three of them a funny feeling as they watched, as if the glowing mix of red, yellow, and orange lured them into a trance. It was Brandon who alerted the other two that the ambulance was arriving as, out of the corner of his eye, he made out flashing blue lights and a large shadow resembling a van turning the corner onto the street.

"Imagine, not even a month after his son's burial and the town may have to arrange another Smith funeral," whispered Jason.

Brandon and Anna nodded as they continued to watch on; two paramedics hopped out of the vehicle and pushed through the crowd to the entrance of Central Church while another two appeared from the back with a stretcher. They lowered the stretcher for the other two to help manoeuvre Clarke onto it. The medics noticed, as they squeezed their way back through the crowd to the ambulance, that Clarke was drifting in and out of consciousness.

Pattison followed behind, hoping that the compressions had at least helped a little.

"What'd we do now?" asked Brandon. He saw Jason slowly rise, like he was eager to either escape without being spotted or inch closer to the scene for a front row view. "Jason," he hissed.

Jason crouched down and headed to the side wall where the entrance to the grounds stood. Gesturing for Brandon and Anna to follow, Jason noticed their unsure faces as they crept to his position. Like a game of Hide-and-Seek, they snuck out onto the main street without being detected.

The three rose and stood up straight, acting natural, watching the paramedics lifting the stretcher and Clarke into the ambulance. The doors slammed shut, and the ambulance drove off. The fire hydrants remained, and the blaze had thankfully begun to be tamed by the remaining firefighters.

"All right! Get back!" ordered an officer.

The small group of officers holding the crowd back from the blaze ushered them out in a calm manner. But Jason, Anna, and Brandon continued to watch on from the street.

"Come on, nothing more to see," another officer said, noticing the frozen three.

Jason looked past the officer, watching Pattison talk to Ton. More aggressively than he had intended, Jason then pushed past the officer and walked towards the chief and deputy, who continued talking. Quickly walking in the opposite direction, was a figure with a zipped-up coat, as if they didn't want to be seen there. The coat was only waist length, and Jason noticed that this figure was wearing priest robes.

"Father Avner?" said Jason.

The man barged past the teen, leaving him speechless. "Watch what you're doing," he added. This surely wasn't typical of Avner.

The priest froze, his head bowed and hood blacking out the entirety of his face. All Brandon and Anna saw was the tip of his nose and faint lips.

"No," said the hooded priest. "Watch what *you're* doing."

Avner proceeded to walk up the road without another word.

Jason walked back to Anna and Brandon, eyes fixed on the priest, who vanished into the dark distance. After that weird confrontation, Jason thought it would've been best to stay away from the chief and deputy for now.

"Come on, leave!" the officer ordered again.

Jason, Brandon and Anna had forgotten for a second that he was still standing there.

"... isn't going to be happy about this," said the chief down the road. It was this that caught his and Deputy Ton's attention. They looked towards the sound of the overlapping voices, and gathered that three students were rebelling against an officer's orders.

"They need to leave!" yelled Ton.

It was when the officer slid out of view that Chief Pattison saw that Brandon was with two of his school friends. In the night, it wasn't possible to see Brandon's face turn a guilty red. He forcibly turned Anna and Jason around, and they walked away from the dying scene.

"Why are we leaving?" asked Jason, feeling Brandon's hand pressed against his back.

"I can't let the chief see me."

Like the hooded priest before them, they descended into the distance, leaving only the chief and deputy on the street, and the remaining fire crew to wipe out the remains of the flames.

"Sir, isn't that—"

"Yeah," snapped Pattison, stroking his moustache. "Friends of Aaron."

Interesting.

All three teens, upon returning to their homes that night, received extremely serious interrogations revolving around where they had been and why.

After the game, Eli and Kelsey had headed back to Eli's grandmother's, bewildered by the amount of missed calls and voice messages they had received from Jason a minute after the game had ended.

The chief tossed and turned all night trying to glue the pieces together. Another fire? Is Clarke recuperating well?

Why were Brandon and that bushy-haired girl and glasses-wearing boy there? All these questions, yet still no answers - only interpretations.

9

There was still the scent of smoke in the air. The fog that appeared the next morning made it difficult for the drivers to see further than five feet, and the Central Church grounds had been closed to the public for the foreseeable future. But that wasn't going to stop the curious Jason from finding answers of his own.

Unable to see a clear way in, Jason looked around for a moment to check if he was in the clear. A bin next to the front entrance of the Central Church grounds acted as a ledge for Jason to climb on, giving him leverage to jump over the wall into the cemetery.

The mist gave the graves an eerie feel, as if something was going to jump out. The stone pathway up to the church crunched under his feet, despite his effort to creep around.

Jason stopped in front of the entrance, which had been barricaded by fresh guardrails and police tape. Although his view had been obstructed by the misty atmosphere, the windows of the church had been boarded up by planks of wood, and, beside the entrance, were piles of earth, wood, glass, and ancient stones from the crumbled building.

Jason wanted to take it all in.

"First Clarke's workplace, now Central Church," he said to himself.

He stood, mesmerised by the carnage caused; not just to Central Church, but everything Castlehead had suffered through up to this point.

"I figured you'd be here."

The sound of the voice had taken him by surprise. He turned around and saw a faint silhouette stepping towards him. It wasn't until they were nose to nose that Jason realised it was Maria, the girl he had met when investigating the first fire that had involved Clarke in some form.

She was as intimidating as she was beautiful; her lips were as red as ever, but she had covered herself up in a large, furry coat.

"As did I," he said confidently, proud it was the first thing he said to her without blushing.

Maria stood close to Jason as they took in the building together. The fog started to clear, and soon they were able to see that the bell tower on top of the church looked like it was dangling by a piece of thread. Newly added scaffolding steadied it, but the bell itself wouldn't function until the tower was completely stable.

"I told you I'd be back, didn't I?" said Maria.

The pair glanced at each other for a split second and then back at the tower.

Jason nodded, secretly biting his lip, trying to hide his wobbly knees.

"Yeah. But I just don't get it."

"Get what?"

"I don't get what Clarke did to deserve this. I mean, he told me about the health inspection a week before the fire, and now he's lying helpless in Oak Castle Hospital, literally on the brink of death."

"Well," started Maria, "can you not think of anyone with a personal vendetta against him?"

Jason pulled a distorted face as he attempted to think if there was anyone out there who may have wanted Clarke dead — or to suffer. But, on instinct, there was no one.

"No, don't think so," he breathed, shaking his head.

Maria sighed, her face serious, and said, "Can I give you a bit of advice? I'm not being crude, just honest. Don't get involved in situations you know nothing about."

That piece of advice did make him think about what he was doing there. Jason would explain that there was something in him that told him to get involved; there was a desire to get roped into a mystery that he wanted to solve. Perhaps it was because of watching too many movies, he didn't know, but this wicked town and its stories intrigued him and made him dive into all the madness the town could not be free of.

"There's something about this town, Maria," he added. "If anything gets released from this town, past those hills, then all this madness is what Castlehead will be remembered for. And I want to help it be free before I go. It's daft, but I love this town. And if we can somehow rid it of its bizarre curse, then this town may for once have a good night's sleep."

The air had finally cleared, the sun breaking through the clouds, and there was a tiny glimmer of blue sky breaking through, too.

Jason and Maria's eyes met, and both felt a sudden exciting tingle spread through their veins.

Suddenly, Maria broke eye contact. She awkwardly looked around as her hand dived into her coat pocket, leaving Jason to feel stupid at the idea that they might have been having a moment just then. Jason glanced down and saw that Maria had pulled out a small white card from her pocket.

"Well…" She grasped the card with both hands. "If you want to get out of this town…" She handed Jason the card, and allowed him to intake what it read. His mouth fell open, and he couldn't have felt more proud as well as shocked and terrified — terrified at how a certain few might react.

"The headmaster wants to arrange an interview with you. Just call the number on the card. You don't have to say anything, just think about it. We're sure you'll fit right in."

She quickly pecked him on the cheek before leaving.

Jason watched as Maria headed to the front gates of the grounds, which she opened and slipped through. After she had left the grounds, cutting off down the street, Jason gently placed the card in his jeans pocket and headed in the same direction. He shut the gates behind him, and began the walk home.

Don't get involved in situations you know nothing about. You'll fit right in. Don't get involved in situations you know nothing about. You'll fit right in. Don't get involved in situations you know nothing about. YOU WILL FIT RIGHT IN.

A reward is given to someone who is recognised for an act of honourable service, effort, or achievement. It is given when one does right, not wrong... not sin. Jason had been rewarded with a chance to set off on the course he had always dreamed of, whereas Clarke had been punished for his sinful ways — no matter how long ago they might have been. These were sins Clarke couldn't erase from his memory, and he had hurt those around him — not just God.

Things were changing. For better and for worse.

CHAPTER FOUR

Halloween

1

The day was finally upon them; children and parents alike would pull out everything in their arsenal to make sure costumes terrified the innocent and intimidated those who handed out jack-o-lantern buckets of sweets and chocolates. Halloween, today, is a fun time for families to scare themselves into mischief. Halloween, originally, was a time when the Celtics would stand around bonfires in costumes to ward off ghosts.

A ghost, however, can be many things. But the one constant that ghosts feed off is memory. And ghosts from Clarke's past might've been catching up with him quicker and quicker with every passing day. But whether that ghost set Thomas Hill alight on Halloween Night was up for the C.C.I.D to decide — not the group who witnessed the blaze.

2

Monday, October 28th, 2019

For Chief Pattison, the week began like any other. He woke up and arrived at the Castlehead Criminal Investigation Department building for 6:00am. The "Good morning" he always greeted the receptionist with was more of a groan, but she always replied brightly, informing him that papers had been placed on his desk upstairs.

A great way to begin the week, he thought, chuckling at himself as he walked up the stairwell to his office. He could see the stack of papers on his desk from the entrance of the offices, and, with every step, he dreaded what the mayor — he assumed — wanted him to sign now.

It wasn't, however, just the leaning tower of papers that he dreaded, but also what would come with this week. On Thursday night, Halloween, children and adults alike would be knocking on their neighbours' doors, hoping for the best kinds of treats — not tricks. There was a tingle that tickled the back of his head as he sat down; it was the thought that this week would be the perfect time for this arsonist to strike again.

He flung the papers to the side, the top two sheets floating down to the ground, and held his head in his hands as he leaned his elbows on the desk.

Stop thinking about it. Nothing will happen this week, it'll all be fine. I mean, what else is there for this person to set alight? Nothing, right? Unless… No… They wouldn't aim for Oak Castle Hospital. STOP THINKING ABOUT IT! Nothing bad will happen. All those dying patients at the hospital… Stop! What if Clarke isn't recovering? Oh, for God's sake, just st—

"Sir, can I come in?"

Pattison jumped back in his chair. The pile of papers flew all over the room as Deputy Ton continued to knock on the office door.

As he rolled his eyes, Pattison gestured at his deputy to enter.

He did so, slowly closing the door behind him. "You all right?"

"Fine," breathed the chief, lowering himself off the chair and onto one knee, beginning to pick up the scattered papers. "What's up?" he added quite impatiently.

The deputy stood nervously, saying, "I just wanted to ask about Central Church and what happened *that* night."

Pattison stacked the papers back on the desk, unaware that he left loose sheets that had landed in the far corner of the office.

He sat back on the chair and was ready to listen.

"I saw your face when you noticed those three kids that night."

The chief's face dropped.

"Would it be my place to suggest that they may have something—"

"I hope not!"

"They were friends of Clarke's boy, you know."

"Yeah." The chief nodded. "I hope to God Brandon's not getting involved. He was good friends with Aaron." Then the thought popped into his head. "Do you know if Clarke's okay?"

"Well, I think he's—" Pattison rose and stormed out of the office, leaving Ton bewildered. "Wait! Where are you going!?"

"Hospital!" he heard from the doorway to the stairwell.

The thud of the closing door echoed through the office, and Ton could make out the rapid stomps his chief made down the stairs. He leapt across to the office window that revealed a majestic view of the town. With his hands pressed against the glass, the deputy looked down and saw the chief run out of the building to a parked car. It pulled away a moment later and sped off down the road.

With a look of uncertainty on his face, the deputy thought there was nothing better to do than finish retrieving the sheets of dropped paper that Pattison left. His back cracked as he slumped over and reached, and cracked again as he straightened up. There was a sudden urge of temptation; he looked around and then glanced at the papers that he knew he shouldn't be looking at.

Ton's grip on the sheets tightened, creasing them.

What has everything come to?

3

There was no panicking about confidential papers at Thomas Hill High that morning; instead, Principal Keeper and the rest of the staff brought their full attention to the school's annual Halloween extravaganza that would be taking place at the end of the week.

It was ten minutes before the first bell when Jason, Josh and Anna walked into the main hall. Jason was in between Anna and Josh. Jason and Anna simply ignored the commotion occurring around them in that moment. Ladders stood high at the sides of the hall, some with teachers almost toppling off the top rung.

"What's all this?" Josh looked up and around the hall, watching members of staff hang streamers and lanterns from the ceiling.

Jason and Anna continued walking across to the round tables in the far corner.

Josh took the preparation in, thinking about how his former school had acted as if celebrations didn't exist. "Are they arranging a party, or something?"

The double doors to the Musical Theatre department swung open like flaps and the trio watched a train of Year 7 students with a variety of pumpkins; big, small, fat, thin. It was glancing at the different-sized pumpkins that made Josh catch on to what was happening.

"Every Friday on the week of Halloween, the school has a party. You come in wearing costumes, and staff vote for the best," explained Anna, brushing her beehive hair out of her eyes.

"Games, prizes, sometimes a disco," added Jason as he cleaned his glasses with his jumper sleeve.

Josh nodded intelligibly. But when the bell rang and the three had made their way to class, Josh couldn't comprehend why the school would celebrate a holiday about ghosts when Castlehead residents had begun to call the mastermind behind these 'accidents' — as Madam Mayor called them — a ghost too. Jason had gone on to suggest that maybe Keeper had decided, after everything they had been through, the students needed a night to forget the harsh reality they were living in…

4

Oak Castle Hospital stood tall, surrounded by a full car park. It had taken Chief Pattison ten minutes to find a space near the entrance. Even with no zebra crossing, drivers allowed the chief to cross. Walking onto the path, Pattison entered into a speed walk and then a hurried jog as he entered one of three reception areas of the facility.

There were no empty seats in the waiting area, and the stern-faced receptionist — her hair in a neat ponytail — typing away on her laptop, ignored Pattison slamming his hands onto the desk. The phone rang and she picked it up, clamping it in between her shoulder and ear.

"Oak Castle Hospital, how may I help you?" she said. "Yes…"

Pattison tapped away on the desk as if it were a drum, making odd glances at his watch. He leaned in and whispered, "Excuse me."

"Uh-huh… Yeah." Her giggly tone as she listened implied to the chief that the receptionist wasn't arranging an appointment. "No way!" She burst out laughing, slouching back in her office chair, and stopped typing. "He really is… No, he is."

"Excuse me," repeated Pattison firmly. He glanced over at the waiting area and saw that the receptionist's casual conversation — and the level of volume she was speaking at — had turned all of the patients' heads. One elderly man with a walking stick by his side, his arm in a cast, shook his head at Pattison, insinuating this was the service that the ONLY medical centre in Castlehead provided.

"Look, I'm in a hurry and I need to see one of your patients."

"Okay… Oh, my God, definitely catch up." At this, the receptionist rolled her eyes as if she didn't mean what she said. "Bye, bitch," she added with a laugh before removing the phone from her ear. She looked up, finally aware of the chief's presence, and asked formally, "Yes? Can I help?"

It was like the phone conversation had never happened.

"Oh, hello Chief."

"Hello," he said irritably. "I need to know which room Clarke Smith is in. It's quite urgent."

The receptionist shifted her focus back to the computer screen and began to scroll through a spreadsheet. It became clear to those waiting that the chief was visibly impatient; he tapped away as the sound of the clicking mouse increased his level of irritation.

"If you go down that hall," she said suddenly, rising and pointing to the chief's left, "and turn right at the very end, it'll be the first door on your left. Room 32."

Pattison nodded and started to walk down the hall, but stopped at the sound of her voice again. "Just to say, he might not be awake, and… someone else is visiting him, too."

He didn't turn back and continued to walk down the hallway, making way for constant stretchers and wheelable trays with needles and capsules of medicine laid out neatly. Signs overhead directed doctors and patients alike to different rooms and wards. But all the chief had to do was head down to the very end of the narrow hallway. Turning right, he immediately glanced to his left, and saw the door labelled ROOM 32.

Before knocking, he decided to press his ear against the door when the hallway was clear. No sound came from inside the room, giving the chief the initial thought that the receptionist had made a mistake when stating there was another visitor. He turned the doorknob, slowly opened it, and froze at the sight; what Pattison saw peering over Clarke's unconscious body could be described as a black ghost, only revealed by the shining lights in the room.

"Sorry, I didn't know anyone was in." Pattison acted natural, beginning to close the door, only to freeze again when the ghostly figure turned. Reality kicked in and Pattison realised that this was no ghost; it was a person wearing nothing but black: hood, jeans, shoes, everything.

"Are you okay?" he asked soothingly to the figure.

The person bowed their head as if guilty of something, clutching the rim of their hood as they darted past the chief and out of sight.

Pattison watched as the figure knocked into a nurse but didn't stop to apologise.

Under the hood, Z barged past doctors, nurses, and patients in a hurried attempt to escape before the chief got suspicious about who she was and why she was there. If she had revealed herself, she wouldn't have been able to form an excuse.

It was at the time of Z leaving undetected through a fire exit that a bemused Chief Pattison pulled a seat across from the back of the room and sat himself next to the sleeping Clarke. Peering over him, he noticed that Clarke had support from an oxygen mask which looked heavy over his mouth and nose. He appeared lifeless, and the chief cautiously tried to look over him for anything that might be classed as a clue. The life support machine beeped; it was the only sound in the room. In all honesty, the chief was disappointed that Clarke hadn't awakened…

That figure, he thought, hoping to spot a twitch or a slight hint of movement from Clarke. *Here to finish the job?* It was plausible. This figure enters the hospital cosplaying as a fake relative of Clarke's, comes in and looks over him, either tempted to bend the mask's pipe or shoot him with a suppressor so nobody would know what happened. *Or maybe not*, he doubted. It was just an interpretation. Then again, the C.C.I.D hadn't brought in any suspects.

5

"Can you give any more factors of—"

The school bell rang for lunch.

Rubbing the pen off the whiteboard, the Maths department leader, Mrs Alnder, heard the scraping of chair legs on the smooth, wooden floor. Like every other student in the school, this Year 9 class was eager to get in the lunch line.

"Before you go, remember homework is due next week."

The students rolled their eyes in unison, apart from Brandon and Anna, who joined Jason in the narrow hallway. Despite, on countless occasions, being told not to run, it was still a race to the finish. Students shoved past, as Jason, Anna and Brandon didn't care for food. They followed the students into the Musical Theatre department, and the crowd grew as more students packed into the area, adamant in their mission to get food.

The three were able to breathe when entering the main hall, like reaching the light at the end of the tunnel. They shifted across to the far corner where *their* table stood, and noticed Josh had beaten them to it, munching away on a crispy chicken burger. As Jason and Anna joined him, Brandon pulled a chair from another table to sit down, too. He looked invested in the possible conversation that was about to start.

But nothing was said.

They all looked around awkwardly, waiting for something to happen. Anything, just anything to break the icy silence. It was clear that they knew what they wanted to speak of, but the possibility of anyone — or everyone — butting in loomed large, and made them talk discreetly.

"So…" said Jason, shrugging.

"What?" asked Josh with his mouth full, chomping on his last bit of chicken.

"Are we just gonna ignore the fact that we were in attendance at the fire?"

Brandon uncharacteristically slapped Jason on the arm, with Anna shushing him too.

"Jason, lower your voice," whispered Anna. "You're going to make it sound like we caused it."

Josh's smacking lips paused and his eyebrows raised. He carelessly tossed the napkin that came with the burger on the floor, and leaned in.

"Josh…"

"Yeah?"

"After you left, Brandon messaged me saying that Central Church had been set alight. The three of us met and… yeah, Aaron's dad got caught in the fire," explained Anna. "Luckily, no one else got hurt, thank goodness, but—"

"It could've been a massacre," snapped Jason bluntly.

"We saw the chief saving Clarke, Aaron's dad, and it just doesn't add up," added Brandon.

"No, it doesn't," said Jason. He rubbed his chin, thinking about that night; the fire was surreal, but the way Brandon had avoided Pattison seemed peculiar. "Talking about the chief…" Jason turned to Brandon, "What was up with you when we saw him? I saw the way you lowered your head, and the look he gave us."

"More specifically, the look he gave *you*," added Anna.

All eyes were on Brandon now. He gulped, but then every head in the hall turned as the double doors swung open. All heads turned back to their respective tables, brushing off the sight of the hooded girl storming through the doors, ignoring everyone in her path as she made her way to a cut that took her to the P.E fields.

Brandon, Jason, Josh and Anna watched intently as the figure quickly shrunk into a single speck the further away she walked.

"I haven't seen her all day," muttered Jason, wondering where she had been hiding up until that moment. He shook the ludicrous ideas out of his head. "Anyways, yeah, we—"

Only the four heads turned as the doors swung open again, this time revealing a group of chattering kids, like a group of seagulls, with similar hairdos, dark — presumably *trendy* — clothing that would commonly be worn just around the house. The last of the seagulls to walk through was the familiar face of Eli. Noticing the three staring kids with whom he had rarely interacted with — until now — and the lad he once considered a friend, Eli stepped back from his clan — which, to many, seemed out of sorts. He walked towards the stunned group and sat himself down.

"What?" He chuckled at the wide-mouthed faces. "I know what's been going on, so... might as well find out the truth." That was his way of admitting that the thought of Aaron had cost him and his team — who still held a grudge — the winning save. "I get that the fires and death could be related somehow. I guessed when Clarke's workplace was on fire."

"It's true," clarified Brandon suddenly. "I heard the chief and my mother talking the other day. That's the theory, and it seems to be true."

"Why would..." Jason didn't finish the question before he figured out the answer. "Why didn't you want anyone to know?"

"It's no big deal. *Uncle* Derek Pattison tells his sister everything," he explained with a single sigh of relief. "But not his nephew. I didn't think the thought of us knowing about the fires came to mind, but since Central Church, I think he may have joined a couple of dots together."

Anna pulled her bag onto her lap, pulling out a sheet of paper with her class schedule on it. Jason, Eli and Josh looked at each other as if they were thinking of the perfect solution. Brandon, however, looked up as his eyes followed a figure walking slowly past them, her hood hiding her face. She was about to enter the Musical Theatre department.

But she didn't walk further than the door, freezing, with one hand on the wood.

Brandon switched his focus to the group again.

The bag the White Shadow wore appeared to be new, as she pulled it off her shoulders and rummaged through it on the ground.

"Then, why don't we lure this guy out before your uncle suspects anything of us?" suggested Jason.

Eli nodded, adding, "Good idea, that. I finish practice every day at five. You could hide somewhere until then, and we meet on the field."

Overhearing this plan, Z rose, whipped her bag back onto her shoulders, and walked through the double doors confidently.

Although the eyes and pale face were hidden, the villainous red lips smiled for the rest of the day.

The plan to meet on the school fields on Thursday, Halloween night, had been set. This obsessed guy was going to be caught, one way or another. Knowing they had a plan, the group, even Eli, felt determined. That night, he would inform Kelsey. The excuses made to the kids' parents would vary, but what they weren't ready for was the surprise that would come with their arrangement.

That would be Halloween, though. They still had Tuesday and Wednesday to get through first.

6

Tuesday, October 29th, 2019

Jason had risen with the sun that morning. He had tossed and turned all night with the range of emotions he felt about the card Maria had given him earlier that month, which he had not moved from his bedside cabinet, and now, with the plan to catch the attempted murderer of Clarke, was something he had not felt before. It was his opportunity versus his possible demise. They were both risks, and he was going to take them head on.

Although waking up at sunrise, he didn't get out of bed until 8:30am, for the previous afternoon he had informed Thomas Hill High that he wouldn't be in until a bit after the first bell as he had an important appointment which he couldn't postpone any longer.

Showered and dressed by the time 9 o'clock had come, Jason paced back and forth in his room, biting the corner of the card nervously.

"Jason!" he heard from the kitchen. "You're late!"

The daunting thought of at some point revealing this to his mother had finally returned. His fingers began to shake as his stomach felt queasy. If only he had been given an inkling of what was going to happen.

His phone sat on his bed. Jason kept glancing at it, hoping it would implore him to pick it up and make the call. He hesitated, like checking if a plate was hot, but then grasped the phone fully. Gulping as his reflection glared back at him through the blank screen, Jason released the card from his mouth and held it with his other hand.

"Just do it," he urged.

"JASON!"

"Two seconds!"

"Two seconds never bloody comes! You're late!"

"All right, all right!" he said.

Jason sighed and rolled his eyes, knowing he couldn't hold Gemma off any longer. He would just have to wait until after school.

Despite reassuring everyone numerous times throughout the day that he was okay, his looks of disappointment and frustration were evident, and it was like talking to a bulldog. It was rare for teachers to question his ability to work, and every time the same question was asked, Jason increasingly lost his patience.

7

It had been said, notably by the rowdy Year 7s who decided to stir the pot of problems just for the sake of it, that Clarke had been in a coma and was unlikely to survive. Once these rumours had started, Father Avner decided to take matters into his own hands and check on his favourite blessed child, as he secretly considered him.

He arrived at Oak Castle Hospital at 11:30am, the beginning of lunchtime visiting hours, in his usual cassock. Beloved by most of the town, wherever he would go, people would politely greet him with a nod and a question of how his day was going. Looking around at the sick patients waiting to be checked, Avner openly blessed all in the reception before the receptionist noticed him.

"Can I help you, Father?" she said with a smile, ignoring the ringing of the phone.

Leaning over the counter slightly, he asked in his common soothing tone, "I was wondering if you could tell me which room Clarke Smith is recovering in?"

"Yes, of course. Room 32. Turn right down the hall, and it's the first door on your left."

The receptionist turned her attention to the computer as Father Avner started to walk down the hall, but then rose from her seat quickly to make sure he heard: "He might be a bit woozy as he's just woken up."

The priest had brought a smile to everyone who passed him as he walked down the hall, giving the doctors, visitors, and the sick some hope. And that was all Clarke could think about when opening his eyes to the bright light of his room: hope...

He had hoped he could've changed his ways before everything that had happened to him.

The knock on the door a few minutes later gave him a fright. He made out, through the blurriness, the door slowly opening and a figure appearing, growing as it stepped closer, until they were overlooking him, in clear view.

"Father Avner," he breathed, smiling as much as he could before it hurt. "I'm so—"

The father raised a hand, forcing him to stop. He saw in Clarke's eyes, which were barely open, the pain he was feeling. It felt like a tide, coming back every so often, the impact in which it returned gradually increasing.

"It's no one's fault. Central Church is under reconstruction, and services are returning to schedule soon."

Clarke smiled again, but a wave came over him suddenly; the smile faded like the pain would soon afterwards, and he squirmed in the bed to get more comfortable. More appropriately, it could be said that the pain would return as regularly as the fires Castlehead had suffered through.

"And... how are you since the fire?"

The priest sandwiched Clarke's hand in between his own, and said calmly, "I prayed. I prayed that you were okay, my child, and anyone else who was there that night."

Remembering what he could, Clarke sat up a touch and looked at Avner with confusion. All he could recall on the spot was thick smoke around him and cries of terror coming from outside the church... and the last thing Father had said to him: *Pray God have mercy on your soul.* Avner would never say such a thing, would he?

"I wasn't talking to you that night," he said as the realisation kicked in. He slipped his hand out of the priest's, and sat upright.

"Clarke?"

"Before the fire..." Avner leaned into a whisper. "I went to the church for a late-night confessional. I hoped you'd be there."

"But Clarke, you know that I only do morning serv—"

"I know, I know." Clarke stroked his hands through his hair with a sigh.

Avner watched as a look of unfeigned fear and panic appeared on Clarke's face. "I think whoever caused this fire is trying to get to me… or worse. They're trying to kill me."

"I'll talk to the chief. I'm sure the C.C.I.D will manage to figure something out."

8

The students of Thomas Hill High raced out of the school like a tidal wave when the final bell of the day rang. Brandon, Anna, Josh and Jason returned to their respective homes, whereas Eli and Kelsey walked along the streets together — not in the direction of Eli's mother's. Lisa had meant what she said the night both she and Eli found out about Kelsey being pregnant; not giving her a chance to explain that, for one, it wasn't Eli's, and, two, she hadn't kept it. However, it was Lisa who — straight after kicking them out — had told her mother, Melanie, to welcome them with open arms.

Meanwhile, Jason was returning home with a secret of his own. He had simply lied to his mother, stating that he had just slept in, still with no idea when he was going to bring up the Desmond School for Creative Arts, or would have the guts to do so. But he was eager to get this call done as quickly as possible.

Jason stepped into his house, taking his shoes off on the doormat, keeping his bag and coat on. Walking through the dining room into the kitchen, he heard the vague chattering of characters on the television in the lounge.

"All right, sonna?" roared a powerful voice with a strong Geordie accent.

"Yeah, Grandad," Jason had replied, his attention on the bag he had put on the kitchen counter. Rummaging through it loudly, he heard his grandfather irritably turn the television volume up, to the point where it sounded like it was blasting out of a cinema screen.

"Where is it? Where is it?" Jason said to himself, chucking loose pens, pencils and papers onto the counter.

Everything had been tossed onto the counter by the time Jason felt the smooth card at the very bottom of the bag, which felt like he had his arm in a tight well.

"What are you doin' in there?" asked Jason's grandad, turning the volume down a bit just as Jason pulled out the card with ease.

"Er… nothing."

Jason piled all of his papers, books, and everything else he had flung out of his bag together before dumping it all back in it as if it were a rubbish bin. He darted up the stairs with the open bag in hand, stomped along the landing speedily, and slammed his bedroom door shut.

"Come on, come on."

Dumping the bag on the floor beside his wardrobe, the card was in hand. Jason clutched it intently, continuously glaring at it as he began to pace back and forth like he had that very morning. Again, like that morning, Jason then took hold of his phone and glanced at both objects. He froze, something clicking in his mind: *Pacing isn't going to get you anywhere. And this opportunity won't last forever.*

A single deep breath was all he needed to calm himself; an exhale of doubt and an inhale of relaxation. But once he had started to dial the number, his hands uncontrollably began to jitter, and he felt his body sweat. It was only eleven easy numbers; how hard could it be? Wait! Did he just misdial? He breathed, relieved. No, he hadn't.

Pressing the phone against his ear, gently placing the card on his bedside table, it felt like his heart had skipped a beat every time it rang. That was until…

"Desmond School for Creative Arts, my name is Jane, how may I help you?"

"Y-ye-yes... H-h..."

"Hello?"

Another deep breath ought to do it...

"Yes, hi," Jason started, silently pounding the air. "My name is Jason Rayne. I received a card with this number from, I presume, one of your students. Maria?"

"Jason Rayne, Jason Rayne, Jason Rayne... Ah, yes, here you are..." Jason could hear many voices in the background and the sound of this Jane woman typing. *"You have an appointment booked in with the headmaster on Friday the 8th of November, is that correct?"*

The statement struck Jason by surprise. He couldn't remember booking an appointment. But then it clicked. The memories of sneaking into both Central Church and Clarke's workplace came back, and all Jason did was smirk. *Maria*, he thought, *you star.*

"Yes. Yes, that is correct," he answered confidently.

"Fantastic. You'll be expected to arrive at 12 sharp with the card and identification."

"Great. Thank you." He tried to sound as calm as possible, for he was ready to burst with joy. "Is there anything else I need to know?"

"More information is on our website."

At that moment, Jason expected Jane to end the call right there, but she added, *"We expect nothing but the best. We're all certain that you'll deliver."*

"Thank you," he whispered as he heard the front door close downstairs.

"Goodbye now."

"Goodbye."

Jason immediately tossed his phone onto the bed and leapt in the air, overjoyed with how simple that had turned out to be. Maria had gone out of her way to make sure Jason had an appointment at the school, and Jane had said they expected nothing but the best from him. Was it certain that he was going to end up there by September? The hints and generous acts said so. He also recalled his and Maria's first encounter, vividly remembering her stating that the Desmond School for Creative Arts had had their eyes on him for a while. Finally, he was being recognised for his talent, not for being *that* kid at school. And, maybe, just maybe, for the first time in a long time, Jason would feel welcome.

All of these joyful thoughts felt so real for once.

This isn't a dream anymore, he thought. *This is actually happening. Come next year, I will be attending—*

"Jason!" came a cry.

The voice was like the squawk of a bird. The sound of his name snapped Jason back into reality, and he realised he was sitting on the edge of his bed, with Gemma.

"Yeah? What?"

"I said how was school?" asked Gemma, aware of her son's dreary face as if he had just been awakened from a dream that felt so real.

"Fine."

He rose suddenly, catching the card in the corner of his eye. He snatched it from the bedside cabinet and cupped it in his hands.

"What's that for?" asked Gemma.

Jason gulped, knowing he had backed himself in a corner. She loomed over him, trying to get a cheeky peek at the card. There was something on it, but she couldn't make it out.

"Son?"

Jason looked up and made eye contact with his mother, who sat patiently waiting for an answer. He knew the consequences of lying, and the wrath he would have to face if he decided to keep this charade up any longer. It was the right time; they were alone, with no distractions, the card was in hand, and it was plausible that Gemma might genuinely be proud of her boy. But he just couldn't muster up the strength.

"Nothing. Just a piece of card I found," he muttered, quickly stuffing the card into the cabinet drawer where everything he didn't use lived.

"Oh, okay." Gemma rose, ruffled her son's hair and began to leave. "We're just going to order takeaway for tea, yeah?" she said in the doorway.

"Yeah." Jason nodded, and Gemma closed the door behind her, smiling.

Phew. He was finally in the clear, and all he could do was fall back onto the bed with his hands on his head, his eyes closed, and instantly regret not telling his mother about his plans.

Jason lay on his bed in silence until he felt the mattress vibrate. Sitting up, he picked up his phone and saw that it was a message from Josh asking if they were still sure about Thursday.

Having been in the moment, Jason had forgotten their plan to lure this maniac out on Halloween Night, of all nights. The plan was ludicrous, thinking back on it. But if anything was going to end this person's reign of terror on Castlehead, it would be gathering Aaron's friends in one place, wouldn't it? The group thought there was a chance it could work.

9

Thursday, October 31st, Halloween

The sound of faint children's laughter coming from outside Oak Castle Hospital brought the first smile to Clarke's face since the last day he had recalled smiling, with Aaron. An orange street lamp light shone through the window, bringing light to Clarke's room, where he sat upright in his hospital bed — which by now was becoming less and less comfortable by the hour. Though, on the upside, he retained a regular breathing pattern without support.

Outside was a grand spectacle of skeletons, monsters, jack-o-lanterns, and — best of all — sweets that the patients were missing out on. The full moon, which was the biggest many claimed to have ever seen, shone a light on the streets below, outshining the street lamps, and cast thousands of shadows of pedestrians on the pavement and road. Spider web streamers hung from the walls of houses and bus stops, and it was impossible for any cars to make it out on the roads through the heaps of children and parents that packed every street one turned onto.

Clarke sighed, reminiscing about past Halloweens with Aaron. Aaron hadn't enjoyed this time of year, Clarke recalled, since one year when he had split from a group of friends he was with and ended up bumping into a clown who towered over everyone in the area. Clarke envisioned the night vividly, on the couch snuggled up with his wife, enjoying a marathon of horror movies, until they heard the door open and slam shut, and wailing. Aaron couldn't catch his breath, drowning in sweat, describing this clown who held a pitchfork in one hand and a flaming torch in the other. The fire reflected in the clown's eyes, and his teeth were like the fangs of a vampire, blood dripping down the side of his mouth, and his puffy yellow suit with large orange pom poms — which acted as buttons — let off a hellacious smell of alcohol and smoke.

"It was like that clown from that movie," Clarke remembered his son crying out as he wrapped his arms around his mother, her chin resting on his head. "I ran. I screamed.

The way he looked at me. I thought he was going to drop the torch on—"

Think about the good Halloweens, Clarke.

But Clarke couldn't. He felt like that night scarred all three of them. From then on, Aaron had spent every Halloween in his room until he started attending Thomas Hill and knew he would be in a safe environment at the school's Halloween extravaganza.

That's better.

The door clicked open suddenly. Clarke snapped his head towards the open door and saw Chief Pattison standing in the doorway, unsure whether to enter.

"Chief, I thought visiting hours were over," said Clarke.

Chief Pattison didn't say a word until he reached the foot of Clarke's bed, holding his belt like a cowboy in a western.

He looked Clarke directly in the eyes, his hands on the frame of the bed, and said quietly, "I've spoken to Father Avner."

Both men took occasional glances at the open door in hopes of not being heard.

Pattison continued. "The doctors think you'll be out in the next week. Two at the very latest. But, until then, I've arranged for 24-hour security on the premises. And when you've recovered and are back home, we'll talk about further arrangements to make sure you're safe."

Clarke nodded, agreeing to the terms — as if he had had a choice.

They stared at each other for a moment before the chief added, "If whoever's causing these fires is out for your head on a stick, then this'll most likely be the next place they'll hit."

This would just be another instance when a member of the C.C.I.D would assume wrong.

10

Although Kelsey had agreed to the plan, Eli could tell by the look on her face that she wasn't too thrilled. Of course, she was grateful for Eli's grandmother for allowing them to stay after the event with Donovan breaking into Lisa's home, but what she had been through over the course of the past two months, she felt, was more important than spending a night on the school's field. Nobody had brought up what the couple — mainly one of them — was going through. She was suffering, and she didn't deserve it. Eli knew he had to be there for his girl, and the pair had come to terms with the abortion. That he could handle. But this was on another level of insanity.

"Are you sure?" Eli asked for the fifth time, tying his shoes.

"Yes, I'm fine."

They had been sleeping in the spare room of Melanie's home. The two single beds made one double as they found a way to join them eventually, thinking at one point that the beds were embedded into the ground.

Eli walked around to Kelsey's side of the bed and put his arm around her as she was doing up her laces. The door to the wide landing stood on her side of the room, and Kelsey kept looking out, her head turned away from Eli. She clearly wasn't fine. As much as Donovan had treated her like a piece of crap, he was still her father. Seeing him in that state the night before was an image she would never be able to erase from her mind.

Eli pecked her on the cheek before ushering her out onto the landing, down the staircase and straight into the sitting room. The plan was to sneak through the sitting room, sneak out of the house, and make their way to Thomas Hill High. What actually happened was that Eli and Kelsey froze when they reached the bottom step.

"Hi, son," said Lisa. She must've snuck in, because she had been nowhere to be seen not five minutes before. Melanie sat next to her, silent. "Where are you off to?"

"Jason arranged a movie night for us all," said her son.

Lisa and Melanie's eyes widened in surprise, struck by Jason actually inviting Kelsey along, too.

"Can you come and sit down?" asked Melanie.

Kelsey sat next to Melanie as Eli sat next to Lisa.

"We've talked, and we think it'll be best if you move back in with your mother." Although Melanie was looking at Eli, she was talking to Kelsey as well.

"Yeah, I do." Lisa looked past her mother and to Kelsey. "We know you must be going through a lot with your father, and I know your family ran out on youse when Donovan began to—" She paused, noticing the look on Kelsey's face, and Eli hanging his head down. Best not to bring that up. "Anyways, I want us to get through this. I should've listened when you were trying to explain the situation. Please come home."

Kelsey let out a little smile.

"Okay," she mouthed.

11

"Where are they?" growled Jason, looking at Josh and Brandon on his left and Anna on his right. They shrugged at him in unison. Jason rolled his eyes.

The group continued to walk; they were curious as to why the street in which Thomas Hill stood hadn't been brightened by the lights and joyous horror mood of Halloween. No lights were on in the houses opposite the school, and it was around this time that everyone apart from Jason started to get cold feet.

"Come on, Eli," he said to himself.

They continued down the street until those black gates, which looked more menacing in the night, came into view.

Jason's phone vibrated.

"Is that him?"

"Yes," replied Jason, looking down at his phone, pushing his glasses up his nose. He explained, "He said they're walking down the street now."

He stuffed his phone in his pocket and joined the rest of the group in looking around for two stick figures in the distance.

"There!" acknowledged Anna, pointing down the street where she spotted the two figures they hoped for.

The group entered a run to the gate, and the figures copied them. They grew closer and met directly in front of the gate. They all looked at each other; Jason at Kelsey's zipped-up leather jacket, skirt, high boots, and leggings, as if it were a night out; Eli at the new kid, Josh, who was in a red puffer jacket; Kelsey at Anna's miraculous hairdo. But then Eli, stuffing his hands in his tracksuit bottom pockets, saw that Brandon had his attention on the gate.

They copied him, looking at the gates that led to their school. It was like the gates to Heaven — or Hell, depending on which group member you asked — and past them, the dormant school. No lights were on, creating an eerie atmosphere for those that wanted to enter, and for those who were already there. Brandon, however, had his eyes on the gate lock. A chain kept the gates shut.

He held the chain in his hand — it was like holding ice — and examined it further.

"It's been tampered with," he whispered.

Brandon's next move was one that none of the others expected from a guy who spent most days studying in his room, his large nose in a book all day, and who wouldn't dare to think about doing something that would be seen as rebelling against the rules.

He yanked the chain off the closed gates and they slowly creaked open, inviting the group in. "See?"

The chain had been passed around the group like it was a parcel as they stepped forward into the Thomas Hill High grounds.

Eli carelessly chucked it on the ground, with no sense to perhaps shut the gate and put it back, in case someone saw it and grasped that people were trespassing.

Jason led the way down to the main entrance, but they all knew they weren't getting in through the main hall. They saw a cut to their left which led them down a cobbled pathway to the sports hall.

But they didn't enter that building either.

Walking around the building, onto the field on which football and outdoor activities were taught and played, the group was stunned to see, in the very far corner, a large pile of firewood.

A figure appeared from around the other side of the building, totally unaware of the group's existence. They watched keenly as the figure walked up to the pile of wood. Jason hushed the group before anything could be said and spread his arms out so no one could take a step closer.

It might just have been the person they were looking for.

Not a moment later, the wood burst into flames, sending the figure tumbling to the ground. Smoke as black as the night sky floated into the air, causing the group to cough and hack. Alerted, the figure turned their head. The group didn't budge as the figure rose to their feet and walked towards them.

"Wait," said Eli. "Is that—"

Z stopped in front of them and asked in a firm whisper, "What are you doing here?"

With her typical black hood on, it was like she was in camouflage with the night. Not even her pale skin was visible, despite the fire burning in the background. She was like a faceless spirit.

"What are *you* doing here, lighting bonfires?" asked Eli, matching her firm tone.

"Are you the one who caused the fires?" asked Josh, who stood at the back of the group.

"Course I'm not," spat Z. "I do this every Halloween."

"Ah, so that's why the lock on the main gate had been tampered with," added Brandon.

Z displayed confusion, and Brandon could tell he was wrong. The rest were beginning to feel worried and predicted in their heads what Z was going to say.

"I don't enter through the main gate," she said, now looking as worried as the group in front of her.

"Then... why—" started Eli.

It was the fire alarm.

"Oh shit," cried Kelsey. *I knew I shouldn't have come here. Got too much on my mind.*

The smell of smoke grew around them, and it had occurred to the group of Year 9s that the fetid smell wasn't just coming from the bonfire Z had lit.

In a huddle, they all ran back around the sports hall and up to where the main building stood. Nothing. For a moment, they looked at one another, none of them taking notice of the main gate.

"Look!" alerted Brandon, pointing up at the sky, noticing smoke in the air which was clearly coming from...

"The Science department!" cried Anna.

The blaze that greeted them after running through the main hall, entering by the side fire exit, left them stunned silent. No one could actually believe that their plan had partly worked. The arsonist had actually struck again. And Clarke wasn't a victim. But how? How did they know? How did they find out?

More and more questions, yet not a single answer — only theories.

Smashed glass was scattered across the ground, and it looked like the fire was moments away from spreading across to the other departments.

Just as Jason had pressed his phone hastily against his ear to alert the fire department, Anna stopped him and said, "Do you hear that?"

The group remained stone still. Apart from the crackling of the burning building, they heard nothing. Listening more intently, however, allowed them to make out the ever-growing sound of relief in the form of sirens.

Like dogs at the sound of food being poured into their bowls, the group raced back through the main hall, which hadn't been touched by the blaze, and out of reception. Instinctively, they ran up towards the main gates, only to find the lock wrapped around them, as if it hadn't been touched. The girls cried for help as the boys rattled the gate. And it was at the point of Z suggesting they try leaving the way she had entered that they were greeted on the other side of the gate by blinding headlights.

Among the commotion, a car door slammed shut and a black silhouette came into view. The panicking kids weren't able to make out the person — but they had a good guess — until they stood in front of them, the gate acting as a barricade between the group and the law.

Chief Pattison, disappointed, took off his police hat and asked rhetorically, "How did I guess?" There was no time for crude remarks. Noticing the looks on all of their faces — specifically Brandon's ashamed glare — the chief added, "Don't worry. We'll get you out." But not without a sigh and a shake of the head.

Nothing was said on the police escort home. After all, they did have the right to remain silent.

"Yeah, we've also got the right to free speech," said Z.

Everyone was surprised that Pattison ignored the sneer that came with the remark. Whatever the chief was insinuating with that sly question when he saw the group at first glance didn't matter to the parents. Jason was grounded for a week upon his return home; Eli and Kelsey weren't allowed out either; it was forbidden for Josh and Anna to see each other until Christmas; Brandon begged his uncle to let him off easy. And knowing what his sister was like, Pattison didn't exactly tell her the truth about her son, stating that he had bumped into him but on their way home had been informed of another fire.

Upon returning Z home, Pattison had been warned by the members of Sunvalley Park to never touch her again. Walking into the trailer to a sleeping grandmother was a huge relief. But that didn't stop her from describing what had happened. Like always, she sat by her grandmother, gently stroking her hand, hoping that she was listening.

"I wasn't going to come home tonight," she said. "It's Halloween, *Abuela*, and I still do the family tradition. It was cut short, though. I set the bonfire, but the school itself caught alight." Listening to her grandmother snore was like hearing someone choke. But Z continued. "It's like a ghost is roaming freely across the town, and it despises everything about it, for some reason. I know we don't like the town, after what it did to us all, but at least we aren't the ones terrorising it."

That's it, a ghost. And a ghost can be many things; a memory, a wish, a figment of your imagination. We're back where this chapter started. On Halloween Night, 2019, Thomas Hill High had been the next victim in the series of fires caused by this ghost. It was unknown if this was it for the foreseeable future, but now, staff and students alike were on guard. Rumours of the seven kids being the cause of the chaos spread quicker than the fires themselves…

Only the Castlehead Criminal Investigation Department had the power to decide.

CHAPTER FIVE

Interrogation Month

1

The Castlehead Criminal Investigation Department, November 2019, was the location of the six interviews in relation to the unexpected fire of Thomas Hill High and Aaron Smith's death. Interrogation rooms under the C.C.I.D building were in rare use, which resulted in the suspects walking into an area of large dust particles, spiderwebs, and mouldy walls. Each room was identical — a single table with a chair on either side — and soundproofed, keeping everything said within the rooms... Well, that's what Pattison claimed to the press on countless occasions.

Suspect one: Eli Lee, born July 1st 2005.

He sat at the table in the interrogation room with his hands cupped together and his head hanging in shame. From afar, it looked like he was praying, but he was too humiliated to be in this sort of environment. Eli wouldn't look Chief Pattison in the eye when he sat down.

Pattison leaned back in his chair, as if relaxed, and waited for Eli to spill.

"Come on, son. You've got to give me something," he encouraged.

But Eli wouldn't budge.

It was odd for Pattison to see a confident kid like Eli in this state; he expected him, by looking at his clothes and overpriced trainers, to be the kind of lad to strut around school with his *cool gang*, hand-in-hand with his girlfriend who — like all the other popular girls — looked like models in their prime and, at first glance, appeared four years older than they actually were. But that wasn't the case when staring at Eli from across the table. What Pattison saw were Eli's true colours, the boy under the mask. Pattison felt an inkling of sympathy for the boy, but he couldn't let his guard down.

"You're not in trouble. All I need to know is what happened the week of Halloween."

The chief knew about Eli and Kelsey, so perhaps he could find answers as to what happened on the Wednesday before that fateful night.

Eli looked up for the first time, but it still took a moment for him to compose himself. He took a deep breath and sat up straight, as if applying for a job. The mask appeared to be coming back on.

"It was on Monday," started Eli, "that we arranged to meet on the field on Halloween. Me, Jason, the smarties, and the new kid arranged it, to host a bonfire. There was no other place to have it, so…" It was when Eli couldn't finish the sentence that Pattison assumed Eli was simply spitting out anything that popped into his mind. "That weird girl, Z, was there before us."

Pattison's ears pricked up.

"Then a minute later, that's when the school was set on fire."

"Hmm… Okay. So, Z was already there?"

Eli nodded and said, "But I don't think she did it, because she had already gathered firewood for her own bonfire."

"Hm-hm."

Eli looked at the chief's serious face.

"Is it true that you're not living at home at the moment?"

The sudden change of subject took Eli by surprise. *None of your business* was what he wanted to say, and would have, if his group had been there, too.

"We're back now," he argued. "My ma had kicked us out because of some… *family issues*." Eli took Kelsey into account, knowing she may not have appreciated him revealing — even to the law — that her father had broken into Eli's home drunker than Kelsey had ever seen him and revealed that she had been pregnant with Eli's child, even though they all knew the truth. "But no, we're back now."

"We?" Chief Pattison just needed the clarification from Eli that 'we' meant him and Kelsey, even though he knew already. "Is it not just you living with your mother?"

"My girlfriend, Kelsey, is living with us for a while," Eli clarified.

"Ah right. I suppose you know of—"

"Aye, I do."

"And what is it that you know about that Wednesday?"

Eli scratched his nose and admitted, "Nowt much. Kelsey wanted to go back to hers to pick up a few things, but she came back all like shaken up. I don't think she remembers much about it, but all she said was that she had found her father dead on the couch."

The chief leaned forward, and asked, "What about Aaron?"

"Aye?"

"What'd you know of him?"

"Weren't exactly best pals, but he was the star player on the school's football team until he went missing. Nice kid, though."

"Was he?" There was a hint of sarcasm in the chief's tone now. "I'm pretty sure you're aware of it, too, but it's come to our attention that Aaron's death and the fires might be related. And finding you and your friends at the scene of Thomas Hill High has dug you a hole that you might not be able to get out of."

Eli hung his head again, his will to talk — and his confidence — lost.

"I'm going to put it bluntly: Were you involved in the disappearance, and eventual death, of your classmate, Aaron Smith? Because, fuelled jealousy is a good motive. You wanted to be top dog, but that pedestal was Aaron's, until he went missing, and then you took that mantle. But the guilt resides in you—"

"No, I didn't kill him!" Eli's face had gone red with pressure and frustration. It may not have been the answer Pattison was looking for, but Eli spoke with truth. "I didn't kill him," he repeated.

Pattison sat there, stunned at how furiously Eli had answered the question. He saw a single tear flow down his face, but he knew it wasn't a tear of guilt. It was sadness.

"You weren't exactly best pals, yet you miss him as if he were your brother," said the chief calmly.

Eli didn't reply, wiping his eyes with his fingers and his snotty nose with the palm of his hand. Pattison flinched at the sight. "You're free to go, son."

Eli immediately stormed out of the interrogation room without a word, hiding his face from Deputy Ton, who waited to accompany him outside where Lisa waited patiently.

One down, only five to go.

This was going to be a long month.

2

Suspect two: Jason Rayne, born October 3rd, 2004.

Today was the day Jason could change his life forever; one step closer to that ultimate dream of becoming a bestselling writer. Friday, November 8th, was here. Jason had secretly booked his train tickets to Valeland online a couple of nights before, but little did he know Chief Pattison and Deputy Ton would surprise him at his front door that afternoon.

"What time did you say you'll be back from Eli's, son?" asked Gemma from the kitchen, partly concentrating on drying the dishes.

"Later," replied Jason from the dining room, zipping up his bag and putting it on his back. They both had to speak louder than usual as Jason's grandfather was using a drill for one of the projects that he said he would get done but hadn't touched in weeks. "I'll text you when I'm there."

"Yes, please."

With his shoes on, red puffer jacket zipped up, and bag on his back, Jason walked to his front door with conviction. But all that positivity was drowned once he opened the front door and saw Chief Pattison and Deputy Ton standing there formally. Jason knew what was coming, and there was no way of getting out of it.

"Jason," greeted the deputy.

"Chief. Deputy. All right?"

"Son, we need you to come down to the C.C.I.D building for questioning." The chief wasn't asking. It was a demand.

Gemma appeared at the door.

"Morning, Gemma," he greeted.

"What's up?" she asked, holding onto her son's shoulders with a kitchen towel over her own.

"We need your son to come with us. All we need to ask are a few questions about why he was there when Thomas Hill was set on fire," explained Ton.

"Can't we just do it here?" asked Gemma.

Jason nodded pleadingly, but, to his disappointment, the chief said, "It's common procedure. Also, nobody is allowed to listen, apart from those in the room. Whi—"

"Will I be allowed in?"

Jason cringed at the thought. He knew his mother was only thinking of him, but he didn't want an interrogation room to be the place he finally revealed the many truths he had been hiding.

Both officers saw the embarrassed look on Jason's face.

"The interro… I mean, the interview will consist only of me and your son. You can, of course, come along and wait."

Mother and son had never ridden in the back of a police car together before. It was daunting for the pair, despite them not having been arrested. The chain-link that blocked them from the two front seats made them feel like animals in a cage. This certainly wasn't the seat Jason imagined being in when this day came. For a moment, he closed his eyes and saw himself sitting on a comfortable train seat across a table from two complete — yet kind — strangers. And on the way, he would look out the window at the beautiful countryside of northern England. Then he would hear the train driver announce that the next stop was Valeland, and a smile would beam onto his face as he knew he had made it.

But in reality, what he heard, in his mother's voice was, "Son, we're here."

Jason looked around. He was back in the police car. The chief and deputy opened both his and Gemma's doors, ushering them out and leading them to the C.C.I.D building. They entered a small reception area. Two leather chairs sat along the wall opposite the smooth reception desk, where a woman in police uniform was writing notes on probably an important sheet of paper.

She didn't glance up from her paper as they passed, heading towards a set of automatic double doors. Past the double doors were three separate hallways; one left, one right, and one straight ahead. Chief Pattison turned left, and Jason and

Gemma knew to follow as Deputy Ton allowed them to go ahead as he took the back of the single file.

Passing a series of doors, with the names of officers written on plaques, Jason wondered how long this hallway was and thought how hollow it seemed, as not a single word was said until they reached the end of the hallway, where a single chair sat staring at them aside a rusty door.

"You can wait here, Gemma, if you want." The chief presented the chair to Jason's mother and she sat politely.

"Come with us, Jason."

Gemma said, "See you in a bit, son."

The chief opened the door, revealing what looked like a never-ending stairwell. Jason looked at the ceiling and saw there was not a working light. What natural light there was in the hallway vaguely showed Jason which side the banister was on and how steep the stairs were, but once the door closed behind the three of them on its own accord, there was nothing but darkness.

With nothing in the stairwell but the clashing sound made by the steel steps, it was like walking down a bottomless pit, spiralling down forever.

They finally reached the bottom, and a series of dying lights flickered to reveal an area of mouldy walls and doors with broken handles, and there was the odd, faint sound of skittering and squeaking.

The last of the doors was the one through which Chief Pattison and Jason walked, entering a claustrophobic, concrete room with two chairs and a single table.

Deputy Ton had shut the door, locking the chief and Jason in. From within, it looked like the door had shut of its own accord, again.

The chief gestured for Jason to sit, and he did. Nerves were kicking in now, and, although Eli had messaged him to say that he had been interviewed, Jason had no idea what Eli had told Pattison. It occurred to Jason that what was said during that interview could be used against him. He had to be cautious.

Pattison sat more upright during this interview than he had with Eli.

"Where were you off to?" he asked bluntly, hands clasped together as he watched the suspect take off his jacket. "Were you meeting up with friends to skip school?" he assumed.

"I've never skipped. They know I'm not supposed to be in today." Jason leaned in closer, and lowered his tone to more of a whisper. "I was on my way to Valeland, because I had an interview at the Desmond School for Creative Arts."

"Where? Sounds made up."

"Only those worthy know of its existence."

As much as the chief nodded agreeably, Jason could tell by his vacant expression that the chief thought he was lying.

Pattison leaned forward, too, and said, "Told your parents? I've seen some of your stuff in the paper. Not bad."

Jason mouthed, "No."

Pattison processed this blunt answer, like he did during all of his interrogations — albeit only having carried out a rare few. He still claimed to be a master of cracking his suspects.

"And... how are you generally?"

"Fine," answered Jason with a shrug.

"Mam okay?"

"Yeah."

"Your dad, too? Have you heard from him since that business a few years ago?"

"No, haven't spoken to him since. This has been the first mention of him since, as well."

Chief Pattison raised his eyebrows at this. Before the case of the blood feud (that's what it felt like) that happened within the

Rayne family in 2016, the chief knew Jason to be close to his dad. When on patrol, he would spot the father and son together walking home from the park, sometimes Jason taking a ride on his dad's back, beaming with delight. They all played the part of one big happy family, so it was to the chief's surprise when Gemma claimed that Jason's father, one night, had left, leaving with all of Gemma's money and debit cards. Jason's father had denied all allegations, and it was at that point that Gemma found out he had lied about putting the house down on a joint mortgage. It was a case that spanned the entire autumn that year; it would've lasted longer if Jason hadn't sent his dad a voice message one night saying that he was a disgrace and he didn't want any contact with him. The next day, his father didn't show up to court. He had vanished from their lives.

"You know of Clarke, Aaron's dad?" The chief didn't allow the suspect to answer. "Of course you do, or you wouldn't have been there when Central Church went up in flames."

Jason gulped.

"I saw you that night. How do you feel about what Clarke has been through?"

"I can't imagine what he's been through, losing Aaron."

"Yeah, you can't, can you?" said Pattison seriously.

"What?"

"Let's not kid ourselves here… you miss your father. That father figure in your life." A grin began to appear on the chief's face. "Maybe, just maybe, the thought of not having a father in your life got to you and you thought that if you didn't have a father, nobody should. Especially those who had the best father-son relationships. Clarke and Aaron."

Jason sat there, not responding, not giving Pattison the pleasure. He knew what the chief was insinuating, but Jason wouldn't lie about something as serious as the death of Aaron and the attempted murder of Clarke.

"Lurking in the shadows, knowing everything and everyone just to write. That's a good character, boy."

It was a good character. But it was Jason. And sometimes, the truth can hurt. It was evident on Jason's face, for he didn't make direct eye contact with the chief for a whole minute, instead glancing at the floor and his trainers.

"You think I have something to do with Aaron's death?" asked Jason. He decided to risk it. He sneered, "Ask your nephew if I was in on Aaron's death. You know he was there, too."

Inside, Jason instantly regretted arguing with a police officer, but he saw the gaping mouth of the chief and became aware that he had made a valid point. There were two other people there that night, and that was something the chief couldn't take away from the case.

"Do you know who might have done it?" asked the chief, finally.

Jason shook his head, and then Chief Pattison freed him from the interview.

3

Suspect three: Josh Anderson, born April 18th, 2005.

Brandon was the one to accidentally inform his uncle of Anna and Josh's whereabouts in the following two weeks, but he had pleaded with the chief to let them off easy, as he knew Anna to be a girl who would never hurt a fly. Josh, on the other hand, still had a veil over him, despite two months of attending Thomas Hill High.

Brandon accompanied both Josh and Anna to their interviews, but left once Josh's had begun, despite staying for the duration of Anna's.

The staircase to the interrogation room creaked hauntingly, and the thought of entering more of a torture chamber than a simple interrogation room popped into Josh's mind.

The room smelled of gas, and it wasn't a light smell, either. It was clear that the smell bothered Josh throughout the interview; he was not fully focused on what the chief was asking and wasn't giving complete answers — nor the answers Chief Pattison desired. This was the interview that turned out to be the shortest of the six, and frankly the most disappointing.

"I need something more than what you're giving me," pleaded the chief, tiredly rubbing his forehead, trying not to grow increasingly impatient with the new kid.

"I don't know what you want," said Josh. "I moved here just before the school year started and didn't realise how messed up this town was until the first day of school."

"What do you know?"

"Mainly about that Isabella girl, and, of course, these fires and the death of this Aaron. I wouldn't have a personal vendetta against him. For goodness sake — I didn't even attend the kid's funeral."

"Then why were you at Thomas Hill on Halloween Night with your group of friends, the school that Aaron attended—"

"Because I got roped into it by Jason!" spat Josh suddenly. "I don't know what it is, but Jason seems to have this obsession with finding out who this crazed person is. I know he writes, so maybe he's looking for a story to tell. I don't know, but what I do know is that weird girl shows up out of nowhere and starts a bonfire."

"You mean Z?"

"Yeah, her."

The chief sighed, and said, "Look, kid, I know you're new and that you want nothing to do with everything you've been dragged into. So, I will let you go, but on one condition."

"Okay."

"If you hear anything else, or witness something that could be related to all this, let me know."

Josh nodded, accepting the condition, and left with the hope of this being the last time he was dragged into all this madness. He knew it wasn't going to be an undercover F.B.I job like in an action movie, which had him cross his fingers in the hope of just being a normal fourteen-year-old boy.

Suspect four: Anna Gardener, born January 2nd, 2005...

4

Suspect five: Kelsey Evans, born December 17th, 2004.

It was common knowledge that Kelsey had been through a lot, yet it wasn't until Kelsey's time to enter the interrogation room that Chief Pattison truly gathered how affected the teen had been by it all. He ushered her in as if with open arms, pulled a seat out for her to sit on and then sat down himself. There was an awkward silence, then the chief leaned across the table.

"Tell me how you are." Pattison spoke with a whisper, more like a soothing and caring therapist than the chief of the Castlehead Criminal Investigation Department. "Kelsey, tell me, please. With the information you give me, I can help you."

Kelsey spat, "I'm fine."

But the chief knew she wasn't; the trauma was written all over her face. "The shit that he put me through... I honestly couldn't care," she lied.

The officer sat back and watched Kelsey's every move; the way she hid her face with her hair made Pattison aware of her vulnerable state. She then began to irritably bite her nails, which made the chief cringe — though he tried his best not to show it.

"Nobody your age, or any age for that matter, should have found what you did." He respected that Kelsey had requested not to specifically discuss what had happened. The chief, however, did need to know what had happened when she had walked through that door on the Wednesday before Halloween. For all he knew, it could be a clue.

He leaned in again and asked after a deep breath, "What happened that night when you found your dad?"

5

Wednesday, October 30th, 2019

Who in their right mind would walk alone on the streets, in the pitch black? Especially in a town like Castlehead? That morning, she realised she had to pick a number of possessions up from the house in which she had been struck — and worse — many times in the past. As much as her stomach felt like it was filled with butterflies, Kelsey walked steadily along the streets to Donovan's house. How she would face her father after not seeing him since Aaron's funeral she didn't know, but she was going to enter strong, and not be the victim anymore.

"It's all right," she kept telling herself as she walked. "He might actually be happy." *Don't kid yourself.*

Seeing the houses on the street blanketed in darkness sent a shiver down her spine; but it was her father's house that stood out most of all. Unlike most of the houses on the street, there was no sign of anyone being in; no lights were on to implore her to knock on the door, and she stood at the small gate, debating whether this was such a good idea.

Kelsey took a deep breath and stepped forward into the garden. It was as she crept closer to the front door that she noticed it wasn't closed. Donovan was usually secure in making sure nobody found out what happened within that house three, four, sometimes five times a week.

There were scrapes on the door, specifically the lock and the handle.

Kelsey stood wearily, looking around in case anyone was watching, before creeping in. She stealthily walked in without a sound, shutting the door as best she could, despite it stubbornly rebelling and staying open just a touch. The door to the lounge was wide open... and that's when the atmosphere changed.

Everything felt cold, as if frozen in time.

Kelsey walked across to the couch and saw her father lying there, unconscious, his hands on his stomach. Yet, it wasn't until Kelsey stood over him that she saw he had something grasped in his hands.

She hesitantly got down on one knee and reached out for her father's hands, for what he was holding. His hands were cold as ice, like he had been kept fresh in a fridge for the past day. Donovan didn't react when his daughter's soft palms met his rough, wrinkly knuckles, though his grip was still very tight.

Kelsey plucked the item from her father's grip and stared at it; the label of a small tub stared back at her as she squinted to read what it said. The tub felt empty. It was then that she glanced up and saw her father's face.

She gasped. She wanted to scream.

His face was as white and cold as his hands felt. There was a vacant expression on his face, his eyes wide and not blinking. Donovan's lips had lost their pink pigment, which had been replaced with white... and a touch of blue?

Chucking the tub on the carpeted floor, she rose and dialled 999 for the Castlehead Criminal Investigation Department.

And that was all she could remember.

6

Present Day

"And then what can you remember?" asked the chief.

Kelsey couldn't help telling the story of that night without bursting into a hysterical breakdown, to the point where it actually hurt to cry. The table in between the suspect and officer had been covered with scrunched-up tissues, with one of the last remaining ones in Kelsey's hand.

"It was such a blur. I can't really remember," she answered, blowing her nose into the tissue and then rolling it up into a ball and tossing it onto the table. "I looked at the tub, and then that was it. I must've called you."

Throughout Kelsey's story, Pattison nodded like he was agreeing with what she was saying. She had, in fact, called the C.C.I.D, and they had brought an ambulance along with them, announcing moments after arrival that Donovan was dead.

"I'm sorry," she said. "This is the first time I've told anyone, apart from Eli and his mother."

Pattison leaned forward and said, "I actually wanted to talk to you about that."

Kelsey sniffed and the tears were finally gone. "I'm staying with them."

"And how well did you know Aaron?"

Kelsey sniffed again and said, "Not very well. I only knew him through Eli and the football team, but we weren't exactly friends."

"Okay, okay," said the chief, nodded lightly and glancing up as he stroked his chin. *That idea's out of the question, then*, he thought. "But why were you at Thomas Hill on the day of the fire?"

"Jason wanted us to try and lure whoever caused these fires out," she said, almost as a whisper. "There was nothing, until we spotted that Z girl."

Pattison nodded again, then allowed Kelsey to leave.

He heard the door slam shut and sat in the room by himself for a moment. His elbow rested on the arm of his chair as his head leaned on his hand. It was the thinking process that all officers had to go through when conducting interrogations; the chief needed to put the pieces together. And if all these interviews had one thing in common, Pattison gathered that it was that Z had also been spotted at the scene... and wasn't with the group.

The chief heard the door behind him click shut again, but he knew it wasn't Z entering.

"You okay, Chief?" asked Deputy Ton. The chief felt his deputy's presence looming over him, and he didn't answer straight away like Ton had hoped. "Sir?"

"We need to bring Elizabeth in."

7

Suspect six: Elizabeth, 'Z', date of birth unknown, surname unknown.

To the chief's surprise, Z didn't try to avoid going into the station for her interview. She claimed to have nothing to hide, so why would she attempt to escape the C.C.I.D when they showed up at Sunvalley Park unannounced during the last week of November? Z understood the park's residents' retaliation when they saw her being ushered to the police car, but before they did something that would lock them up, she told them to stand down.

The handcuffs weren't exactly necessary, thought Z when being shoved into the back of the police car. It was an interrogation, but the chief had acted as if it was an official arrest... like he had already made up his mind. Nevertheless, she didn't argue it.

As the residents of Sunvalley Park watched furiously as the police car took Z away, the girl in all black sat calmly without a word being said. This wasn't the reaction that Pattison expected at all.

By the time they had reached the Castlehead Criminal Investigation Department building, Z's hands were numb and the cuffs around her wrists had begun to dig into her skin. She pushed through the increasing pain, and although she needed help getting out of the car, she was still able to walk on her own. Still the chief insisted on pulling her all the way to the interrogation room as if she were a bag of rubbish.

Through all this, Z did nothing. This type of behaviour by the authorities is liberally exerted towards those seen as lesser; the minorities. Those at Sunvalley Park always received grief in Castlehead. Nevertheless, all those assumptions made by those who owned opulent homes (compared to the rundown caravans) didn't matter. All that mattered was that the Sunvalley Park residents knew the truth. It also didn't matter how hard they tried to turn the town's views around, because of one simple, continuous virus: Tabloids.

Chief Pattison uncuffed Z before they entered. She strutted in first, her hands in the pockets of her hoodie. From the chief's point of view, it looked like she was trying to grasp something. As she sat, legs crossed sophisticatedly, she revealed a cigarette and put it in her mouth, objecting the law. Her arrogance towards the chief clearly angered him, and Z couldn't help but let out a smile.

Pattison locked the door behind him, and sat down at the table too, leaning in close. It was like a staring battle. Who was going to break first?

The tension in the room made it feel more like a battle for dominance.

Z saw the chief biting his lip, and, with a grin, she leaned in and blew a streak of smoke in his face.

He didn't react. All he did was ask, "Why'd you do it?"

Z flung the remainder of the cigarette into the corner of the room and said, "What? Kill Aaron?"

The chief nodded, desperate for her reason.

"Easy... I didn't."

Pattison grunted.

"How is Clarke, anyways?" added Z with a snarl.

"He's home. Still having regular check-ups at the doctors but is recovering well," answered the chief with barely any interest.

"Good."

"Explain to me, then, why you were at the scene at Thomas Hill on Halloween."

Z said, "I set off a bonfire every Halloween on the field. You can ask the staff there. After everything they've done for me, why would I set the school on fire?"

"Funny you should say that, 'cause your attendance at Thomas Hill is the lowest of any student in the school's history. If they've done *so much* for you, why do you repay them by never going in?"

"My grandma. She's sick. Castlehead Council and Oak Castle Hospital would know about that, if they answered my goddamn calls instead of prescribing her meds that don't work." They were only making Willow worse. Z's tone grew passionately. "I didn't know the others were going to be there that night."

The chief rested his chin in his hand as his elbow leaned on the chair's arm, following up with, "Talking about the hospital, how come I bumped into you when I came in to see Clarke?" As he recalled, she had scurried off. "Hm?"

"I was... praying."

Pattison scoffed at her answer.

"I was praying for the Smith family, because they don't deserve what happened to them."

"Bu—"

"*And* I scurried off because I had to get to my grandmother." Then something clicked in Z's brain. "Actually, come to think of it… Why were *you* there?"

"To check up on him, of course."

"Or to finish the job?" Pattison's eyes widened, and his heart began to pound. "You're Madam Mayor's little puppet. So, let's assume you didn't start the fires but had a grudge against the Smiths and wanted to take the credit." It was as if the roles had been reversed. "I saw you find the body bag a couple of months ago. But I noticed that you didn't open it to see if it was actually Aaron himself. You just took it in, then it was the poor kid's funeral just weeks later. You—"

"ENOUGH!" Chief Pattison hadn't felt so much pressure since he first got appointed chief of the C.C.I.D. He rose, his chair skidding across the room. If he could, the chief probably would've flipped the table, like how a family game of Monopoly ends, and arrested Z right then and there.

The girl simply retained her cool and sat there.

"I understand that Aaron was close to all of you in one way or another, but do not — and I mean DO NOT — mistake you lot as the only ones who care about what happened to Aaron and the Smiths."

The chief watched Z slowly rise to her feet, and shockingly almost match his height, still standing at opposite ends of the table.

She placed her palms firmly on the table separating them, and whispered, "Whoever killed Aaron and started these fires is out for blood. Out for Clarke. And now… those close to him."

The chief was aware of the situation, but it was when he heard it from Z that it truly began to sink in.

As she walked past him, Pattison sulked, and it felt like his heart had sunk while his guts were almost in his throat. All in all, he was back at square one, and the case of Aaron Smith was now at a stale-mate. Nobody could predict how this was going to pan out.

CHAPTER SIX

The Countdown to Christmas

1

Interrogation month slid into December like skaters on an ice rink. Decorations were being retrieved from the attics of the many Castlehead households, and kids began to get giddy as they wrote out their wish lists for the one and only St Nick. This was a special time of year, and there was hope of this next month sucking all the darkness out of the town — even if just for one moment.

The lack of snow made it easy for the girl in all black to head to Thomas Hill one morning in early December. Without the tidal wave of students walking into the school building that morning, it felt eerie, and the dark, winter clouds cast a blanket of black over Thomas Hill, making the front resemble a haunted mansion. From here, it was impossible to catch where the school had been set alight, but, because of the lack of facilities due to the fire, all students were forced to work online until — approximately, as stated by Madam Mayor — the new year.

Z heard the faint mechanical sounds of cranes and tractors in the distance as she stood at the school gate. Drivers passing were perplexed as they drove past Thomas Hill to see the black silhouette of a figure frozen in front of the gates. But Z didn't care about that; what she cared about was getting into the school grounds without attracting any attention. Nobody could know.

She looked around then dug around in her baggy trousers for a moment before taking out a small, golden key. Z then walked forward and focused on the chain and lock around the gates. Jamming the key into the keyhole easily, Z twisted it until she heard a click. Doing this every Halloween, and every other day since Year 7, was a piece of cake.

The chain collapsed to the floor and Z pushed the heavy gates open with that very same screech that had made her cringe for the past two years. She didn't bother closing them behind her, as she was focused on predicting what sights she would have to witness on the school premises.

Nobody was working at the reception, and the main hall was deserted.

Z turned towards the doors that led to the Musical Theatre department, but kept glancing outside to the Science department, which had been blocked by the cranes, yellow police tape, and piles of grit and dirt. Walking into the Musical Theatre department almost felt normal, apart from the lack of students barging past her as if she didn't exist. Instead of walking straight through, however, Z cut off and headed for a door that had mainly been ignored by students and only used by technicians and cleaners.

With the coast clear, Z walked through the doorway, shutting the door behind her, entering a narrow, unlit hallway. She spread her arms out until her hands reached the brick walls on either side of her. As she walked, she brushed her hands across the walls and froze when she felt something a little smoother than a brick wall. It was a light switch. The hallway lit up and Z was standing in front of a wide storage area.

Shelves with loose stage lights and boxes of costumes covered the side walls; but as the lights flickered on above her, it was what was against the far wall that she couldn't take her eyes off. A flat pillow from Sunvalley Park, boxes filled with unused props acting as a mattress, and two pairs of coats tied together as one lying on top of the boxes was what she was staring at. She continued to look at the made-up bed, sighing every so often as she knew she just had to accept that this was her life. Some of those nights in Sunvalley Park were unbearable, never able to drift off into a deep slumber as she was constantly on edge, anticipating her grandmother's hacking and need for medicine. It was the only place Z could think of.

"Had a feeling you'd be here."

Z jumped and turned to see who else but Principal Keeper standing there with a sincere smile on his face.

"I know the situation you're in is tough, and I understand the deal we made when you started here. It had begun to get too much, and I know that." Keeper wrapped his arm around Z's shoulders and ushered her to the makeshift bed. They both sat, and Z waited for the headmaster to continue. "We're a good community, although it appears that nobody realises it. But even good communities have to do things they regret."

"What're you saying?" said Z flatly, her arms folded.

Principal Keeper took a deep breath and said, "We've been able to hide you here, but now, with the fire happening recently and Castlehead Council around my throat, I can't risk everyone finding out that this is where you stay when you're not at home."

Z looked down at the floor and replied, "It's fine, I get it." She rose and started to head towards the narrow hallway and the stairs. "Thank you for everything you've done."

Keeper remained seated, beginning to watch her leave, but stopped her with an alerting "Hey."

Z turned around and looked at the headmaster as he walked towards her. "Don't try to find another place to stay. Live fulltime with your grandma. She needs you. You never know when she'll go, and I know it's scary to think about when or how it'll happen, but I guarantee the last thing you want to do is leave her alone for sometimes days, having told her to ring you should anything happen. And one day… that doesn't happen, because she couldn't."

Despite Z being expressionless, she took in and embraced every single word of what her principal said.

She nodded unconvincingly and whispered, "See you later."

"Wait, Z."

The girl turned around again.

"Can I just ask… did you really have something to do with the fires and Aaron's death?"

Z grinned and asked rhetorically, "Why would I? Hm?"

The principal didn't reply and watched as the girl in all black blended into the dark hallway, before returning to Sunvalley Park — her rightful home.

2

From one who constantly moved back and forth to one who hadn't moved house since he was born, Jason shivered every time he thought about having to ring the Desmond School for Creative Arts about missing his scheduled interview back in November. He paced around his bedroom like a caged animal, phone in his tight grasp, and he just knew he had let this once-in-a-lifetime opportunity slip through his fingers.

Jason double-checked that his door was shut and listened out for his mother or grandparents. *Yes*, he thought, *they're downstairs*. And he dialled. The more the phone rang, the more Jason became certain — and worried — that his call was going to be ignored.

"Come on," he said through gritted teeth.

"*Hello*," he heard from the other end of the phone suddenly, "*Desmond School for Creative Arts. My name is Jane, how may I help you?*"

Oh, thank God, thought Jason with a breath of relief.

"Hi, my name is Jason Rayne. I had an interview scheduled for the eighth of last month. But I—"

"*I remember you. We were so looking forward to seeing you.*"

Jason knew where this was heading. Nevertheless, if he wasn't able to do anything about missing the interview, then he wouldn't have to speak of it to anyone, would he? No! He wasn't letting this chance pass by like a speeding driver who wouldn't even take a glance at him.

"Yes, I'm sorry about that." He began to rub the back of his head with his free hand, distorting his face. "Listen… I was… wondering if…" He took a deep breath, hoping to muster the courage to ask the simple question. "I was wondering if… I could reschedule?"

Jason tightly shut his eyes, his face now scrunched up in scared anticipation, like waiting to receive a grade for an important exam. The sound of computer keys in the background didn't help.

The sigh he heard from Jane the receptionist made his insides sink, and she added to the pain by saying, "*I'm sorry.*" She sounded sincerely apologetic. "*But the Desmond School for Creative Arts shuts next week for the Christmas holidays and doesn't reopen until the new year.*"

Jason held back the tears; working so hard for something only to trip at the finish line is the worst feeling for people with a passion. He expected the "good luck in your future endeavours" speech that employees get after they're fired. Jason imagined it for that single moment, no other road to take to get him to riches and fame, no successful books published. Just a ludicrous fantasy.

"*But*," started Jane again. A glimmer of hope, maybe? "*I'm certain we can get you in for the new year.*"

If only he could've jumped for joy without attracting attention. Jason pounded the air, thanked Jane and said he was looking forward to his visit in the new year. Ending the call with a wide smile on his face that showed all of his teeth, Jason tossed the phone on his bed and collapsed onto it freely, as if he were gently ascending through fluffy clouds into space. There was light at the end of the tunnel for Jason; he could only dream of the opportunities given to him when he would walk through the doors of a school where he felt he belonged.

3

The joyous weekend came to a close and it was back to weekly learning for the Thomas Hill High students. But it was a type of learning students had to adapt to during these strange times.

Dear Parent/Guardian and Student

Thomas Hill High was unfortunate to suffer a fire on Halloween Night, and I am aware that there is speculation on what the future will hold for staff and students. Although only the back of the school caught alight — including the Science department and parts of the Humanities and English departments — for the wellbeing of everyone at Thomas Hill High, we have decided that, after much consideration, students will

continue to learn from home until further notice and the school will remain closed.

Lessons will commence from 10:30-15:00 every day Monday to Friday on Microsoft Teams. This way, we can communicate and have the closest thing to a normal school experience. We comprehend that this will be a big change for both staff and students, but we think that this is the most stable way to move forward. When something like this happens, the safety of the Thomas Hill High family comes first, and you have my personal guarantee that we should be returning to normal face-to-face lessons after the Christmas holidays.

Stay safe everyone.
Yours faithfully, Principal Keeper.

It was like an extended school break, working from home, especially for the younger years, who saw it as an excuse to just act as if they were listening. Put yourself on mute, answer odd questions to stay relevant, and that's you sorted. Many would agree that the best part of working from home was no more pre-heated school meals that tasted of cardboard. It was the perfect opportunity to head to a place with decent food: Carl's Cafe.

Jason rang up that morning and made lunch reservations; a table for six. Of course, Jason was there first and Carl ushered him to the biggest table in the cafe.

"Want a drink, Jay, while you wait?" asked Carl as Jason sat. He wiped his hands on his sauce-stained apron as Jason considered the beverage options. "Water? Tea? Coffee?"

"Just a water."

"How's your book going, anyway? I haven't seen you here in ages."

"With everything happening, Carl, I've only had the time to write at home. But apart from the fires, everything is peaches and cream."

Carl nodded, heading across to the counter and into the kitchen. Jason watched as Carl did so, and tapped his fingers on the round table.

A few minutes had passed and the ringing sound of the bell told those in the cafe that more customers were entering. Jason glanced over and saw Eli, Anna, Brandon and Josh walk in, in single file. It was Eli who noticed where Jason was sitting, and they walked across.

"Areet, mate?" he asked as he sat.

Jason nodded with a little smile and watched the others sit, too.

"Where's Kelsey?" asked Jason directly.

Eli shrugged and said, "She said she'll be late."

"How's she holding up after her dad… you know?"

For a second, Eli thought it was Jason that had asked the question, but glanced over and saw Josh's hungry expression. It took Eli by surprise.

"Oh… She's fine. I think," he answered unconvincingly.

"Ah right," said Jason. "So did she say why she would be late?"

Carl returned with Jason's water, placed it on the table and took a miniature notepad and pen out of a small pocket in his apron. He stood over them in silence, patiently waiting to take orders for the others.

Eli shrugged again, eyes peering at the phone in his hand, and said, "Something about picking up her da's possessions," as if he wasn't invested in the conversation. "To be honest, she's been very blunt about it, pal."

The other four glanced at one another without Eli catching on. Even Carl had his suspicions as he still didn't speak a word to them. But looking up from his phone, Eli finally caught on to the perplexed looks of everyone around the table. He had to work it out for himself in silence, allowing the possibility that Kelsey was keeping something from him to slowly seep in. When it eventually did, Eli snapped a look to his phone again and the others watched his fingers tap away.

"Eh-hem," coughed Carl.

4

It wasn't home.

As Kelsey stood, handbag over her shoulder, in clothes unsuitable for the chilly December weather, she knew the house in front of her had never felt like home. A decade and a half of being raised by an abusive father does things to you, and the feelings trapped within — it could be said — correlated with the traumas that happened within those walls.

If she was being completely honest with herself, there were no possessions she had to pick up; all she wanted was to bask in the past that could be erased. Long overdue. *Let the past be in the past*, she had thought during the walk to the house.

The clearest change to the house was that the door had been replaced by yellow police tape in the typical 'X' shape. **Do not cross**. She had to, to see what was left of the house. That last walk around the house, she hoped, would be a huge weight off her shoulders — and off her life, too — and a new chapter could finally start without Donovan.

She stood in front of the tape, looked around warily, then tore it down, making way for herself. Stepping into the house, she felt nothing. The wallpaper had been torn and the carpets had been removed, along with all the furniture.

Kelsey walked into the lounge, expecting nothing but a large room where, for once, she could feel free. But seeing a woman standing in the centre stunned her to an immediate halt.

The woman had heels on, which made her taller than she actually was. Her fashionable clothing made Kelsey aware that this woman had money, and lots of it. At first, Kelsey expected this to be a construction manager planning to dismantle the house, or perhaps renovate it. It was, however, the woman's strands of brown hair and blood red lips that drew Kelsey in most of all.

They looked directly at one another as if in opposing corners of a boxing ring.

"Who are you?" asked Kelsey finally. "Why are you here?"

"Really?" asked the woman sarcastically. Her tone was smooth, the type of smoothness that intimidated others. "How can you not recognise your own mother?"

Kelsey stumbled back, trying to steady herself. The wind had just been taken out of her, and it took a few deep breaths for her to compose herself.

Her mother? The mother that ran out on the family when Kelsey was just a baby? But why did she leave? Was this even her mother? All of these conflicting questions, yet no answers; her insecurity got the better of her and she debated whether or not she should embrace her mother.

Kelsey crept forward, and it was the lips and hair that confirmed she was the offspring of this woman. It was like looking at her future self. Yet she still couldn't decide whether to smile or cry, and it ended up being her mother who made the first move. She hesitantly wrapped her arms around Kelsey, unsure, likewise, of how her daughter would react.

"Mam…" whispered Kelsey, feeling the succulent touch of her mother's hands on her back. *So this is what being loved by a parent is like.* "I—"

"Shh." Her mother released the hug, and they locked eyes. "I know I should've called, but I was scared. I didn't know if you would answer. I came up when I heard about your dad, and the chief told me this address."

Something within told Kelsey that this wasn't false; her mother meant every word, and when she promised that they would sort things out between them and have a relationship, Kelsey broke down in tears. This time, her mother didn't hesitate to hug her daughter. Kelsey embraced her mother as a child should, and didn't hold the tears back.

In between sniffles, Kelsey said, "I wish you'd come back sooner." Maybe, just maybe, things could've been different. But both Kelsey and her mother saw this as the perfect way to start to redeem themselves because of the lack of communication between the two during Kelsey's younger years. It didn't help that Donovan had told her that her mother had abandoned them and moved to Spain.

"Why did you do it?"

They released the hug again, and her mother led Kelsey to the doorway and into the small garden.

She explained, "I left because I couldn't handle the pressure that your father put on me. He hurt me. He really hurt me, and one day I had enough. I packed and moved to London, changed my name to Melissa Snave, and had a fresh start. I started my own business in fashion design, and it became massive. I headlined shows all over the world. I swear I intended on coming back for you, but I got caught up in everything. And for that—" *And for everything*, she should've said, "I'm sorry." Melissa didn't expect anything from Kelsey after her explanation. "I am willing to be the mother I should've been… if you'll have me."

Kelsey sighed, and gave her answer: "Okay then."

A bright smile appeared on Melissa's face. Her teeth had clearly been whitened by a dentist. She wrapped her arm around Kelsey's shoulders and they walked out onto the street as mother and daughter.

"Kelsey." An idea came to mind. "Do you have any friends you'd like to invite to a party… as a way to celebrate *us*?"

After everything she had been through, Kelsey knew immediately that a party would be a great way to release some steam. She had suffered at the hands of her father, through the death of him, and many more things she couldn't dream of revealing to anyone. And if anyone deserved a party, it was her. Oh wait! That meant she would have to invite Jason and his friends. She groaned at the thought, but considered that it could be worse: *Imagine if that Z girl came. Not telling her.*

"Yeah. I do. I think a party would be great," she finally answered as they continued down the path, turning onto a fresh street.

Melissa's arm was still wrapped around Kelsey's shoulder, and she asked, "So what's been happening lately here?"

Kelsey scoffed, chuckled, and said, "Believe me, you don't want to know."

5

The group sat patiently, a stack of plates in the centre of the table that were on the verge of collapsing. They were aware of the time and had accepted that Kelsey wasn't going to show up. Jason continuously tapped his fingers on the table while Eli pressed away on his phone, most likely messaging Kelsey, asking where she was. Anna, Brandon and Josh, on the other hand, sat awkwardly, glancing at one another, expecting one of them to break the silence with a conversation starter.

"She just said she's walking up the road now," mumbled Eli, eyes still fixed on his phone.

No one responded, but the bell above the cafe door rang sweetly. In came Z, walking directly to the counter, her head not turning to the group or anywhere else in the cafe. She leaned on the counter somewhat uncharacteristically, waiting for Carl to turn and notice her.

"Here for your order?" he asked as he faced her. She nodded once without moving her lips, her eyes drenched in darkness by the hood she wore. Carl turned back around and lowered himself to match the level of a shelf. On the shelf sat a medium-sized takeaway coffee cup; he clamped the lid like a claw and placed his other hand under the cup, the strain in his face evident as he tried not to scream because of how hot it was. "Here you go."

Z snatched the coffee from him and tossed a pile of loose change on the counter. She turned 90 degrees, facing the exit. She aimed to leave, but the sudden entrance of Kelsey stopped her in her tracks. As Kelsey walked past Z, she gave the coffee-holding girl in all black a withering gaze. Z shook the look off and walked out of Carl's Cafe, taking that deadly first sip of the scolding beverage, never acknowledging the group of her fellow students — who half expected her to join them at the table — in the process.

Eli *actually* looked up from his phone as his girlfriend strutted in. She placed her hands on her hips and looked the group over. It was the most confident Eli had seen her in a long, long time.

"I have a proposition for all of you," began Kelsey as if this *news* was a royal decree.

Jason rolled his eyes at her powering voice.

"As a way to forget these past few months of hell, you are all cordially invited to a party I…" Kelsey directed her look towards Eli, "am hosting. Alongside my mother."

"What?" said Eli.

"Even you, Jason."

Jason exaggerated his smile at Kelsey.

"I will send the details later on."

Eli couldn't find words; all that came out were frequent sounds that resembled a buffering video. "Bye-bye," added Kelsey with a cheesy grin.

Her hair whipped the air as she turned and strutted towards the exit.

Eli jolted to his feet and followed, leaving Jason and the rest of the group in further awkward silence, speechless. Eli couldn't decide if it was just being told that Kelsey's mother had miraculously returned out of the blue, or this unforeseen, new-found confidence (*ego*, some like Jason would say) that had made him trip up on his words. More confidence she already exuded.

"Kelsey, wait. Hang on, hang on just a sec," he called as he ran to catch up with her. Kelsey was nearly at the end of the road. "Kelsey!"

"Woah!" cried Kelsey. "What ya doin'?"

Eli cut her off like a roadblock until she gave him answers.

"Why didn't you tell me that your ma had come back? Instead of announcing it in front of all of *them*?" It was then that it had occurred to Eli that he hadn't used 'them' as an abbreviation for the likes of Anna and Brandon in a while. "Huh?"

"I literally just saw her like ten minutes ago," she answered. "You were meeting here anyway, so I thought it'd be easier."

"And a party? Thanks for telling me about that, too," said Eli a bit too forcefully.

"Don't come, then," snapped Kelsey.

Kelsey barged past Eli as if he were a total stranger, not looking back.

Eli growled and regretted everything he had just said instantly.

He headed back up to Carl's Cafe, where the rest of the group stood at the entrance, hoping to return to their online lessons in time — and forget about this slight disagreement.

6

CRASH! BANG! BOOM!

"Steady! Steady!"

"Frigging hell, be careful, Gemma."

Thankfully, Jason's teacher didn't ask the students to turn their cameras on for the remainder of the lesson, or they would've all seen Jason biting his bottom lip, unfocused, constantly jolting after a bang or a crash. At this time of year, it was the norm for households across the entire United Kingdom to scurry around in the attic to get the many boxes of tinsel, baubles, candles, calendars and cards out to begin preparing.

"Any questions?" asked the teacher.

No one replied, but Jason had one he didn't ask out loud: What are we doing?

"Okay, get to work," added the teacher.

There were a couple of knocks on Jason's bedroom door which he also didn't respond to, for he knew Gemma and his grandparents were expecting high-quality work from him, even when working from home.

He lay on his bed until the end of the task he was meant to be doing, but all he could think about was the new year.

"Is that everything?" yelled Gemma from outside his bedroom door.

Jason heard thumping above him, with dust sprinkling from the ceiling.

"Aye, that's it," said his grandfather from within the attic.

"Be careful," squealed his grandma, thinking the worst.

Jason shook his head as more thumping from above distracted him, though it wasn't long until the school day ended. *Ten minutes. Nine minutes.* Counting down the minutes appeared to make the day go even slower; if working on Microsoft Teams was the foreseeable future, then the future was as bland as a packet of ready salted crisps.

The time to complete the task concluded, and it was like a breath of fresh air.

Jason quickly picked up his phone and left the Team's call without warning. *The teacher won't notice*, he thought. He couldn't have left the chat any quicker, leaping off his bed and walking out onto the landing. His mother nor grandparents were in sight, but clear traces of dust and box lids scattered across the landing all the way to the stairs lay in their place. Stepping over them felt like an obstacle course.

Jason walked down the stairs where he met a small hoover purchased from the Dyson range. It leant against the wall and didn't budge as Jason chose to go into the sitting room, which resembled more of a garage, with all of the boxes lying around.

Sitting on the arm of the couch, Jason watched Gemma at the far end of the room fiddling with tape and a long, red box which had a picture of a Christmas tree covered in sparkling lights on it. He turned his head and saw his grandmother doing the same as she sat on the couch, but his grandad digging into a box.

"Jason," his mother said without looking up from the box, "help get the tree decorations out."

Jason did as he was commanded; he leaned over towards a blue box filled with silver baubles and other tree decorations that reminded people of this joyous occasion, and started to rummage through it as if looking for gold.

By the time an hour had passed, the tree was partly up, many of its branches still needing to be stretched, and many of the decorations within the box Jason started to look through had been placed on the sitting room floor in an orderly fashion, from smallest to largest. The most attractive and spectacular ones would be placed at the front of the tree for all the guests to see, whereas the small would be plopped at the back or bottom of the tree to be ignored. By this time, Jason's grandmother had got his grandfather out of the house, with him reluctantly agreeing to help her find more Christmas lights at the Wilkos that had recently been added to the newly-built retail park.

"So… how was today?" said Gemma, breaking the silence.

Jason sat on the couch properly, untying two knotted decorations, and said bluntly, "Okay."

"*Okay?*" Gemma turned and saw that Jason's head was down, his eyes fixed on the joined baubles, his tongue sticking out of the corner of his mouth slightly.

"I get that working from home isn't great, but you still have to look at the bigger picture."

Jason desperately wanted to groan.

"Your GCSEs aren't far away, and to get the ones you want, you're going to have to put your head down."

"All right," mumbled Jason. He didn't want to hear another typical pep talk at this moment. "I will," he added, finally separating the baubles once again.

"Good. If not, then you're never going to get into college or university."

College or university, he thought. *How about the Desmond School for Creative Arts?* As much as Jason would deny it, he still didn't have the courage to speak up about his secret application to the school of his dreams. He shrugged it off and decided that today simply wasn't the right day. *Let's wait until after the interview*, he thought proudly.

7

Yes, it was unjust and unfair for Chief Pattison and Deputy Ton to make this decision, they thought, as they walked up the many steps leading to Clarke's front door, but it was a decision that had to be made, considering the extremity of this case. Clarke had escaped certain death by not even an inch, and, for all the C.C.I.D knew, the person responsible for these fires could be scouting their next attack.

"You know he won't like this," asked Ton for the fifth time.

"Yes," snapped the chief. "But it's for his safety. We can't let him roam about the town when there's someone actually out to kill him."

They reached the top step, and the chief pounded on the door. "Clarke, it's Chief Pattison and Deputy Ton. We were wondering if we could have a few words."

Pattison had spoken with fury as if he were about to make an arrest.

Deputy Ton looked at his boss' face, and knew this wasn't the right way to handle the situation.

The deputy knocked, and said soothingly, "Come on, open up. You're not in trouble."

As they waited for a response, a wave of wind came over them. Then they heard footsteps coming from within. The door lock clicked, and Clarke appeared as he opened the door. A befuddled expression remained on his face until he gestured for the officers to enter his small, yet warmly, home. With his comfy shorts and hoodie, it was clear that Clarke hadn't made plans other than to lie on the couch watching awful daytime television; drowning in sorrow, grief, and regret, as he had been doing since 'this curse' came over him.

Clarke's home sat on the corner of a street not too far from Carson Estate — and everyone knew how rough that place was — but when in that house, the street rats, the drunks and druggies didn't matter. With two small bedrooms, a narrow kitchen, a reasonably sized sitting room with a TV and an electric fire, and a bathroom downstairs, this house was big enough for a family of three. Not bad for £70,000 at the time.

But now two members of the family were gone forever.

"This way," said Clarke plainly as he led the officers past the brown carpeted stairs into the sitting room. The floor matched the stairs; the TV sat in the corner on a stand next to the electric fire, and the leather couch sat opposite.

"What's up?" he asked as all three of them sat down.

"Clarke," started the chief, his hands clasped in front of him, "we've been looking into this case for a good while now, and safety is — and always has been — the department's main priority. An—"

"And," said Ton, unexpectedly butting in, "we, as a unit, have made the decision to put you under strong surveillance."

A puzzled look appeared on Clarke's face.

"Not as cruel, but it's like house arrest," added Pattison. But straight away, he knew that wasn't the best way to put it. "What we mean is that you'll only be allowed to leave for essential reasons. Like shopping. We can't risk any more accidents happening to any more residents." Clarke knew the chief was making reference to the six suspects at the school fire. "You avoided death by only God knows how much, and even Madam Mayor has agreed to this. She was actually the one who insisted on the idea."

Before Clarke could come up with a response (if his mind could formulate one, that is), the deputy added again, "Three out of the four fires have been related to you, in one way or another. Your workplace—" *Don't bring back the memories*, thought Clarke as the deputy listed the incidents, "you were a part of the Central Church catastrophe… and Thomas Hill High, even though you weren't there—"

"You attended Thomas Hill as a student," said the chief.

It took a moment for the deputy to silently forgive his boss for butting in, and vice versa, but it was Clarke's guilty, embarrassed look that made them aware that he had previously thought this person was out to torture him, and him alone. Clarke didn't have to be told that the kids Aaron knew had been dragged into this, too, and it was then that he reflected on all the times his son would return home from school, carelessly chucking his expensive school bag at the foot of the radiator beside the front door (as much as that wasn't appreciated at the time), and tell him of these classmates with whom he surprisingly got along very well — despite not being in the same friendship group. Nonetheless, it was comforting to know that his son had friends.

This was the relationship they had beforehand, before the accident in May, and before Aaron's disappearance and untimely death. The Smith family became the light in a very dark neighbourhood, and Aaron, many claimed, was the centre of that shining light. But at some point, notwithstanding the people who hated this fact, every light must go out eventually. And in Clarke's eyes, the light went out between May and his son's disappearance, causing a strain on the once kindled bond between father and son.

It wasn't his fault, thought Clarke during every passing day, it just wasn't. *Accidents aren't anybody's fault*, he thought as the officers stared at him. *All I wanted was to keep the family in line, and not sin.* But it wasn't admitting in Central Church that he had sinned that ate Clarke up alive, it was that he sinned in the first place.

No! I didn't do it. IT WAS AN ACCIDENT.

"It was an accident," muttered Clarke.

Chief Pattison and Deputy Ton glanced at one another, thinking the same thing: *What's he on about?*

The chief smacked his knees with a deep breath, rising, as Ton copied him. For a moment, Clarke didn't know what was happening. He tilted his head upwards and saw the officers towering over him.

"Right, so," said the chief, clapping his hands together, "we'll keep in touch and get cameras installed around the house at some point before Christmas."

Clarke nodded at this information and rose, leading the chief and deputy back to the front door, instinctively blocking the sight of the radiator.

"I hope this won't be a huge adjustment."

"Oh no, don't worry," answered Clarke as he held the front door open.

"It'll feel like they don't exist, after a day," said Ton in an uplifting manner.

Clarke chuckled, and there was a little bit of reassurance now. Both officers saw this on his face, and Ton said on behalf of himself and Pattison, "Goodbye. Stay safe."

Once the door had clicked shut, all Clarke's body could do was collapse onto the bottom step of the stairs. He rubbed his head and caught sight of the radiator. But the heat beaming off it didn't bother him. It was the bottom left corner. He didn't need to squint to see a drop of red covering not even a centimetre of white; he knew it was there, because he witnessed what happened that night in May.

The scream came flooding back. It had all happened so quickly; he was sure he had blacked out after the clang between head and radiator. Aaron was asleep that night. *Wasn't he?* Did that mean he knew what transpired beforehand? This would haunt Clarke — he knew it — and it had done for months.

8

Saturday, the day of the party, had come, but it wasn't until midday that everyone received a text.

"Mam," said Jason, glaring at his phone as he sat in the sitting room with Gemma, "the party's now at Gill & Susan'z."

Jason couldn't be certain if Eli or any of the others felt the same way, but he was sure there was going to be an eerie atmosphere upon first entry, as the last time any of them had been there, it was for Aaron's wake. "Can we still go?" he asked.

Gemma breathed, "Yes."

Jason's grandparents made the decision not to go to the party, but everyone else within the inner circle was adamant to make the most of the night. Hiring out one of the most successful pubs in town wasn't exactly normal, and everyone supposed Kelsey's mother had made sure it was worth the cost. Kelsey, on the other hand, didn't have a say in the matter — nor did she intend on getting her hands dirty. All she cared about was impressing Eli after their little mishap earlier that week with a brand new, sparkling dress the colour of the night, matching the heels bought for the occasion by Melissa.

The lads didn't seek out anything smart for the party that night, remaining in casualwear. Eli, looking back, thought it was ridiculous to have had that argument outside Carl's Cafe; he had just wished Kelsey had told him about her mother. Aren't people in relationships meant to tell their other half everything? But he focused on making it water under the bridge, wanting to apologise straight away.

Gill & Susan'z was like a winter wonderland, having been decorated with silver tinsel, false snow sprinkled on all the tables, and with a magical tree shining brightly by the bar. Christmas tunes played as the guests walked in at different times. Kelsey and Melissa were the first to arrive, arriving an hour early, whereas Eli and Lisa arrived an hour late. The rest arrived in between.

When everyone had arrived — all who had been invited — the party really started. Gill and Susan amped up the volume on the Christmas tunes, switching off the main lights and turning on the disco lights that had been installed; as suggested by Melissa. Although there were only a handful of people in attendance, with the flashing lights, loud music, and — since no one could remember — smiling faces, it truly felt like everything outside those pub doors could happily be forgotten.

But it was when the pub doors swung open that all heads turned.

Since the main lights were off, only footsteps could be heard. The music continued to play, but the upbeat Christmas song didn't fit the sudden spread of uncertainty. Amidst the darkness, they all saw that hood.

"What is *she* doing here?" asked Kelsey, not caring who would answer. She hadn't invited Z. As the group watched by the tree, Z took no notice of their gawking faces when walking up to the bar like an unknown cowboy entering a saloon full of turning heads. "Eh?"

"I invited her," said Jason.

Kelsey snapped her head towards him; the rest, however, didn't seem too bothered.

Jason looked at Kelsey, leaned in and said soundly, "She's been through all this, too."

Kelsey strode off, saying nothing more, with Eli trailing behind her.

Anna and Brandon joined Z and the group of parents by the bar, leaving Josh and Jason by the tree.

"What's her problem?" asked Josh, watching Kelsey and Eli sit down in a booth, with Kelsey evidently in a sulk.

"She needs to remember that the world doesn't exactly revolve around her," said Jason with a sneer.

At the booth, Kelsey said, "Look at her."

Eli secretly rolled his eyes but didn't say anything. Kelsey kept her eyes on Z, watching the girl in all black sitting at the bar with a glass of Coke on the counter. She ignored the muttering from the parents by her. "I didn't—"

"Kelsey!" spat Eli, knowing Kelsey's next move. She had placed a hand on the table, as if ready to rise; if Kelsey had it her way, she would've darted over to that *thing* people call Z and had Melissa throw her out.

"Don't! Just leave it. Maybe Jason's right. She has been through as much as we have."

Not as much as me, Kelsey thought as she gave her boyfriend a dirty look.

Not a single word had been said directly to Z, and she stayed at the bar until it was almost time to leave. The bar stool began to hurt her backside, but she didn't express the irritation when Gill or Susan walked over to take her empty glasses away and replace them with filled ones.

"Here you go," said Gill sweetly, handing Z another glass of Coke. Gill expected to be thanked, but Z didn't say a word. She was wrinkling her nose and it looked like something more than the bar stool was irritating her.

"Are you okay?" asked Gill.

Again, Z didn't respond. She rose from the stool, leaving her drink on the bar. She looked around — everyone seemed to be enjoying themselves — and then back to Gill.

"What's wrong?"

Z said, "Do you smell that?"

Gill sniffed, and looked at Z shaking her head.

"Really? Smells like… smoke."

Gill shifted across to the end of the bar and walked around the pub, pushing her glasses up her nose. Admittedly, the more Gill moved around, the more the unusual scent of a BBQ began to take over. But the smell wasn't as strong as Z had made it out to be, Gill thought. It could have been something burning in the kitchen. It *could* have been.

Kelsey glared at Z shuffling around the bar, wondering what she was up to. It was her intention to kick her out herself if Melissa wouldn't do anything about it.

She cocked her head towards Eli and Jason chatting away — with Jason suddenly raising his eyebrows — and then turned to Brandon and Anna. They too raised their eyebrows while chatting away. Their ears had pricked up like a pack of dogs'.

"Do you smell that?" said Jason to Eli.

"What's that?" asked Anna to Brandon.

"I don't—" started Brandon.

"OUT! EVERYBODY OUT!" cried both Gill and Susan. Susan must've accompanied Gill and Z to find out what the smell was, but as they continued to cry out, it was Kelsey who noticed that Z was nowhere in sight. "NOW! THE PLACE IS ON FIRE!"

Everyone panicked as smoke soared down the stairs from the rooms upstairs. All made their way through the exit, pushing and shoving.

Not again, thought Jason. Gemma had her arms tightly around her son as they made it outside, this being her first experience of a fire, like the rest of the parents. They reached the parking area and saw the powerful flames smash the glass windows above.

"Wait!" yelled Jason. "Where's Z?" He stared at the blaze. She had to still be in there. Faint sirens echoed in the distance, but Jason couldn't wait for the fire brigade. "Someone's got to get her."

There was a roar of "No!"'s as he took a couple of steps forward, with Gemma reaching out for him. She reached out further and clamped her hand around her son's arm, yanking him back as Jason anguished at the thought of nobody helping Z. He should've taken the chance. It's what he had started to do.

Fire engines pulled into the car park. The firefighters stepped off the side of the trucks and ran inside with a hosepipe. The driver of the first hydrant leapt out of the driver's seat and ran towards the worried citizens. They looked awfully familiar, but he couldn't quite put his finger on it.

"Is everyone out?" he yelled over the loud spraying of water.

"No, we think someone's still in there," said Gill, her hands over her mouth, withholding anxious tears.

"Okay." The chief of the fire department turned his head to the second truck. "Go in! Nobody is left behind!"

Time had slowed down. It was only two minutes, but felt more like two hours before the firefighters came out again...

... empty handed.

The fire was finally dying down as the firefighters walked out, wearing expressions of disappointment under their protective helmets.

"Nobody's in there," said one of them.

No, thought Jason, lowering his head into Gemma's shoulder. She reacted with a hug, instinctively knowing her son's sick feeling. Eli and Lisa felt the same way. Kelsey showed sadness, but how can you feel sad about losing someone you didn't even like? She hugged Melissa, thoughts kicking in already.

9

Everyone, including Kelsey and Melissa — because they didn't want to make it too obvious they had more important things to care about — headed to Eli and Lisa's. They convened in the kitchen, most of them holding cups of tea and coffee; Lisa and Gemma shared a glass of vodka to steady their nerves.

Shaking her head at the floor, Kelsey said quietly, "I can't believe it…"

"I know," agreed Anna. "She's actually gone."

"I can't believe she would actually do it," Kelsey added.

Jason gave her a dirty look, disapproving of her ludicrous statement.

Eli caught his gaze and couldn't think of anything worse than his oldest friend and current girlfriend clashing, especially on a night like this.

"Kelsey," he said warningly.

"Are you actually taking the piss?" said Jason. Nothing could be contained anymore. "You really think she did it?"

"Jason!" said his mother. "Calm down, please."

"NO!" he barked defiantly. "She actually believes Z caused the fires, and I'm guessing killed Aaron too." He stepped forward, almost nose-to-nose with an uncomfortable Kelsey.

Melissa just stood there, oblivious as to why Jason was being so defensive.

Jason grinned, believing he could see straight through Kelsey. "I bet she's just framing Z because *she* is the one behind all this shit!"

"Woah!" roared Eli, as Kelsey stepped back, hurt.

"Jason, calm down," ordered Gemma.

Eli pulled him back a bit too forcefully and said, "The fuck do ye think you're doin'?"

Anna, Brandon and Josh stepped in between Jason and Eli. Eli's allegiance was with Kelsey, for sure, but they could see this escalating more than it should if they didn't do anything.

"Get out the way!"

"What? Were you in on it, too? Wouldn't surprise me."

"Jason, that's enough!" cried Lisa.

"You've always been good at hiding things, being a backstabbing bastard!"

Eli launched himself at Jason. Jason just stood there, as if sacrificing himself. Fighting wasn't going to solve this, Jason thought, as he grinned when being shoved into the wall by his former friend.

Brandon shoved Eli back as a way to restrain him, to calm him down.

"I had nothing to do with that! And you know it!"

"RIGHT, STOP! NOW!"

All heads turned to Melissa, and the silence that was needed finally came over them. Steam had been let off, but apologies weren't going to be made anytime soon. But with the tension settling, perhaps they could go back to working together.

Then there was a knock on the door.

"Urgh, what now?" said Lisa, walking towards the door and opening it.

"Can I come in?"

Lisa stepped aside and allowed the smoke-covered Z in.

Jason leapt towards her into an embrace, not caring about the smoke; Z, however, raised an eyebrow at the action, not wrapping her arms around him in return.

Kelsey overdramatically spun around behind Melissa, cowering from the girl in all black.

"You see! She's here to finish—"

"Shut up!" barked Jason. Releasing the embrace, he said, "We thought you didn't make it."

"Well," she explained, "when me and Gill went up to check on the smell, I told her to make a run for it once we saw the flames. She gathered all of you while I was able to sneak out the back."

Lisa shut the door.

"But why didn't you join us straight away?" asked Anna from the far side of the kitchen.

"I was going to, but I didn't know where you were going. So I kept my distance and followed you."

Kelsey kept a straight face. It was clear to Jason that she didn't believe a single word of it. They needn't guess what the next step of this investigation was going to be: another interrogation and more pointing fingers. The parents thought that fingers had been pointed enough that night; *Year 9 students shouldn't have to go through this*, they all thought. They managed to retain their array of emotions, with none of them speaking another word of the incident for the rest of the night.

A couple of hours had passed. Taxis were ordered for 11pm, and the exhaustion was visible on all of their faces. They moved into the lounge, with music playing faintly in the background. Lisa seemed to think they should at least try to retrieve some of that night's party feeling, but Kelsey and Melissa were the first to leave; a private car had been requested to pick them up. Jason secretly gave them the finger when they left.

"Jason," snapped Gemma. It hadn't been that much of a secret.

When 10:30pm arrived, Z glanced at the clock on the kitchen wall. She walked into the lounge where the others sat and stood in the doorway. All of them felt her presence and turned their heads.

"I'm going to go," she announced.

"Do you not want a taxi?" said Jason. Gemma gave him a slight nudge as if to tell him to stop talking.

"No, I'm okay. I like the walk."

Jason smiled, with Z surprisingly reflecting the smile back at him. He liked it.

"Okay, just be safe," said Lisa.

"Before I go, I just want to say… Merry Christmas. I know it's been crazy, but try to make the most of it. And—"

"What are you actually doing this Christmas?" interrupted Jason, with Gemma giving him another nudge.

"Same as every year. I'm with my grandma."

"Well—"

"She needs me."

Gemma smiled in relief, as if she approved of Z's caring manner.

"Oh… Err… Okay," stuttered Jason. "Well… okay. I-I… Okay then. See you in the new year."

"See you in the new year. Bye everyone."

"BYE! MERRY CHRISTMAS!" replied everyone in unison.

They heard the door slam shut.

Jason turned around and saw Eli slouching on the couch, giving him a look. He saw the way Jason and Z looked at each other; he and Kelsey did it all the time. All of them looked at one another, too, but not with the same thought; Z wishing them Merry Christmas had reassured all of them, and it had definitely lifted their spirits. Despite the terror the town had experienced, Christmas was going to be jolly.

10

But Christmas isn't always a jolly time. For some, like Clarke, it can be a haunting time; a time when memories are repressed.

Clarke unlocked the door to his gloomy house, the radiator clanging as he placed his hands on it in search of the light switch. In the end, he didn't bother. He walked through the narrow hall to the kitchen. This time, he found the light switch. It flickered on. Not a sound was made inside the house, but outside, crickets could be heard.

Even with Clarke in it, the house was empty. Not a single decoration was up this year, and, as if on instinct, Clarke opened one of the drawers next to the rusty, mid-90s oven. Under the kitchen utensils, loose paper, bottle tops and scissors was a single strip of paper with an illuminating headline on it.

He clenched it to his chest as streams of tears flowed down his prickly face. Nobody heard him cry. He didn't want anybody to hear him, in fact. Especially not before Christmas…

Especially not on that day in May.

THE CASTLEHEAD CHRONICLE:
DATE - 19/5/2019
Local Wife Found Dead After Falling
Down Stairs and Hitting Radiator

CHAPTER SEVEN

A Castlehead Carol

1

Christmas was right around the corner; the time to rejoice, to spend time with family and friends. The only problem was, Clarke had neither of those things. The thought of this being his first without both his wife and son haunted him. He would've much preferred to skip this year. Maybe the next, too… And the next… And the next… And so on and so forth until he was in his grave.

The calendar above his bed said it was December 1st, when really it was the 22nd.

Clarke kept the curtains shut that morning, slouching as he walked downstairs in a brown-stained white vest and boxer shorts. He rubbed his head as it pounded, making his way into the kitchen to rummage through the cupboards overhead in search of paracetamol.

Two should do the trick.

The divine voice of his wife had always told him that after a night of heavy drinking, whether it be out at Gill & Susan'z or if the pair had decided to stay at home. The pricey wine they would sip in the dim candle light tasted more exquisite when they were together. A trail of rose petals would lead upstairs to their room for an epic conclusion to a great night, and the next morning they would suffer together, while Aaron returned home after a night at a friend's or aunt's.

"Always take two," she would say.

"Always take two," he said to himself, finally finding the tub of painkillers. He spilled two out onto his hand and chucked them into his mouth, swallowing them at once without water. There had been many — countless — times when this had been his morning routine.

"Thanks, babe."

They always kept each other in line.

2

The Past

Husband, wife and child. That's all that was needed in this household. Of course, every Christmas had been cherished by all three of them, but if you had to ask Clarke yourself what the family's best Christmases had been, he would say the ones when Aaron was growing up. Lights would hang from the ceiling above, the delectable smell of turkey roasting in the oven in preparation for Christmas Day, Aaron eager to at least sneakily open one present before the most wonderful day of the year. All of it was to die for.

Aaron never did open presents early. He was good like that, knowing what his father would do if he ever found out. Their Christmas Day was like an unplanned routine. Clarke anticipated Aaron to jump on their bed at around 7:30am so that they could open presents.

"Okay, okay," said a drowsy Clarke. "We're up, we're up."

A ten-year-old Aaron cheered and ran down the stairs as fast as he could, jumping from the third bottom step. Clarke heard the thump below.

"Come on!" cheered his son.

"Babe, come on," said Clarke as he swooped his legs off the bed. There was no response. "Babe?" Waiting for a reply, Clarke scanned the bedside cabinet for his cross. It dangled on a chain on the corner. He picked it up and kissed it, closing his eyes for a moment and thanking the Lord for everything he had done. But there was still no response from his wife.

Downstairs, Aaron sat cross-legged in front of the tree and pile of presents. He couldn't wait any longer, he had to at least touch one. And he did, poking the big, shiny red package in front of him.

"Ma—" he started, but a crash from above stopped him.

"BABE, FOR HEAVEN'S SAKE, WAKE UP! HE'S WAITING!"

Aaron gulped and began to grow nervous. He never liked it when either of his parents yelled. It was scary, and the thought of the yelling primarily being his fault slipped into his mind a lot of the time. Never explained and never understood, Aaron always saw their happiness. They even renewed their vows when he was five. He assumed that they just didn't want to reveal their anguish in front of him.

These thoughts, however, disappeared, once his mam and dad entered the lounge at the same time. He saw their happiness, as always. The smiles they put on were believable, but Aaron knew by his mother's chilly gaze they were not on good terms. He had to be happy. For them.

His mother sat down first, keeping her eyes on him, whereas Clarke sat a moment later, with a video camera, and at the far end of the couch.

"Which one do you want to open first, son?" his mother asked.

"Ooo, I don't know. I can't choose."

Both parents pretended to laugh, meeting each other's gaze, Clarke rather apologetically (he didn't see a reason to apologise) and his wife icy.

"How about this one?" It was the one Aaron had secretly poked. "Please."

His mother snapped, "Yes." She didn't mean it, but that didn't stop Clarke now giving her a look of distaste. How dare she. "I mean, yes," she repeated more calmly.

As Aaron tore the glowing red paper to shreds, Clarke scooched towards his wife and said, "Look, I'm so—"

"I know, I know," she said, keeping her eyes off him.

"It's just you were—"

"Out of line?" Her fiery hair fell in front of her face as she turned to him. Then it went silent.

The wrapping had stopped, and Aaron sat patiently again, waiting for them to give him the all-clear to continue opening presents.

"Don't," she toned down to a whisper, "be giving me lectures when I have to remind you every time you get pissed to take two paracetamol."

Clarke fell back, his face turning red. *Yes*, he thought, his face scrunched up like a pug, *you are out of line.*

"Wow, thank you!" said Aaron, leaping up into both parents' arms. "It's the one I wanted."

The three, like a happy family, smiled down at the neatly packed PlayStation, which came with a pile of games Aaron hadn't been able to keep his eyes off when in the shops. "Love youse."

3

The Past – May, 2019

Many altercations had happened since that Christmas, when Aaron was ten, between Clarke and his wife, but unlike that time, they were always able to reconcile their dispute — verbal or physical. Aaron *knew* it was both. *Things* commonly took place at night, when the pair thought Aaron was fast asleep. If he had been, he was always woken up.

The stuff going on in town with that Isabella girl was finally dying down by the time May had come around. Both Isabella and Sharron were dead, and Anthony had turned himself in, but what wasn't dying down were the constant clashes between Clarke and Aaron's mother.

It was a sunny Sunday afternoon when Aaron's mother made the decision to go out... to Clarke's displeasure. May 19th was the date, and Aaron walked into the lounge to see his father sitting on the couch, a can in one hand and the television remote in the other. He watched him for a moment, occasionally glancing at the news on the screen.

"Dad..." started Aaron nervously.

"Yes, son?"

"You know Mam's going out soon, right?"

"What?"

"She said last week..."

Clarke planted his can on the ground and rose, exclaiming, "No, she didn't."

"Yes, she did."

"No, she didn't! Okay!"

There was no winning against his father.

Aaron huffed and stormed off.

Clarke heard Aaron's bedroom door slam shut and carelessly sat back down on the couch, resuming his previous position: a beer can in one hand and the television remote in the other. In line with the TV, Clarke was loving the peace.

Early evening came and the sun was still shining brightly, glaring through the window. Clarke shut the blinds at one point and it was like being in a cinema. The splash of fresh air that hit the room when Clarke's wife entered hurt his comfortable position. He turned back to the TV again, seven cans down, completely ignoring his wife's radiant appearance.

She had placed curlers in her hair earlier that day, and had worn a face mask for the majority of the day too. Her nails matched the tight black dress she wore, revealing three-quarters of her long legs. Over her shoulders was a leather jacket and a small handbag containing cash, her phone, and her card. She didn't seem impressed by the man sitting on the couch, whose eyes were almost closed.

"Have you actually sat here all day?" she asked, hands on her hips.

Clarke looked up, his head dangling as if by a thread, scoffed and said, "Maybe."

"Right. I don't know what time I'll be back but don't wait up."

Her husband didn't reply, his eyes fixed on the TV.

She shut the door forcefully, not to be seen until midnight.

Walking up the stairs to the front door to the sound of ear-aching gunshots wasn't exactly pleasant for the missus. At first, the ridiculous thought of someone breaking in popped into her mind, but then when she heard the voice of a famous actor she could not remember the name of, she came to terms with Clarke being awake still.

She stumbled through the door. It swung easily into the wall. The sound of gunshots continued to echo throughout the house, and she was surprised that the noise hadn't disturbed any of their neighbours.

She locked the door behind her after eventually finding the right key, and walked into the sitting room. The image of a man with his throat slit appeared on the TV, making her gag. With a range of drinks in her system, however, she wouldn't have been surprised if it was just the alcohol making its way back up.

There was the television remote on the couch, but no husband. Crushed cans were scattered around the floor, with carpet stains scattered too. *He's frigging spilled some*, she thought angrily. She would switch the TV off, but she was going to save the rest for Clarke when he would eventually wake up the next morning.

She shut the sitting room door slowly behind her, and even more slowly, walked up the stairs. No noise was made until she reached the top of the stairs. To her left was the door to Aaron's room, and to her right, the door to hers and Clarke's. She turned left and poked her head around her son's door. The bed was in the far corner, and Aaron wasn't stirring, *lying* on his side facing the wall. His mother let out a small smile, but he didn't see it.

Shame.

No further noise was created when she shut the door, hoping Aaron wouldn't wake. She sighed as she shifted across to the right door, but what stood in its place was a noticeably infuriated Clarke.

He had his hand on the wall, keeping him steady, and was in his boxer shorts and vest. He was almost hunching over, and one eye was open while the other was closed. She didn't say anything to him, looking at him distastefully, knowing all too well that he wouldn't remember this night.

"Time do you call this?" he said, slurring his words. "This… is bullshit," he spat. "I let you leave the house, only for you to come back in this state?"

"I told you what time I'd be back," she argued, keeping her voice low.

"NO! YOU DIDN'T!"

"*Shhh*. Your son's asleep," she whispered harshly.

Clarke scoffed, now swaying from side to side, and said, "Everything that I do for this family—"

"Go back to bed!" she ordered bravely.

Shock spread across Clarke's face, and she was surprised at herself, too.

Clarke stepped forward, towering over her. A drunken fire was in his eyes, his eyebrows narrowed, and he snatched her arm.

"DON'T YOU TALK TO ME LIKE THAT!"

With every word, she took a step back, nearer to the stairs, while he took a step forward, his hand still wrapped around her arm. "EVER AGAIN!"

And all Clarke could remember from that point was the chilling scream of his wife as she lost her balance and fell down the stairs, and the *clonk* the radiator made when the back of her head cracked against it. Blood immediately splattered all over the carpet and radiator.

Clarke didn't know what had happened in that moment, frozen at the top of the stairs like a terrified sculpture.

In their son's bedroom, Aaron lay there trembling, tears in his eyes.

"Mam had an accident last night," Clarke told Aaron the next morning, arm wrapped around his son's shivering shoulders, as paramedics examined and eventually took a loving mother and wife away in a body bag.

BROWNING MEDICAL INSTITUTE
CASTLEHEAD
AUTOPSY REPORT

- **Deceased:** Mrs. Caroline Smith
- **Height:** 66 Inches
- **Weight:** 128lbs
- **Date of Birth:** 20/01/1982
- **Date of Death:** 19/05/2019
- **Cause of Death:** Severe Head Trauma After Falling Down Stairs and Hitting Head on Radiator

It had made Clarke physically sick, when reading the report that came back on the 21st, but it was the manner of how it happened that made him wonder who was really out of line.

"What was the manner, Dad?" Aaron asked, his head on Clarke's shoulder as he read alone.

"Erm…"

Aaron jumped from how quickly Clarke pressed the report against his chest when his eyes met the bottom category. He never got the chance to read it.

"It's unknown." Clarke caught Aaron's gaze. "Son, this isn't really for your eyes. Why don't you go upstairs for a bit, and I'll call you down for food? How about takeaway?" Clarke forced a smile out of himself, mustering all of his strength.

Aaron loved a takeaway, yet wasn't completely sure how to react this time. He did as his father said, still secretly contemplating if what his father was telling him was the truth.

"Love you, son," he added as he watched Aaron leave.

Once he heard his son's bedroom door shut, Clarke rose and scrunched the report into a ball. He took it into the kitchen, opened a cupboard under the sink, and chucked it into the full bin. But as Clarke shut the cupboard door, on top of the rubbish pile, the autopsy report for Caroline Smith unravelled, revealing the possible manner of death.

- **Manner:** Potential Homicide

4

The Present

Then, just like that, Clarke Smith woke up and found that it was the 23rd.

Since it was two days before the big day, this was a hungover Clarke's last chance to get fresh food in, for Madam Mayor had announced the previous week that everything would be shut for three days: Christmas Eve, Day, and Boxing Day. He checked the fridge to find only half a carton of out-of-date milk, two cans of Pepsi Max, and mouldy cheese.

He wrote out a list straight away, knowing that he had ruined his own plans of doing nothing once again. Leaving the shopping list on the kitchen bench, Clarke miserably walked up to his room to decide on his untidy, non-ironed clothes for the day. *That will do*, he thought, pulling out some jeans and a black top with a mustard stain. The shoes he chose needed a good polish, along with a scrape, as there was dry faeces stuck to the soles. *That'll do.*

Bathed and changed, Clarke stood at the front door, list in hand. He zipped up his winter coat, expecting the wind to hit him once he opened the door. Before doing so, he glanced up at the top corner of the ceiling, aware of the recently installed camera's presence. They were watching.

"Shops," he said.

And then he left.

Walks to the local Tesco by Liberty Street felt essential for the grieving man, not just because he had nothing in the house most of the time, but because it got him outside, even if it was only for half an hour. Although sometimes Clarke had to will himself to get out of bed and onto the streets. Some who passed by would avoid eye contact, hearing the rumours and truth about his wife and only child, while others...

"Clarke!" said a voice. Clarke tried to ignore it. "Clarke, it's me!" He knew the voice, but it would just bring back more memories of the past he would rather hide away from — memories of attending Thomas Hill High. "Clarke!"

Clarke finally reacted and looked across the road. A man stood, waving embarrassingly at him. The man sped across the road to Clarke.

Clarke hated these moments, awkwardly seeing someone from school whom you obviously didn't like — and still don't — and having to put on an exaggerated smile and act as if you're glad to see them again after so long of trying to forget.

"Wesley County," said Clarke, partly enthusiastic, partly kicking himself inside. "It's been so long."

"Yes, it has," said Wesley, running in for a hug instead of the handshake Clarke offered. Wesley released the hug and stood tall in front of Clarke. Lean and blond, nowadays Wesley was eye candy for the ladies, but back in the days of 90s Thomas Hill High, he had countless spots that made his face a dot-to-dot puzzle, a chipped tooth, and arms long enough that people called him a wacky air dancer tube man you see outside car dealerships. Well, at least he didn't have the spots.

"How you been? I've heard what's been happening."

"The whole town knows what's been happening," said Clarke rudely.

Wesley didn't take offence to his former classmate's tone.

"I just want to get on, mate, to be honest with you."

"And how's Aaron?"

Are you for real? Clarke thought as he said, "Still dead."

"Oh mate, I can't imagine everyth— "

"Look," snapped Clarke, "I really just want to get what I need done, so I can go home and drown in my sorrow. Is that okay?"

"Oh... okay," answered Wes awkwardly, not expecting, well, that. "I guess I'll see you in a bit, then."

Wes began to slowly walk away, head down, hands in his pockets.

Clarke groaned and knew this time Wes had taken offence to what he said.

"Hey!" he called.

Wes turned as Clarke walked towards him.

"After the new year, how about a drink?"

Wes let out a smile and nodded. "Good, looking forward to it… mate."

Clarke allowed Wes to walk off, but as he watched his old schoolmate, he thought: *Never goin' to see him again.* And then Clarke continued on by himself to Tesco. Many would describe this megastore as an island, where what you were looking for was treasure, yet for Clarke, he knew this island too well, and was in and out. He only required his bare hands; no basket or trolley, unlike most of the other customers, heading in all directions, sometimes bumping into one another. Regardless of the lack of time Clarke spent in that shop, leaving via those automatic doors and feeling the cool breeze was a breath of fresh air.

The thought forced itself into mind: *Why did it feel… jolly?* Other customers caught Clarke's eye — or just his peripheral vision, he would lie — and the last-minute gifts, decorations and booze in the many trolleys entranced him. The smiles of both parents and children warmed him like a toasty fire, and yet he had none of that. Anymore.

On his way back, switching his plastic bag from hand to hand every so often, Clarke saw the rows of houses, their decorations. Some with lights at the windows and others lit up like an airport runway. In contrast, he saw his own house on the lonely corner. In the light, it was like any other home: a place where someone lived. But by night, it felt out of place. From a distance, because of the glistening lights of the other households, Clarke's home couldn't even be seen.

The grey clouds made it seem later in the day than it actually was. Clarke struggled up the stairs to his front door, where a newspaper sat waiting in the letter box. Placing the shopping bag by his feet on the top step, Clarke tugged on the paper, trying not to rip it. All he could muster the enthusiasm to read was the front-page heading:

THE CASTLEHEAD CHRONICLE
The Castlehead Curse Strikes Again

Instantly, Clarke gathered what it made reference to. He hadn't been at Gill & Susan'z that night, but he was still able to feel the pain the owners were currently going through. Not invited to attend... yet a fire still occurred?

"Curious," he said to himself, planting the paper in with the shopping so that he could unlock the door. The door jerked open, with Clarke having to put a bit more force in than usual. He took a step in, and felt something under his feet. Glancing down, he saw a pile of red envelopes — Christmassy, red envelopes. "Curious," he repeated as he bent down to pick them up.

With the door locked and the bag of shopping by the stairs to be taken care of later that night, the bags under his eyes weren't going to stop Clarke from seeing who these unexpected letters were from. He sat on the couch with them firmly in hand, and couldn't help but genuinely — for the first time in what felt like a lifetime — smile, with a little chuckle.

Dear Mr Smith,

I understand that this is your first Christmas alone, but realistically you're not. Aaron's death has affected all of us, he was so thoughtful and caring. A genuine friend, something I rarely say about anyone. I just want to wish you a Merry Christmas and here's to a better 2020.

From Jason Rayne.

Clarke placed the card on the couch and ripped open the other envelopes.

Dear Clarke,

First of all, I want to apologise for barging in on your son's funeral a few months ago. I didn't mean to cause a scene like that, I was just late. It's not fair, what you're going through, and what the town has gone through too, to a lesser extent. Even though she's lost her mind, my abuela always tells me to try to find the light in the dark. And maybe Christmas is that light. I hope everything gets better soon.

From Elizabeth

Dear Aaron's Dad,

I didn't know Aaron at all, but after spending a few months in this town, I have heard a lot of things about him. I wish I could've met him. Basically, I don't know you and you don't know me but almost everyone else was doing a card so I thought I'd do one too. Have a Merry Christmas, and a Happy New Year.

From Josh

Josh's card made Clarke laugh out loud. At least he had made the effort.

There was only one left, and it was from both Brandon and Anna. Now, these two Clarke remembered. As he read, another letter slipped through the letterbox and landed on top of the Home Sweet Home mat that Caroline had made.

To Clarke Smith,

It's only Anna writing this, but I know Brandon expects me to sign his name on it too. Firstly, it is absolutely heart-breaking about Aaron. You remember what we had, and I didn't get the chance to tell you that your son was, and will always be, a shining star in a dark universe. I bet he's looking down on you proudly, along with Caroline. I loved him... and still do. Writing a letter was much easier than actually coming over. I think it would've been too much for me to handle. But you are more than welcome to come over any time to have a catch up or if you just ever want to talk.

Merry Christmas and have a Happy New Year.

Love from Anna and Brandon xx.

The bags under his eyes didn't stop him from reading that last one, but the tears definitely did. What Aaron and Anna had in Year 7 was lovely. Seeing them together had always brought a smile to Clarke's face — just like the card. He sat there, wiping away the ongoing tears as if he didn't want people to notice.

A bit later, after cleaning himself up and sorting the shopping, it brought him joy to place the cards he had received neatly on top of the electric fire.

If only Caroline and Aaron could see.

The smile faded. Those who were there for him in the present weren't the ones there with him in the past. Knowing the past couldn't be changed, and with the scolding memories returning when his wife and son came to mind, he hurried into the kitchen and pulled out a £16 bottle of Jack Daniels Tennessee Whiskey. He didn't need a glass, twisting the bottle top off and drinking — drowning — his regrets as he collapsed on the couch.

If this is my life, he suddenly thought, *people feeling sorry for me at every turn, then I don't want any part of it*. With that thought — and with only a drop of whiskey remaining in the bottle by 7:30pm — Clarke was in a state that made him seem lifeless. But the thoughts still seemed to circulate.

5

The Future

There I stand, in the garden of my house, taking in my surroundings closely, as if through a pair of binoculars. But something seems different about Castlehead. It is strange, stranger than before, and I don't know how it has happened. I am struck with a sense of deja vu. Above me is nothing but polluted black clouds; no sun, no light, nothing but a corrupt Castlehead.

After contemplating what I should do with myself, as I am aware that there is nothing I can do, I decide to leave my garden and head out onto the streets. I think a bomb has hit, but then I see a sheet of ripped paper gliding through the air. I snatch it and see that it is an issue of The Castlehead Chronicle *from 2021. Now I have grasped what year it is, I need to find out what happened.*

Windows are either shattered or boarded up, as if the buildings are being refurbished. I cough profusely, as if I've been poisoned. The rare faces I catch when walking along the barren streets all look awfully similar, either their arms dangle off their shoulders as they sway back and forth with nothing to help stabilize the pain, or they are covered in deep wounds that ooze sickly substances. Teeth are missing and clothes are torn, revealing cuts and bruises on their torsos and legs. Their faces, however, are the worst, streaming with blood, which I can only assume is flowing from their eyes. Some people have bits of their ears missing, while others look as normal as they can in this different Castlehead...

Wait! Did I notice a regular human? Not someone who resembles a zombie? YES!

I run and scream out to them. They don't notice me at first, but I get their attention by hesitantly tapping them on the shoulder. I think about whether they are affected, too, but I courageously take the chance. The person turns and I am stunned to see that it is Chief Pattison.

"Chief?" I say.

He glares at me devilishly, also hesitant, and says, "*Clarke?*"

When I nod, his face lights up and he adds, "*You're back.*"

But I never left?

I raise an eyebrow and take another good look around. I hear gunshots in the distance, but neither I nor the chief react. He is accustomed to this life, but I'm not.

"*What do you mean? What's going on?*" I finally ask, my heart pounding.

Chief Pattison looks at me, his face tilting like a confused dog, and asks, "*Wait, you don't remember?*" I shake my head furiously, and he leads me down the street.

"*After my departure from the C.C.I.D, the town went to shit. I came back to a town I once knew.*

Apparently, it was the mayor that issued all the riots—"

I am understandably confused; I don't know how I went from reading cards to a scene from Zombieland. Stroking my hands through my hair, trying to gather my thoughts, I come to a stop. The chief hasn't noticed.

"*Riots? Quitting the C.C.I.D?*" I repeat.

The chief stops and finally notices that I am stationary.

While he walks towards me slowly, I add, "*I don't understand.*"

"*Well, you should!*" bellows the chief suddenly.

I jump and notice how distorted his face is now, I don't know what I have done, but it appears he is angry with me.

"*YOU STARTED IT ALL!*"

"*What?*" I say.

"*It's your fault. If you had just… What is it that you say? Remained in line? Then none of this would've happened.*"

"*No…*" I realise what the chief is blaming me for. One act can always lead to something drastic… "*This can't be my fault. I'm never out of line.*"

"*It is,*" repeats the chief, his hands on my shoulder. I see his sincere look, and there is silence for a moment.

"*It is,*" he says again.

No… Never."

I don't say another word and leave the chief on the street on his own; though I keep hearing his voice replaying in my head like an old record player.

Rain begins to fall from the coal clouds but I actually don't care, acting as if it's not there.

It is. It is my fault. All this is because… I was the one out of line. It is my fault. It is. IT IS.

"It is," I say out loud.

6

Clarke jerked up from the couch, drenched in sweat, somehow with the empty whiskey bottle still in hand. For a moment, he had to gather where he was. Not in a post-apocalyptic Castlehead, that was for sure. He was back in his sitting room, with light blaring through the window blinds, though it wasn't sunny.

Peeking through them, he was mesmerised to see that the roads, gardens, cars, and roofs had been blanketed in coats of snow. It was a sight to behold, and placing the empty bottle on the television stand, Clarke ran to the door in his clothes from the previous day. Before unlocking it, he did a double-take after spotting one of his Christmas cards. There was a warm feeling inside him, and it wasn't the whiskey. He wasn't sad. For once.

Unlocking the door, cheers and uplifting children's laughter gently drifted into his house and filled the Christmas air. The laughter was infectious and Clarke laughed at a group of kids in fur coats, dressed in hats, scarves and thermal gloves, having a snowball fight — with one kid hitting another square in the face.

Bullseye, thought Clarke.

"Hey!" he yelled gleefully.

All the kids on the street, maybe around ten or eleven years of age, looked up at him.

"Do you know what the day is today?" he asked.

"CHRISTMAS EVE!" they all answered.

But Clarke imagined them saying, in innocent posh accents: *Why, it's Christmas Eve, sir.*

He laughed at the thought as the kids went back to their snowball fight. This wasn't a Charles Dickens book; it was a day when Clarke hoped that all those children would put cookies and milk out for Santa, a carrot for the reindeer, and then afterwards, sit with their parents, toasting by the fire in Christmas PJs.

Something was in the air, and it gave Clarke the one thing he hadn't had since the beginning of summer: hope. He hoped that the new year would bring new opportunities, which was what New Year was all about. 2020 was right around the corner, and things had to change. And those changes were in the form of resolutions.

CHAPTER EIGHT

Changes and Resolutions

1

2020 had finally come. What a year people envisioned it would be. Year 9 students across the country were mere months away from choosing their GCSE options, Clarke promised to involve himself with the town more, and the Castlehead Criminal Investigation Department became intransigent in solving any cases but the town's arsonist.

"We're not having a repeat of last year," the chief told his team on January 2nd.

But then Clarke stormed in spontaneously with an envelope tightly gripped in his hand. He darted for the chief, who stood at the door of his office, but Deputy Ton cut him off, ushering him back into the stairwell promptly.

"You can't just come in here unannounced, Clarke," warned Ton in a snappy whisper.

"Well, I think this is a much bigger matter than a pep talk," argued Clarke in the same tone. Then he held up the envelope. "Here…" he spat.

"What's this?" asked Ton, snatching it from Clarke. He held it up to the light to see if it had an address on it, or a name, but none of those things appeared. "When did you get it?"

"I—"

Clarke was cut off by the roar in the chief's voice as he said, "... And nobody is going to argue about it. They caused all this havoc, out of pure jealousy. Because we apparently hid them away—" But Clarke brushed it off.

"I found it on top of my doormat, at Christmas," Clarke told the deputy.

"Uh-huh. Did you get any others like this?"

"No, just normal Christmas cards off those kids."

"Okay." The deputy tore the envelope open and pulled out the folded sheet of paper inside. In child-like writing, it read *Happy Holidays, Daddy* with an awful drawing of a smiley face in the corner.

"It could just be a prank. Is there anyone you know who might've done this?"

Clarke shook his head and said, "I guess the kids, but they sent me cards, so why would they do such a thing?"

"It might not be those kids. Just kids trying to be funny. Probably scum who hang out in parks and get drunk and high because they have nothing better to do."

"You think?"

"That's most likely the answer," said Ton with a smile.

But then a thought came to mind, and Clarke said coldly, "But say, hypothetically, what would be the chances of it being the arsonist?"

This caught Ton off guard. Handing the letter back to Clarke, he looked up and thought for a moment. *That is a possibility.*

"Very little," he said instead. Ton then walked back into the main office, leaving Clarke in the cold stairwell.

"Sorry about that," heard Clarke. "Chief, I need to talk to you. Urgently."

2

No one was exactly elated to be returning to scheduled school days once Thomas Hill High reopened. Principal Keeper sent a letter out on New Year's Eve — very short notice — stating that he and the staff were more than ready to bring the students back.

Attendance was high on the first day back, so much so that Anna, Brandon and Josh (who all walked into the main hall together, chatting away) didn't notice Jason's absence until they reached their first class.

Their form teacher sat at her desk, her green eyes locked on her laptop. Not even she was aware of Jason's absence over the rumbling chatter until she looked up when the first bell rang.

She rose proudly, and said with forced glee, "Welcome back, everyone." She looked at her class; they either stared back at her with their chins resting on their hands, or had their heads on the tables, hoping for that extra five minutes of sleep. The three empty chairs (two at the back, one at the front) got under her skin. "New term, new year. Change is coming."

No one bought her enthusiasm, so she stopped trying and sat back down at her desk to take the register. "Beth—"

The door swung open suddenly; Eli appeared. He looked careless in his act of being late, and the teacher's annoying admonishment went in one ear and out the other. Walking — slouching — across to his designated seat at the back of the room, normally next to Kelsey, Eli glanced to the front, where Jason would normally sit. He caught Anna, Brandon and Josh's eyes. They looked equally curious.

"Soz, Miss," he remembered to say.

As the teacher continued reading out the register from her laptop, Eli continued to match the *smart kids'* gazes. They nodded at each other, as if knowingly making plans to meet at their usual rendezvous point in the main hall at either break or lunch — or maybe both, if Eli's mates didn't catch him red handed, sitting with the 'other' kids.

"Kelsey?" announced the teacher, looking out at the sea of students.

"She'll be in later, Miss. She didn't say why," explained Eli.

"Ah… okay. Ale—"

"Miss?" Brandon butted in. "Sorry, but do you know where Jason is?"

"I don't see what business that is of yours, Brandon."

"Oh, sorry," said Brandon, hanging his head.

Eli's ears pricked up at his old friend's name, but he remained slouching so that nobody would notice his interest.

Glancing from the register to the three sitting in the front row and seeing their slightly worried faces, the teacher sighed.

"He's at an appointment of some sort. I don't know the ins and outs but he said it was very important."

The row of three blocked out the teacher calling out the remaining students, leaned in towards one another, and Anna said, "What important appointment?"

Josh and Brandon shrugged.

At that moment, exactly one-hundred miles due west, Jason Rayne was on a train, continuously debating in his head if said *appointment* was a good idea — especially having not told anyone… still.

3

The 8:30am North2West Express train to Valeland was a peaceful ride. Jason had booked a table seat, and those sitting in the other seats gave him odd looks during the journey, which he ignored. He relaxed his head, leaning back in the seat, and gazed out the window vacantly. The soothing sound of the rails clickety-clacking as the train made its way across the country caused Jason to zone out at points; he couldn't fall asleep, not on this train ride, aware that Valeland wasn't the final stop.

"The next stop is—" the train driver would announce just before arriving at every station. He would add, "This train terminates at Derryman, Scotland."

No turning back now, Jason thought. Everything had been arranged via his phone; the tickets, the interview, everything, and regardless of Gemma knowing his passcode or not, Jason never let his phone leave his side. In another world, he thought, if he had been just that little bit careless with his device, his secrets would be revealed, and then he would face his mother's wrath. Up to now, his plan had unfolded neatly; the last steps of this plan, though, had not been plotted yet.

Just continue looking out the window, he told himself. *You're going to play a game. Yes! A game, a game where you have to spot something different. Sounds simple.*

On the other side of the table, a shrivelled couple glared at what appeared to be a cold, blank stare from a kid who didn't know where he was.

Bushes. Trees. A field. Bull. Calf. Farmhouse. Trees — Dammit. He grunted.

Okay, here we go. Field. Horses. Flowers. A cabin. Trees—

"Excuse me."

Jason felt a kick from under the table, but it wasn't from a foot. Shaking his head, he noticed the old couple opposite jerking their heads towards the aisle. He looked up and saw a trolley of snacks, sandwiches and drinks. Pushing the cart was a plump woman with short, curly hair who appeared to have had her fair share of train journeys over the years. "Anything off the trolley, my dear?" she asked politely.

"No thanks," Jason answered tiredly.

"Two coffees, please," said the husband. "Black."

"Very good, love," complimented the lady.

The wife looked bemused and pulled up a silver cane from under the table.

There was a point of realisation from Jason: *That must've been what kicked me.*

"Two minutes," said the apron-wearing lady with assurance, preparing the black coffees.

The wife rested the cane on her lap, staring at Jason, her faint brown eyes expressing curiosity. The husband, on the other hand, watched the lady intently. As the coffee machine did its magic, the husband felt something he hadn't felt since his wedding day — which Jason could only assume happened in the early 60s (at the latest).

"The next station is Harrington," the driver announced over the tannoy.

"Family trip?" assumed the lady, looking at Jason and the couple with a smile.

"Oh, no, no, no," said Jason. "I'm here..." *Be careful what you say, Jason.* "My mother is meeting me at Valeland Station."

A beaming row of white teeth spread over the teen's face in the hope that everyone around would believe him. "I have family in Castlehead, so I visited them for Christmas and New Year," he added.

"My apologies," said the woman, handing change back to the couple.

She strode off, wincing at her assumption.

The couple sipped their coffees together as Jason went back to gazing out the window, a platform coming into view.

A little after five minutes had passed and the North2West Express train was back to moving at full-speed towards its next stop: Valeland.

Jason rose and headed down the aisle, knowing he had all of his possessions, and waited by the automatic doors. He didn't want to waste any time in getting off; the meeting was at 12:30pm and it was already coming up to 11am. The thought of getting lost instantly came to mind — he wasn't exactly good at navigation, even in Castlehead — and his legs began to tremble.

"Come on, Jason," he said through gritted teeth.

Determined, that's what he had to be. Not scared stiff.

"We are now arriving at Valeland."

The train slowly pulled up to the platform. A bustling crowd awaited. Jason denied the jitters in his stomach, for now.

His legs went stiff as the door slid open, and it became evident quickly that he was the only one getting off. Stepping onto the platform with planks as legs was difficult. He had to steady himself and act as if he were fine.

Ticket booths probably made in the 40s or 50s sat by the station's main entrance and exits. Staff in neat navy blue uniforms attended travellers in need of tickets or directions. The analogue clocks overhead, with Roman numerals instead of numbers, read dot-on 11 o'clock in the morning. Perfect timing.

Jason froze at the majestic archway that was both the entrance and exit. He took it all in, and he was desperate to step forward into Valeland. But it felt like something tugged at his back, like a force beyond life, holding him back. Was it the thought of Gemma? No, because she wasn't his main worry — yet. It wasn't his friends at Thomas Hill High, because they hadn't come to mind, either. Jason couldn't put his finger on it.

Stepping forward, out of the archway's shade and into the blaring sunlight, Jason froze again in disbelief. What stood in front of him was a view that he could only describe as a postcard town.

No way I'm still in England, he thought. And then he walked on to the Desmond School for Creative Arts.

4

Thomas Hill students barged through the flapping doors as the bell rang for lunch. Like every previous lunch and break time, the main hall was crammed with students in a matter of seconds. It didn't surprise Brandon, Anna and Josh that the only table remaining — reserved — for them was the small round table in the corner.

Scanning the hall, Josh unintentionally caught the eye of Eli, who sat at a long table that could seat a dozen students. Eli blended in with the hoodie-wearing, football-loving group as he switched his focus back to his mates.

"What ye lookin' at?" said a round-headed pal of his, scanning the room, too.

"Oh…" He couldn't really admit who he was looking at, when in reality he genuinely would've much preferred to sit with Anna, Brandon and Josh.

Josh saw this in Eli's shy look and the way he sat, looking away from his group.

"Nothing, mate," answered Eli finally.

"So, what do you think Jason's really doing?" asked Anna.

"You know what he's like, probably still on the case, like the detective he thinks he is," said Josh.

Then the doors to reception opened wide.

Every head turned. The boys tried not to express their rising testosterone levels by charging towards her like a pack of drooling dogs fighting over a bone, and the girls secretly admired the glistening white dress — the quite revealing white dress — and the heels that went with it. Kelsey strutted in, her fiery lips entrancing Eli, especially, and it was clear that curlers had been used in her brown hair.

"Really? Could she be any more full of herself?" remarked Anna.

Brandon, Anna and Josh glanced up and saw Z appear out of what seemed like thin air, standing over them, rolling her eyes at Kelsey. They jumped at Z's sudden arrival, but switched their focus back to Kelsey instantly.

"She thinks it's a catwalk," joked Brandon.

Kelsey walked across to the table Eli sat at, and he couldn't take his eyes off her — like the rest of his group... and the school. She placed a hand on her hip and stood confidently over him, letting everyone bask in her presence. Eli knew how extremely lucky he was.

"Don't tell me this is why she wasn't in form this morning," spat Z, her arms folded.

"Her mother's back, isn't she? She probably has her wrapped around her pinky," suggested Brandon.

They continued to stare at her distastefully, whereas the rest of the school mostly resumed their own conversations (most of them about Kelsey).

Kelsey evidently wasn't planning on taking a seat, for she knew the value of the dress and heels. The dress was smooth and silky, and, on closer examination, Eli spotted Kelsey's pierced ears and didn't want to guess how much it had cost to purchase those diamond earrings, not to mention the manicure.

"What'd you think?" Kelsey asked, whipping her hair in the air just so that the boys could get a close look at the earrings.

"You look great," said Eli.

"Good," said Kelsey with a smile. "Because Mammy's treating us to a meal tonight at Cheryl's Italian."

"Sorry, where?" coughed Eli, his mates just as surprised as he was. One of them had to pat him on the back so that he could catch his breath. "You know that's a place for the poshies, aye?"

"Mammy said she's paying, so it's okay," argued Kelsey.

That was the last Kelsey was going to have of her boyfriend's reluctance.

5

These were uncharted streets Jason was walking on. Maria had given him the address for the Desmond School for Creative Arts, but where it was actually located was still a complete blur.

As he walked, Jason learned very quickly that Valeland wasn't Castlehead. There were seagulls instead of crows, genuinely nice people instead of criminals, and... no friends or family.

Jason thought, *Don't have second thoughts now.*

The streets weren't crammed with people; more or less only a few passed when Jason decided to stop at a small shop on a street corner. When he entered, Jason was almost blinded by the darkness of the store, given that his eyes had just adjusted to the bright Valeland sky.

At the back of the store was the counter, and Jason headed straight for the cashier, ignoring the shelves of snacks, newspapers, magazines and milk. The cashier glared at this new boy, waited a beat to see what Jason would do, and then went back to pressing buttons on the till.

"Excuse me," said Jason shyly.

The cashier glanced back at Jason on the other side of the counter.

"I've just got here and I don't know where to go."

Through gritted teeth, the cashier said, "Buy a map."

"What?"

"I said, what are you looking for, my friend?"

Jason pulled out his phone from his coat pocket, scrolling hurriedly through his Notes app. There was another beat before he presented the cashier with the address for the Desmond School for Creative Arts.

"Oh, yeah, I know the place. What you wanna do is follow the road until you reach a large roundabout, take the third exit to Main Street and it — *I think* — is at the end of the road."

Jason nodded and said "Okay, thank you," with a small smile before leaving.

The sun blinded him again as he stepped back onto the smooth pavement and did as he had been instructed. The buildings he walked past and the street he walked upon reminded Jason of an old English town which had kept its rusty charm for as long as it stood. Continuing up the road, passing narrow backstreets, Jason knew that this town had history, and he was certain that it was definitely a tourist destination — unlike Castlehead. He saw the sparkling sea at the ends of the backstreets, and heard a blend of faint conversations that told him that families were making the most of their Spain-like weather.

Valeland had been completely unknown to Jason before now, and he had never expected a rusty, north-western coastal town to feel like paradise.

Home.

Jason had finally reached the roundabout the cashier told him of and froze at a green sign informing drivers of each exit. *Main Street. 3rd exit.*

When the road was clear, he rushed across with his heart pounding; the worst was always in the back of Jason's head. But he made it onto Main Street and started to walk alongside a seemingly never-ending brick wall that looked like it continued beyond the horizon.

What was beyond the wall filled Jason with curiosity. He couldn't peek over it, for it stood about 20 feet. The fading colour on the bricks made him think it could be a sacred — maybe restricted — field of ancient ruins.

A museum? A prison? He scoffed at the thought. A prison? Really? Jason couldn't help but laugh at himself for even thinking about it. *Or how about a mansion owned by a billionaire mobster?* In his defence, that last idea was most accurate, given what he had read in old library books about Castlehead. Valeland might not be much different after all. Now he was kidding himself. This wasn't Castlhead; this town had a completely different story of its own. Something inside made Jason feel adamant to find out what it was.

However, shortly afterwards, he finally had an answer to all of his speculation while walking along Main Street. He came to a stop at a set of majestic steel gates. A crowd of about twenty stood there, peering through the bars of the gates, getting a glimpse of what their future would hold. Jason did the same, squeezing through the crowd — who all roughly looked the same age, or a tad older — and peering through the bars. Beyond the closed gates was the campus for the Desmond School for Creative Arts.

Home.

The anticipation was getting to the crowd. Students of all different ages were walking through the campus with bags strapped to their backs, ignoring the crowd, eager to get to their next lesson. There were concrete pathways splitting off in many directions like a spider's web, and — from what they could see — many patches of grass, home to park benches. But the crowd's attention suddenly turned to a young, smart woman walking towards them.

Jason smiled.

It was Maria, in a knee-length skirt and blazer, holding a clipboard, standing formally on the other side of the gates. She glared at the suddenly silent group, knowing that only a fair few would get the chance of a lifetime.

The group took a step back and the gates opened smoothly, with Maria greeting them with a smile. Her eyes were on Jason.

"Welcome, all. You have been specifically chosen to fight for a chance to study something you desire." Maria ushered the group in, and they entered in a neat, single file. All stayed silent as Maria spoke. "We here at the Desmond School for Creative Arts search for the best students from across the U.K. You are all very lucky." Leading them deeper into the campus, Maria presented them with the main courtyard, which was surrounded by three intimidating buildings — all of which had a rich feel to them. In the middle of the courtyard was a bronze statue of a man in a suit and hat, holding a cane. "We remember those who came before us, and this man right here—" Like a tour guide, Maria pointed at a plaque on the pedestal the statue stood upon, "is the founder of Valeland: Lord Alfred Vale."

A wave of "wow"s came over the group. That was the reaction all new applicants gave when entering the school grounds for the first time.

"So, what is the specific curriculum?" said a woman, 18, in a white shirt, as if ready for a job interview.

They continued around the courtyard as Maria explained, "As well as having Maths and English departments, which are located at the back of the campus, the three buildings surrounding us are the main reasons why people study here." Each word made Jason thirsty for more. "Art, Creative Writing, and Performing Arts. Like every subject and course, there are many components, some of which are optional. Others are compulsory. But that's okay, because everyone comes here for the same reason." No members of the group needed to be told said reason; they instinctively knew it. "Now, when I call your name, you will join me to head to the headmaster's office." She looked down at the clipboard and scrolled her finger down it while calling out names. "Jessica Collins." The shirt-wearing girl stepped forward, nudging past Jason. "Sam Dylan." A young lad in baggy bottoms stepped forward. "And…" For a second, Jason's heart sank into a void. "Jason Rayne."

"Oh my God," whispered Jason, breathing the relief out of his system.

He joined the other chosen ones behind Maria. She looked up from her clipboard and didn't react to the hurt faces of the candidates who thought they had just wasted their day.

"Just because you haven't been picked today, doesn't mean it's the end of the line for you," she said. "And should you get another chance…" Jason knew that was meant towards him. Maria added, "take it. But remember that we don't want average, here. We don't want to be satisfied. We expect excellence."

Dismissing the rest of the group, Maria turned around and, without looking back, gestured for just Jason to follow her.

The other two fell behind, with large grins on their faces.

Something was going on.

"Why aren't they coming with us?" asked Jason.

Maria kept her eyes forward and answered, "Because they already study here."

"What?"

What was right. Did she mean to say that this open day was all a ruse just to get Jason in? Why him? And he thought Castlehead was crazy…

"Imagine the complaints if I had only chosen you," she explained.

"So, you get students to pretend to be applicants to make it more realistic?"

"Exactly." *This is why we need you*, she thought. "Follow me."

Walking back past the memorial statue of Alfred Vale, they stopped in front of one of the buildings. The great silver dome upon what Maria told him was the Great Hall resembled London's St. Paul's Cathedral. It was the building where professors had their offices and where exams took place. Entering, Jason caught sight of the crystal chandelier that lit the Great Hall, with both his and Maria's reflections visible in the floor looking back at them like a mirror.

Maria led the curious boy up the golden-banister staircase, taking him to the second floor, which was nothing more than an everlasting hallway filled with doors leading to exam rooms and offices. A string of lights lit up the hallway this time, and the sound of their footsteps echoed throughout.

"Why am I the only one the head wants to see?" Jason finally asked.

As they continued down the hall, turning a corner, Maria explained quietly, "People will stop at nothing to get a place here. For those out there, they'll be waiting years…"

Jason gulped at the thought of suffering the same fate if he hadn't asked to reschedule after the Thomas Hill fire.

"You, however, might get your place today."

But that didn't answer his question.

Regardless, Jason tried not to express his giddiness.

They stopped abruptly at a dark brown door that read: **THE HEAD'S OFFICE – KNOCK AND WAIT**.

Jason took a deep breath in an attempt to reassure himself.

"Okay, I think I'm ready," he said.

"You'll be all right."

And just like at the ruins of Central Church all those months ago, Maria healed him with a peck on the cheek before leaving.

Jason did as the door instructed. Twiddling his fingers in silence, it was only now that he began to get those jitters in his stomach again — butterflies. Excitement and nervousness blended together.

"ENTER!" A powerful voice shot through the door and walls; Jason wanted to believe it was actually the forceful voice that made the door click open.

Jason left the door ajar as he entered the grand office, but as he was taking it all in, the door clicked shut of its own accord. Shelves containing books and trophies of vibrant gold and silver stood against the walls all the way up to the ceiling, the large throne-like chair on the other side of the stable office desk faced the admittedly lovely view of the campus, and on Jason's side of the desk was a single wooden chair expected to collapse under too much pressure.

"I–I just want to say thank you for the opportunity."

Slowly lowering himself into the wooden chair was like entering an intense game of chess. Jason was unsure if he had made the correct first move — the first move sets any game in motion. After all, he was up against the master.

"Consider yourself extremely lucky, Master Rayne." The principal remained staring out at the school he ruled. "Second chances should only come once in a blue moon. A lot — in fact, most — people take them for granted. But you…" The chair spun around and there Jason sat, face-to-face with the principal of the Desmond School for Creative Arts: Master Desmond Edwards. "You're different, aren't you?"

Who Jason saw across the desk from him — if he had to estimate — probably outweighed him by 300lbs; his Santa Claus beard hid his mouth, but his deep voice told everyone he spoke to that his mouth was very much there. Jason's initial thought was that the principal was slouching, but it was his belly, and it was with this realisation Jason assumed that the chair had been specially reinforced. Sweat patches showed under his stretched suit, but it didn't seem to bother the principal one bit; his attention was firmly on the applicant, and Desmond saw by Jason's expression that he was unsure what his next move was going to be.

"Um… I guess so," answered Jason.

"You *guess* so? No, no, no. We don't guess here. You either are or you're not. That's it."

"S-sorry, I'm very nervous."

"Don't be," the principal said more calmly. He clasped his hands together, planting them on his rotund belly, and continued. "Now, as you know, we've had our eye on you for a good while."

With a slight nod, Jason agreed, "Yes."

"There's a simple reason for that. We know talent when we see it."

Jason felt pride in that moment.

"But…"

But? Jason repeated in his head. *Why does there always have to be a 'but'?*

"Yes?" he said, anticipating the worst possible outcome.

"We haven't exactly told you the full story."

Okay, that was an unexpected move.

The game was firmly in Desmond's favour, and with that statement, the perplexity Jason felt increased drastically. Jason was as nervous as ever, all the excitement drained from his body.

"What do you mean?" Jason asked, leaning forward as the chair creaked.

"Your talent has been noticed, as much as you may not think it has. And your talent is great. Your book will definitely show that."

"How did you know about—"

"There's a place you've been going to write, and we have an informant on the inside to scout for possible recruitments for our program."

"Carl," guessed Jason.

Desmond gave him a look.

"Wow."

"And he sends us all the information he finds out about your town—"

Jason gave a look of impressed realisation, and said, completing his sentence, "and that's how Maria knew about the fires and Aaron. She came to investigate."

"Correct again, boy."

Jason imagined Desmond smiling under his bush of a beard. "You see, to the rest of the U.K., Castlehead doesn't even exist. The meteor that struck before the town was formed hid all of its inhabitants from the rest of the country. The Valeland Council fund Castlehead on top of themselves, but your mayor has been trying her best to get Castlehead back on the map."

From under his side of the desk, Edwards handed the applicant a pile of tabloids.

THE GUARDIAN
Crazy Lady Appoints Herself Mayor of Fictional Town

THE SUN
Daughter Left Homeless After 'Crazy Mayor Lady' Imprisoned at New Mental Institute

THE TELEGRAPH
Could The Craziness Be Genetic?

"So, what does this have to do with me?" asked Jason, tossing the papers back onto the table.

"I have," started Desmond, "direct contact with the V.C.P.A—"

Jason butted in: "V.C.P.A?"

"Valeland Citizen Protection Agency. Anyways, our school has formed a partnership with them. Our school can get you into any university or any job in the arts. Your specialty is writing, but your life recently has been devoted to finding out Castlehead's mysteries. Should you accept our offer, we will also offer you a place as a junior detective at the V.C.P.A, alongside Maria, and some other possible candidates."

"Are you saying...?" Jason didn't need to finish the sentence. "God." His body went numb with joy and a hint of worry. *Finish your GCSEs, son, you're going to go to university. Do something proper.*

"What do you say?" demanded Desmond calmly. *Please say yes,* he thought.

"I... I..."

Principal Edwards grasped Jason's range of emotions, and said, "I get that this is a lot to take in. But, son, at this rate, if things keep happening, there won't be a town left; never mind not being on the map." Desmond saw Jason was battling himself inside, trying to make a decision. "Okay, I get it. Nevertheless, we will send you a letter..." The principal caught Jason's small, thankful smile. "Just in case."

"Thank you."

Jason stood up and headed back to the door. Placing his hand on the handle, his body froze. Perhaps second thoughts?

Desmond said, "Why not use a gift that God has given you?"

On the way home, that question — in that deep voice — repeated constantly in Jason's conflicted head.

6

"Mother, I'm home from school," called Anna, locking the door behind her. But all she could hear was the echo of her own voice. "Mother? Father?"

The lounge and dining area joined as one, and her mother and father sat silently on the lush white couch. As she sat down too, they all sunk into it. Then Anna noticed why they were acting weirdly. On the coffee table, by the unlit scented candles, was a torn envelope. The same wave of curiosity her parents had experienced came over her.

Why is there no address label?

Anna slowly picked the envelope up, noticing that there was a folded piece of paper inside. She looked at both of her parents, who glared back — her mother with tears in her eyes and her hand over her mouth, and her father, who appeared more angry than scared — before reading what the sheet said.

"It came for you today," sniffed Anna's mother.

Anna read:

DO YoU MisS HIM, AnnA?

Anna's face grew pale. It was like all of the breath had been sucked out of her.

"Sweetie?" said her father, now looking worried.

Anna said nothing, frozen, dropping the sheet of paper; the memories of Year 7 came back, all the laughter, picnics, joyous kissing behind Thomas Hill High's P.E building during lunch… and the arguments. There was this vacant stare, nothing like her parents had seen before. Anna's head began to jitter, and she clutched her chest. She felt nothing; everything was in slow motion. She couldn't help herself falling backwards into the couch.

"Get her some water," ordered her mother to her father.

His footsteps were like drums in Anna's ears, rattling her head even more. Her father, a moment later, stormed back in with a glass of ice-cold water. Anna's mother snatched it off him and put the glass by Anna's lips, almost forcing her to take a sip. It was painful seeing their daughter in that hyperventilating state, and they couldn't bear to imagine what was going through Anna's mind.

Aaron, I'm sorry. I do miss you, Anna thought. *Take me back… Take me with you.*

Swallowing that excruciating first sip of water, Anna came back around, and as the afternoon carefully slid into early evening, she couldn't help herself by constantly staring at the question: *Do you miss him, Anna?*

Then it hit her, after looking at it long enough. The question was a statement, a statement being made.

A clue? Anna wondered. *Possibly. Mind games? Undoubtedly.*

7

Deja vu struck as Z walked up to Sunvalley Park after school, seeing flashing blue lights in the midst of all the trees. *Oh what now?* Z thought. She didn't acknowledge the crunching leaves and twigs beneath her, nor the rustling branches and bushes. Gaining speed, Z's walk turned into a full sprint. *Please don't be Abuela*, she thought. Without seeing the vehicle, it was near impossible to tell what department the lights and sirens were from. *What if it's a fire?*

She came to a sudden halt as she reached the welcoming Sunvalley Park sign. Surrounding the normally lit campfire on site were not only the caravans, but also a series of C.C.I.D police cars.

"Shit," she said through gritted teeth.

As she stepped forwards onto the site, all heads turned; everyone must've been forced out of their caravans, for the park's residents had their hands raised, with the officers going as far as to aim guns at them. They stood like statues, eyes on Z, but it was the two officers that stood straight as logs in front of her home that caught Z's attention.

"Elizabeth!" called Chief Pattison as Z inched nearer.

But she ignored her name, her eyes widening at the sight behind the two officers. It was like she had been filled with utter fury; seeing an officer pushing her grandmother in a wheelchair was unforgivable. They obviously weren't aware of the gravity of her health issues.

"What'd you think ye doin?" she growled. "She's sick!"

The chief and deputy glanced back at the chair-ridden, fragile lady for a second then grinned back at Z.

"Put her back where she belongs!"

The residents remained silent, but Z could tell that they were just as scared and confused as she was.

Pattison stepped forward and said, "You see, that's not our job. Our job is to put tramps *like you* back where you belong, not look after dying souls."

Z was well above boiling point now; it was clear in her eyes and face.

"Elizabeth…" Deputy Ton walked around behind the girl in all black, forcing her hands behind her back. "I am placing you under arrest for arson…" Z scoffed. "And for the murder of Aaron Smith."

She scoffed again, the handcuffs immediately rubbing, saying firmly, "Are you serious?" She looked around at the other residents, who were also being abusively handcuffed. It was when she caught the chief's gaze that she eventually realised what was going on. "Oh, I get it," she said with a grin. "The solution is to arrest Z, because you don't have anyone else to blame. Why not? It's the simplest way to dig yourself out of the hole the *actual* arsonist created."

She saw the worry on the chief's face as he spat, "You have the right to remain silent, Eliz—"

"YEAH? AND I ALSO HAVE THE RIGHT TO FREE SPEECH, SO SHUT UP!"

"Z?" her grandmother said, startled by the roar in Z's voice. "Is that you? Why are you upset, honey?"

"But…" She lowered her tone as she continued, "say, hypothetically, it was actually—" she looked around, "Ton who did it." She smirked. "Honest mistake, right? Let him off with a warning? But when you suspect — *blame* — the likes of us, throw away the key and a life sentence."

"Take her away," ordered the chief.

Being forced into the car by Deputy Ton, Z's rebellious — and possibly true, thought Ton in the back of his mind — words were: "You haven't found a solution. Basically, you're still on the hypothesis."

People — not the Sunvalley Park lot — would argue that Z's pride got the better of her, smiling as they drove away to the C.C.I.D offices, but others would say she did the town justice for bringing up a problem with mainstream society. Madam Mayor just brushed it off and acted like nothing had occurred.

8

Another arrest, assumed Jason as he heard police sirens on a nearby street. In spite of the light shining through into the house, there was something off about the atmosphere as Jason returned home from his interview.

"Mam? Grandma? Grandad?" he called as he shut the door. There was no response from any of them, leading him to believe something was wrong. "I'm home."

He took his shoes off and left them by the door, walking through the kitchen to the stairs. But that's when he stopped. Sitting with their heads down, Gemma and Jason's grandparents were on the couch. It was like they were comforting one another. The pile of used tissues sitting on the arm of the sofa was a giveaway.

"Oh, Jason," sniffled Gemma, reaching out for him. Her eyes were sore and red from all the crying. Jason stepped forward into the sitting room — back to the way it was, without the Christmas decorations — and he sat in between his mother and grandparents. "We've got some news."

"What?" he said nervously.

At first, noticing them in the sitting room, Jason suspected they had found out about the Desmond School for Creative Arts. Perhaps Thomas Hill had called, to make sure Jason hadn't been fibbing. But by the distressed looks on his family's faces, Jason knew that this was a more serious situation.

"What is it? Tell me." He started to grow scared and began to feel sick.

"When you were at school, we received a call," explained Gemma. "It was from a man who turned out to be your father's boss. Apparently, he was on his way to sorting himself out, but then they went out one night — your dad and his work colleagues. He wasn't drinking because he was the chauffeur for the night. It was late, too late. Driving along the motorway the car in front came to a sudden stop, forcing your dad to stamp on the brakes. But... he wasn't quick enough."

Jason knew where this was going. The sickly feeling got worse.

"Son... he didn't make it."

CHAPTER NINE

Early Days of Spring

1

As the season began to shift into spring, Castlehead residents received more and more cryptic letters from this anonymous source. It had to happen to everyone eventually, many supposed, so it was no surprise to Jason, on April 1st, when he too received a letter. If nobody else had been sent them, Jason would most likely have shaken it off as a sinister April Fools prank, but nobody knew what to believe anymore, and the wickedness of this little north-eastern town was eating everyone alive.

The letterbox bit into the sheet of paper strongly. Jason released the letter with a tug, but didn't read it until he was sitting at the dining room table. The blinds were shut, yet the orange evening sky still shone through.

"Mam, come here!" called Jason as he unfolded the paper to read it.

Gemma ran in and didn't need to be told what Jason had in his hands. She leaned over Jason and took an intense look at what the letter said, her wet hair dangling by Jason's cheek. There was a moment of silence before Gemma snatched the sheet from her son. Walking around with it, she gazed at the messy bold writing.

"We have to go to the C.C.I.D," Gemma said, looking up from the letter.

Gemma felt her heart race. Why things happened to good, honest folk like themselves was unbeknownst to her. Time was running out for Jason to settle on his options for his last years at Thomas Hill High, and she was on the verge of a promotion, which included a pay rise, but all that, she thought, was forced to be put on hold because of the things they were being unwillingly dragged into.

Jason huffed and rose, knowing it was the only *legal* option. But the thought of just doing it himself, like he had done alongside his fellow friends, did race through his mind. It was tempting, but doing it himself meant he had to bring Gemma into it. And with Gemma more paranoid than ever after being a part of the blaze at Gill & Susan'z, there was no way he was going to get rid of the letter without getting caught.

"Okay then," he agreed grudgingly.

2

Kelsey sat, panicking, as she held the sheet of paper in her hand. She had been itching to check her phone for the last five minutes, urgently wanting a reply — from anyone. Eli, her mother, anyone; all she wanted to know was why she would be sent such a disgusting letter.

Her phone sat by her side on the couch, blank.

Kelsey glanced from the paper to the front door, waiting for the lock to click open.

She read:

HOw's YoUR DaDDY?

"Dead," she said aloud.

The door began to shake, the lock clicking as a key jammed its way in. Then the handle turned and Melissa entered, putting the bags she held on the floor, forming a mountain, and the leather jacket she wore. Melissa dropped them at the bottom of the stairs and entered the lounge.

"Hi, honey," she greeted excitedly. "This isn't exactly a rich town, but I'll tell you there's some cracking shops around here. You got to see what I bought. Kelsey? Kelsey, honey? Kelsey, what's wrong?"

Kelsey remained seated as Melissa moved her phone and sat next to her daughter. Kelsey passed the sheet to her mother, who at first glance shook it off as a silly prank. But then she saw her daughter's hurt, almost tearful expression.

"It came through the door this morning just after you left," said Kelsey quietly,

"Could it not be someone being stupid?" asked Melissa.

"No, not many people actually know about Daddy."

"Okay…" Melissa contemplated other options. "Well, why don't we go to the C.C.I.D?"

"They're useless, Mammy," said Kelsey bluntly.

"We might as well try."

Kelsey rolled her eyes and said, "Okay. But I'm telling you, you won't get anything out of them."

They hugged each other warmly, which calmed Kelsey down a touch, and Melissa said confidently, "Honey, *I* will get something out of them."

3

It had been a week since her arrest, but for Z it felt like a lifetime. The bitter cell was getting to her; she wanted chalk to begin marking down how long she had been imprisoned. Sleepless nights in a prison cell hit differently to sleepless nights attending to her abuela. At least her bed at Sunvalley Park had a mattress and a duvet, and the pillow didn't feel like cardboard.

As night turned to day, Z began to appreciate what she had in life more and more.

Birds began to tweet outside, but the joyous, sweet sound was run over by the opening of the door that led to the cell. Chief Pattison stood in the doorway with a plain look on his face, his arms folded. Z glared evilly back at him, both of them knowing the truth.

He leaned his head back into the hallway and his voice echoed as he said, "You may go in."

The chief fully entered the room, standing out of the way of a small fraction of the Sunvalley Park residents.

Z jumped up and ran towards the cell bars, reaching out through them, overjoyed to see them again. "You have five minutes. THAT'S IT."

Their voices overlapped but predominantly asked the same thing: "Are you okay?"

"I'm fine." Z held onto the cell bars as she spoke. "How's my grandma?"

The man in front of her, who had a scraggly beard and was balding, answered calmly, "She's fine. Ef is looking after her. She was fine after—" His voice turned into a whisper, "this bullshit department invaded us, she was just exhausted as we helped her back into bed."

"That's good," Z breathed. That was a lot off her mind.

A greasy-haired woman in a vest and a jean skirt stepped forward and involved herself in the conversation, asking, "So how long are they going to keep you locked up?" Her voice was scratchy and didn't sit well with anyone who hadn't heard it before.

"If the jury come to a verdict, and say I'm guilty, which they will 'cause no doubt the chief or the mayor will pay them off, then I'm looking at a life sentence. With the offence being murder and arson, and stuff."

She sounded like she was just shrugging it all off, which didn't sit well with her Sunvalley Park family. They either rolled their eyes or scanned the room for a camera via which to flip the chief and deputy off.

"Absolute bullshit," growled the man. "Just because we aren't exactly kings and queens eating off a silver platter, and we actually fought for our home. The only reason why we're still up in the hills is because the town simply doesn't care. What difference would it make to them? None. But it would to the council and Madam Mayor. Replace our homes with what? A new, rich estate? A hotel, maybe? Z, getting rid of you and your grandma as Sunvalley's oldest residents is the beginning. It'll only be a matter of time before we get either arrested or killed, too."

"We've got to think of something, then," suggested the greasy-haired woman.

Everyone in the room thought for a moment, stealing glances at the door, just in case the chief or deputy decided to waltz in.

A minute passed and Z suddenly clicked.

She leaned forward as far as she could and whispered, "You know what the authorities hate most?" The others shook their heads cluelessly, making Z grin.

"Rebellion. Backlash. A simple, non-violent — yet *demanding* — protest."

4

Later that day, after the Sunvalley Park residents had finally left, Ton sat in the chief's office upstairs, typing away, answering an email that had been sent a few weeks prior.

A once scalding — now freezing — coffee sat on the desk on top of a pile of A4 sheets of paper. 'Misplaced documents' is what Ton called them, when asked about them by other officers.

As he typed, Ton kept glancing back at the papers. It wasn't a neat pile, and you might say that that was getting to him, but it wasn't the untidiness at all. With Chief Pattison away, Ton had to consider all types of solutions on his own. That was easier said than done.

Then came frequent banging, very distracting, and the echo of the stairwell. Ton closed his eyes as if a shooting star passed and wished that it was Pattison.

The stairwell doors swung open violently, and two females — one older than the other, both looking particularly glamorous, like they were ready for a night out — stormed towards the office. Ton anticipated the smashing of his boss' office glass door.

Melissa and Kelsey entered, Melissa looking furious and Kelsey looking slightly scared of her mother. and Ton scooched back in his chair.

Melissa hunched over the office desk until she was uncomfortably close to the deputy.

"Can I help?" asked Ton.

"I don't know, can you? My daughter received a letter the other day and I want to know right this second what you're going to do about it," growled Melissa.

Ton sat upright, smartly, taking another glance at the pile of papers.

Kelsey caught his eye.

"Well?"

"I'm sorry that this is happening—"

"You're sorry? Oh, well, that just fixes everything."

Ton bit his lip — and Ton wasn't one to get overly frustrated — and exhaled. "Look, we're all in the same boat here. We're doing all we can."

"THAT'S NOT GOOD ENOUGH!" Melissa roared.

Kelsey timidly stood in the corner, allowing her mother to get on with it.

Melissa picked the letter out from her pocket, unfolded it, and planted it on the desk immensely. "Where's the chief?" she added, a bit more calmly, but her anger still evident.

"He's away on business."

Ton then cocked his head a touch to see past Melissa. The stairwell doors swung open again and walking towards the office were Jason and Gemma. Gemma had a handbag hooked on her shoulder and didn't look happy with how the C.C.I.D had been handling the situation.

Ton slouched back in his chair again. *Oh, what now?* Ton thought as the mother and son entered the office. Neither of them said anything, with Melissa and Kelsey looking at one another in confusion, while Gemma rummaged through her handbag as Jason stood, arms folded and eyebrows narrow.

After a silent moment, Gemma pulled out a folded sheet and placed it on the desk in front of Ton, matching Melissa's immense force.

"Explain this," said Gemma.

"Okay, look, I understand the stress of the situation. Believe me, most of the town has come here with the exact same problem. All we can do now is—" Ton picked up the sheets of paper, unfolding them to place them on the pile, but then he stopped and his eyebrows rose. "Wait a second…" Placing them flat on the desk, he looked up and asked, "Kelsey, Jason… tell me how your fathers died."

"Overdose," said Kelsey quietly.

"Car crash," said Jason, wonderingly.

"What sort of a question is that to ask to Year 9 students?" spat Melissa.

"Look…" started Ton.

They all looked at the two sheets of paper, and then gasped.

"They're the same."

Identical writing, same question… the same message being sent — making them tremble.

"Which could mean—"

"They weren't accidents," Jason finished.

Everyone looked at Jason. He took a closer look at the letters, and then cocked his head towards the pile of papers. Without asking permission, he picked them up and flicked through them, as if this were a giant flipbook. *I knew it*, he thought.

"But how can we be sure?" asked Gemma, the muscles in her neck tensing as she tried to breathe steadily.

"'Cause all of the letters have the same writing. Not just ours," Jason explained.

Deputy Ton opened a drawer on his side of the desk, pulled out two sticky notes, found a topless pen on the desk and scribbled.

He rose, handing a note to each of the parents, and said, "Here's a number I want you to call. His name's Doctor Medica."

"Doctor Medica?" snickered Kelsey.

"Yes. If there's anyone in this town who can tell you what happened, it's him."

5

Around this time, near Carson Estate, Clarke was sweating as he finished hoovering his bedroom — and then the rest of the house. *You haven't done it right.* The words of his wife laughed in his head, making him smile. There was no doubt who the cleaner out of the two of them had been. Clarke did attempt to clean, on numerous occasions, just to give her a break, but it always resulted in her taking over, regardless of how much he did.

He wiped the sweat off his forehead with his bare hand as he stopped vacuuming. But as he pulled the plug out of the socket, he could've sworn he heard screeching from downstairs.

Clarke left the hoover leaning against the doorway of his room as he steadied himself to tiptoe down the stairs. Superstitious; that's what people get a lot of the time when they're in a house all alone, sometimes hearing things that aren't there. Perhaps a bang, or a knocking... but never the screeching of a door. Having lost Aaron and his wife in the space of only a few months, Clarke was used to his ears playing tricks on him. *Can't be too careful,* he thought as he descended the stairs.

Reaching the radiator, he poked his head around towards the kitchen. Nobody there. Then he turned to the lounge where the door was open wide; he rarely shut it nowadays. *But you can't be too careful,* he thought again. He rested against the door, making sure it didn't make a single creak. He shuffled inward, just enough to poke his head around the door into the lounge.

Clarke gasped.

A thin figure in a black ski mask and hoodie charged towards him. They forced him against the wall, their hands on Clarke's shoulders, slowly edging towards his neck. The figure stood almost eye-to-eye with him, and they breathed heavily. As the figure began to wrap their claw-like hands around Clarke's neck, Clarke had to think quickly and desperately.

With a kick to the kneecap, the figure stumbled back, releasing their grip. Clarke never saw himself as gutsy but it was the adrenaline, he thought, that made him grab the figure by the hoodie and chuck them by the front door. It was then when Clarke spotted a few tufts of hair poking out the back of the ski mask. Whatever, that didn't matter. The figure was lighter than Clarke thought they would be.

Recovering instantly, the figure leapt forward and grabbed Clarke by the collar of his shirt, swinging him into the radiator.

Clarke collapsed to the ground, groaning, aware of the bruises that would soon appear. The figure was merciless, now standing over him, grabbing Clarke by the back of the collar and — even though it was a strain — managed to drag him all the way into the kitchen, tossing him against the cupboards under the sink and drainer. The dishes drying on the drainer clanged as Clarke hit the cupboard doors.

The figure didn't give Clarke a chance to gather himself, kneeling down and once again wrapping their hands around his neck (handprints had already begun to show) in the same way. They began to squeeze, deflating Clarke like a balloon.

Clarke glanced up on instinct as the figure began to tighten their grip. Slowly slipping away, Clarke made out the items above them on the drainer, one of which was a pan. With one hand, he pressed the figure's face in an attempt to gouge their eyes out. The figure let go, remaining silent, but Clarke knew he had wounded them. And with the other hand, he reached up for the pan's handle.

Clarke choked the handle as if it were the figure's own neck, saw the pained eyes of them and sought to add more pain. The figure stared at Clarke, and with a bonk to the side of the face, before he knew it, the figure began to stumble towards the front door. Clarke couldn't go after them, for he still had a shortage of breath. He relaxed himself, dropping the pan, as he heard the front door slam shut.

Clarke coughed and wheezed, but all he could think about was who and why.

6

Browning Medical Institute, opened by Doctor Medica — real name, Doctor Steven Carlson — in May of '71, and since then, has been the only place in Castlehead that carries out autopsies. The doctor had this fascination with human anatomy, and he looked it, too; his eyes were wide and appeared to never blink, the years he had lived had caught up to him, and the white hospital coat was still a perfect fit, given the fact that he was never seen without it on.

Jason and Gemma parked up outside the facility just as Kelsey and Melissa arrived. They stood in a row in front of the entrance, Jason full of intrigue, Melissa and Gemma full of nerves, and Kelsey, who would rather have been anywhere else.

"Do any of us think this guy is legitimate?" asked Gemma.

Jason pulled out his phone and said as he opened the Google app, "According to this, apparently he's never been wrong." He put his phone away. "Let's hope that streak continues."

The automatic doors opened and the four of them walked into reception. They stood at the reception desk, which had a young, glowing girl sitting behind it.

"Yes, can I help you?" she said cheerfully.

"We need to see Doctor Medica," said Gemma.

"Of course. Deputy Ton told me that you were all on your way." Next to the laptop was a telephone, and on the dial, the woman pressed a button. It beeped. "Sir, the customers are here."

She released the button and sat quietly, smiling at Jason, Kelsey (who didn't notice because she was on her phone), Gemma, and Melissa. They stood looking at her for an awkward moment, the smile prolonged by the time Doctor Medica himself entered from a door in the corner.

"Ah," he breathed. His missing teeth were evident, and the ones that remained were stained. It made Jason evidently queasy, and he tried to avoid the doctor as they entered the room. "I've been waiting for you." When they all entered, the doctor pulled the door shut slowly. In this room was a single overhead light shining onto a hospital bed. Chairs stood against the wall, which Kelsey immediately went for, whereas the others remained standing. Shelves of medication, plastic gloves and tools for operations shook them; they had to take a moment to adapt.

"Now, I—" The doctor noticed Kelsey sitting. "Missy, you may want to listen."

Kelsey looked up, rolled her eyes, and went to stand at her mother's side.

"Doctor Medica," started Gemma, "do you think you know the answer to these letters?"

Gemma and Melissa simultaneously placed the letters on the bed for the doctor to look at. His frail arms held them up to the light.

"They're in reference to—"

"Your husbands, I know," the doctor breathed irritably. "Now, of course, I can't re-examine Donovan's body, as it's decomposing six feet under at Central Church. However, I do have his report. As I do for your husband, Gemma."

He shuffled over to the corner of the room where a filing cabinet stood. As he opened it, Jason couldn't help but go over to snoop — like something was pulling him in magnetically.

"Jason," called Gemma.

But Jason ignored her, peering over the doctor's shoulder.

"That's a lot of reports," said Jason observantly.

"Ah, here we are." Doctor Medica pulled out two documents, shuffling back over to the bed. "The reports state that Donovan Evans died of an overdose on his couch. That's what they *want* you to see. After close examination, the day after he died, I found handprints on his wrists and a scar the diameter of his entire body."

"Christ," gasped Melissa, looking at Kelsey.

The night Donovan was found lifeless on his couch came back to Kelsey painfully. Her stomach twinged.

"Your father, Jason… he did in fact die in a car crash while on the motorway. He was brought to me with a lack of blood in his system, his two front teeth in each nostril, along with shards of glass, and a broken leg. All of it due to the impact of the crash."

Gemma wrapped her arm around her son, her other hand over her mouth in shock and terror.

"Hang on," said Jason, brushing his mother's arm off his shoulders. He stepped forward and said, "Why did *you* have to do the autopsy, Doctor? Why not the doctor wherever he was living?"

"Because, Mr Rayne, your father didn't live anywhere else. The only recorded place was here in Castlehead."

Gemma put her hand over her face in pure disappointment, and embarrassed that she had ever married him.

"There is something else you should know. When being asked about the scene by the authorities, the remaining survivors said that the car in front stopped in the middle of the highway, not at a traffic light, and not because another car stopped in front."

"So…"

"So, regarding the reason you are all here today... it is very, very likely that your fathers' and late husbands' deaths were staged as an accident and a suicide."

Jason, while the others tried to absorb this information without breaking down, continued to glare at the filing cabinet.

"Doctor, you wouldn't mind if I had a look in that filing cabinet, would you?"

"Jason!" spat Gemma, giving him a warning glare.

"No, it's quite all right. I'm sorry, son, but that's classified information. May I ask why?"

"I just wanted to look for someone."

Kelsey gazed at Jason, for once not with anger or hate.

"Who?" asked the doctor.

Jason looked at his mother, Kelsey and Melissa, and said, "Aaron Smith."

The atmosphere in the room changed drastically. There was a wave of gasps from Gemma and Kelsey, as if to ask why he would think of asking such a question. The doctor had said that it was classified information.

"Jason," sighed the doctor, "when somebody dies in this town, I receive their body to examine them. But I can assure you..."

"Assure me of what?"

It slowly seeped in as to what the doctor was going to say.

"That Aaron was not one of them."

7

It had dawned on Principal Keeper that very day that these absences from Jason and Kelsey were becoming more frequent. Z being absent he was used to, but not a student who was deemed one of Thomas Hill's best. The news regarding Z's arrest hadn't been released yet to the faculty, only Keeper and

Thomas Hill's Board of Directors. Looking out his office window to the main hall that day at lunchtime, Principal Keeper couldn't help wondering if any students had found out.

The hall filled up, and the lunch queue — as usual — extended all the way up to reception. The three students, however, that caught Keeper's eye, were those in that lonely corner, sitting on that round table, looking very distracted. Aware of their friendship with Z, Principal Keeper looked around his empty office, deciding if he should head over casually or if he should just let them be.

He grabbed the door handle, began to open it, and stood there for a second. *They've been through enough*, he thought. Best not interrogate them and put them under more stress.

Up in that lonely corner, Josh, Anna and Brandon sat silently. They were all thinking the same thing: *Should we bring Z's arrest up?* None of them was very confident around others, but it was odd for Keeper to see the way they looked at one another from afar. He knew they were the best of friends, and best friends never looked at each other like that.

"Brandon…" started Anna, saying his name sweetly. She didn't want this situation to cause a rift within the group.

Brandon glanced up at her.

Josh gave her a sideways look, waiting for her to continue.

"We were thinking…" Anna looked at Josh; he matched her gaze and nodded, giving her the all clear.

"What?" said Brandon.

"We were wondering if you know about…" She toned her voice down to a whisper and leaned in. "Z's arrest?"

Brandon leaned in too, placing his finger on his lip, hushing her as the double doors nearby swung open.

Obnoxious laughter filled the hall.

Josh made eye contact with Eli, who stood at the back of the group. He glanced back and forth between his mates and

— agreeably, he thought — Jason's friends. They weren't his friends; they couldn't be.

He sighed and ultimately joined Brandon, Anna and Josh at the table. His group didn't notice his absence. Sitting, Eli immediately noticed their looks — mostly Brandon's

"What's happening?" he asked.

With a nod from Brandon, Anna leaned in closer to Eli and whispered, "Z's been arrested."

Eli looked around the main hall, perplexed, wondering if anyone else knew. It took him a moment to compose his thoughts. No, he didn't know Z well, and no, they weren't friends — none of them sitting at the table were his friends — but after everything that had transpired, he couldn't quite believe that it all circled back to Z.

"What? Why?"

"I—" started Anna.

"Threatening behaviour," interrupted Brandon.

Threatening behaviour was an understatement. He gave Eli, Anna, and Josh a look. They all caught on instantly.

"Yeah," he whispered. "The C.C.I.D believe she did it all."

"But how?" snapped Anna. "We know she didn't start the fire. Everyone said that at their interrogation, right?"

Brandon looked away, visibility guilty.

"Brandon?" said Josh curiously. "None of us said anything to the chief, did we?"

Brandon finally looked up, knowing he had to admit it to them at some point.

He sighed and admitted, "Okay, look, no, nothing was said. I know, because he told me. He didn't tell me why specifically they arrested Z, but apparently, she put up a fight. The Sunvalley Park people tried to fight them off, too, even pointing guns at them. It was going to get very bloody."

"Bullshit," said Eli. He didn't know why, but Jason came to mind; he thought about how he stuck up for Z when Gill & Susan'z caught alight. Although, he and Jason hadn't exactly talked since the dispute. "They just arrested her 'cause she lives in that trailer park."

Brandon hadn't wanted to believe it, either, when he was first told. In fact, he *knew* it not to be true. In his room on the night of the arrest, Brandon constantly thought — and even dreamed — about why Castlehead had such a personal vendetta against those in Sunvalley Park. They were rough, nobody could agree more with that statement, but they weren't animals. Watching Jason sticking up for her when Kelsey was being a brat and pointing the blame made him realise that, and he had begun to wish he had been interrogated, too. *Your mother wants you safe, and not to get involved.*

Sitting there at lunch was a weight off his shoulders, telling them he hadn't been interrogated and allowing them in on the truth about Z's arrest. For years, Brandon always saw his uncle do bad things for the right reasons. But pure hatred wasn't the right reason; there were bigger things to think about, and he couldn't help salivating over ending this madness with his friends for good.

8

Gemma was okay with her son having the rest of the day off — just this once — as GCSE options day was drawing nearer by the second. The letter, and finding out Doctor Medica had not received Aaron's body, was a lot to take in, she would gladly admit that, but she just begged for things to go back to normal. *Normal,* she thought. *That's a distant memory.*

Jason stood behind her as she unlocked the door to their house upon returning from Browning Medical Institute.

The door swung open and they entered. As Jason was taking his shoes off, Gemma walked into the dining room. She stepped towards the table and noticed a letter waiting for someone.

It wasn't like the message. It was formal, uncreased, and was addressed to Jason. Raising an eyebrow, she held it forward so Jason could see.

"For you," she said. She took another glance at it, and it was then that she noticed a symbol — a school emblem — in the top right corner.

"Jason…" Her tone switched suddenly, as if to the opposite side of a spectrum.

Jason slowly walked in.

"Is there something you haven't been telling me?"

"I… don't think—" he started. But then the emblem came into focus. *Shit*, he thought. "Mam, listen—"

"Listen? You've been lying to me this whole time, son. The Desmond School for Creative Arts, really? All this time, your family has prepared you for life beyond school, your GCSEs, everything, and *this* is what you want your life to be?" She looked disgusted, outraged, and like she wanted to spit all over the envelope. "All of our support…" She grimaced. "For *this*."

All Jason could do was stand there, humiliated and upset. *Support?* Jason thought as his mother took the envelope into the kitchen. *If you really supported me, you would let me go, not force me to be something I'm not.* He was hungry to spit all this anger out, but he thought better of it and knew it would just make it worse. He continued to watch Gemma head to the sink. She opened the cupboard under it, and there was the bin.

"Mam…" he cried.

She ignored him, scrunching the envelope up and tossing it into the bin.

Jason's heart sank and he stormed upstairs, not to be seen for the rest of the night, his dream torn apart.

9

Eli and Kelsey had their arms wrapped around one another as they stumbled back to Eli's that night. It was beginning to get dark later now, but they were tired after an evening out on a field with their many, many friends. Times like that helped Kelsey escape, and after the day she had had, she felt like she deserved it — and so much more.

Any time Lisa knew Eli and Kelsey wouldn't be back until late, she left the door unlocked. And today was no different. They knew Lisa was already dozing off as no lights were on downstairs.

As they entered the kitchen, Kelsey switched on the light.

"Err... Eli," said Kelsey, looking back for a second to shut the door.

"Aye?"

Kelsey shut the door, but then kneeled down. Turning around as she rose, Kelsey presented Eli with a folded note.

"This is what I was talking about."

She handed him the letter, and he looked at it, scoffing. He flung it on the counter like a frisbee, causing Kelsey to pick it up again.

"It's nothing, Kelsey," he said confidently.

But Kelsey gulped as she unfolded the note.

"Eli..." Her voice shook. "Look."

Eli rolled his eyes and snatched the note off her more forcefully than he had intended. Up until this point, he had only heard of these letters being sent around town. *It's just some sad kid trying to scare you*, he thought, even after Kelsey telling him about the identical ones she and Jason had received.

Coincidence. But that's not what he thought when he read this note. He regretted saying it was nothing. Goosebumps appeared on his arms and he had trouble keeping a hold of the note. Of course, Eli couldn't show his worried look to Kelsey.

"Do you think they're talking about... you know?"

"What? That you were pregnant? That was ages ago, Kelsey. What else could it be?"

Everyone had their secrets; Jason and the Desmond School for Creative Arts, Z once living at Thomas Hill, Eli and his appreciation for Jason — if that friendship still existed — and Kelsey with... well... she'd rather not say.

"Nothing," she said, pecking Eli on the cheek before heading upstairs.

The peck was reassuring, but the silence before Kelsey had finally answered was worrying. Eli thought they told each other everything; that was a part of the love he had for her. He had secrets, too, but he considered those to be minor, meaningless secrets.

With that thought in mind, he placed the note — unfolded — back on the counter and followed her up.

WHat HaPPEnS in ThE Dark cOmES Out IN tHe LiGHt.

CHAPTER TEN

The Calm Before the Easter Storm

1

Although the country was in the depths of spring, it felt like summer, with the clear sky and glistening sun bringing joy to Castlehead after months of anarchy and lacklustre weather. They say spring is the season of rebirth, a time when animals mate, and students across the country began to count down to the two-week Easter holidays. What the town had been through up until this point, and the current April weather, seemed to be corresponding. The amount of letters and notes people were receiving had finally started to die down, so perhaps something was about to change. Perhaps, for once, something good was about to happen.

Just one more sentence, that was all Jason needed to finish his first ever full manuscript. The lights in his room were off and the curtains were shut, as if he were a bat. He wasn't accustomed to writing in the light. *Make it count*, he thought as he looked over the final paragraph. One thing he had learned when releasing his snippets of writing to the paper and from learning the craft was that the two most important parts of a story were the beginning and the end; the beginning, to make the reader continue reading, and the end, to make the reader feel satisfied with what they had just read. The ending was the moment that the previous 200+ pages build up to.

Make it count, he thought again.

But the memories and stories that we pass down are what keep them and their spirits alive in our hearts.

Perfect.

There was this feeling inside him, writing that last sentence. Satisfaction. Yes, that was it; he was satisfied with this manuscript. Where this book could take him if he were to attend the Desmond School for Creative Arts, well… he knew that the possibilities were endless.

Consent was all he needed. As if that was going to happen.

2

The next morning, Principal Keeper was not surprised at all when he saw roughly 90% of Thomas Hill High students enter on what was the hottest day of the year — according to the weather forecast — in shorts, caps, and sunglasses. Thank God it was a Friday, many of them thought. And it was only going to get hotter.

It was becoming a natural instinct for Principal Keeper to catch sight of that lonely table in the corner. He would spend hours after the school day was done glaring at it, constantly wondering what those kids were talking about — and what they knew. The mornings were no different. He watched from his office as the main hall began to fill, his students walking in all directions and at different speeds, like cars on intertwining motorways, but not even the students could obscure his view of the table. He may as well have placed a 'reserved' sign on that table, as he was never surprised to see Jason, Anna,

Brandon and Josh. Eli voluntarily sitting there, however, was an eyebrow raiser.

They all waited for someone to say something about anything. Jason clasped his coffee from Carl's Cafe with both hands as he gently sipped it, but the others knew something was off about him. By now, it had pretty much been established that Jason was the ringleader of this group and the mysteries they had encountered over the past year.

Why isn't he saying anything? Eli thought.

He gave a light smile towards Jason, and said, "Jason—"

"Something on your mind, Jason?"

Eli snapped his head towards the other side of the table, as if offended by the interruption. It was Anna who had finally asked the question, noticing Jason's dipped shoulders and lowered head.

"No," he chuckled unconvincingly.

Anna struck him a look which made all the boys gulp. What was it about women staring deeply into a man's soul until they revealed what was bothering them? That was the question, and Jason had to cave weakly.

"Okay, yes," he sighed truthfully.

There was silence again.

"Well?" said Eli, nudging Jason.

"It's stupid." Jason rolled his eyes. "But… I may or may not have been accepted into the Desmond School for Creative Arts."

The others looked at him as if he were talking about a fictional place.

"Only a fair few know about it, and a representative came to me just before the school's fire."

They all leaned in, apart from Eli, who leaned back with his arms folded.

"But my mother isn't too happy."

"Well, where is it?" asked Brandon.

It was like trying to explain his opportunity to his mother; he had to face it. It was also just as hard to tell them.

Jason took a deep breath, and eventually said quietly, "Valeland."

Eli's expression changed significantly. Anna's eye caught his hurt — and angry — look. After a moment of taking it all in, Eli huffed, picked his bag up as he rose and stormed off through the doors to the Musical Theatre department.

Jason was left befuddled. Had he done something? Or was it what he had said?

Likewise, it took the others time to process what Jason was saying. They realised the impact this loss would have on them; coming into Thomas Hill High and him not there. Having this moment, the group also thought about the impact it would have on the school in general. Yes, they could all admit he wasn't the most popular, but everyone knew that even the littlest of errors or smallest piece of a puzzle could damage the whole operation.

"That's great, Jason," said Brandon.

"Yeah, you should definitely accept the position," added Josh.

"Jason, no offence," said Anna, "but your mother would be stupid not to let you go." Jason shrugged and sipped his coffee again as she added, "This school won't help you in any way to get where you want to be."

Jason shrugged again, and said, "Well, thanks, guys... It's not just the school, though."

The other three leaned in, their elbows on the table.

"What do you mean?" asked Anna.

Jason looked around observantly, leaned in also, and explained, "Last week, me and Kelsey received the exact same letter from this nutter. Anyway, we went to get the autopsy reports on our fathers, but I also managed to get a little bit of information on Aaron."

"What about Aaron?"

"Doctor Medica didn't receive his body after it was found by Sunvalley Park," Jason revealed.

"And?" Josh shrugged.

"*And,*" Jason continued, "apparently all the dead bodies go to him straight away."

"Are you saying…" began Anna nervously.

"It could be a cover up," said Jason.

Anna breathed deeply and said, "My brain is actually hurting."

"That's saying something," joked Josh with a grin.

"I mean, can't we just take a minute to relax?" she suggested.

They all caught each other's gaze and nodded.

"All right, then," she added with a smile.

"But what should we do?" asked Josh.

"How about Jaxson Bay?" suggested Jason.

They all looked at each other and again agreed with the idea, with simultaneous nods.

Jaxson Bay, what a place. Small but comfortable, the beach itself looked out towards the North Sea (as did the likes of North and South Shields, about an hour or two away) and was famous for being trapped between two cliffs resembling the historic White Cliffs of Dover. In other words, a perfect break — a perfect escape — from life, and the madness that came with it.

But imagining the gentle ripples of the sea brushing up against the shore didn't keep the group from hearing "WHAT IN THE FUCK?" coming from the other side of the main hall, where the long stretch of tables stood.

In a second, the entire school had rushed towards the scene.

Jason, Anna, Brandon and Josh couldn't squeeze to the front of the crowd surrounding the long table. Among the crowd were Kelsey and Eli, who were both crimson.

"What's happening!?" roared Keeper. He shoved students out of the way to get to the table and stood by Eli and Kelsey, examining the situation.

"Whose idea of a joke is this? Huh? Step up now or suffer the consequences. Your choice."

But no one did.

Keeper scoffed and said, "Fine. Eli, Kelsey, come with me now."

Keeper forced himself and the couple back through the crowd and led them up towards his office. Once the students heard the door slam shut, that's when the mumbling began. A hall monitor disbanded the students away from the scene, allowing Jason, Anna, Brandon and Josh to get a closer look at what the problem was.

On the table, it was like reading one of the notes.

Jason stepped back, losing his balance as the images of the note he received came back to him. The day in Browning Medical Institute, the note, the uncertainty of attending his dream school, it all came to him at once.

"Jason? You okay?" asked Anna, holding him up.

The bold writing, the message this person was trying to send… everything made Jason turn visibly white and made him sick to the stomach. The other three grasped this upon first glance and ushered him away from the table, leaving the words to sink in as the day went on.

It read:

YoU DEseRve NOthING, SLUT

3

Chief Pattison didn't know why he had even hired anyone to join the Castlehead Criminal Investigation Department in the first place, because every single officer (apart from Ton, the only one he seemed to always rely on) hadn't come in. Sitting there at his office desk, Pattison slammed his laptop shut as the raucous noise outside was getting to him more than it should have. *Kids*, he thought.

But then Deputy Ton rushed in, panting.

"Chief, you've got to come quick," the deputy said as he tried to regain his breath.

The chief rose and followed the deputy down the stairwell. The noise became fainter as they descended towards the ground floor, but once they had entered reception, the noise was as loud as ever.

"They're not shifting."

Outside, a mass of people wearing shaggy, stained clothing had formed a semicircle around the entrance. Most of them held up signs reading **INNOCENT** and **FREE Z** on them. But not a single member of the crowd budged.

"FREE Z!" the crowd chanted. Those who didn't hold up signs stood their ground, arms folded, not taking their eyes off Pattison and Ton. "FREE Z! FREE Z! FREE Z!"

The chief and deputy turned to one another, Ton looking uneasy while his chief smirked. They stood there, allowing the crowd to continue pathetically chanting for the one thing they weren't going to get.

A moment passed and over the chanting, the chief could hear a siren — or sirens. His grin grew as a herd of C.C.I.D cruisers pulled up; some blocked the road while others parked up carelessly, screeching to a halt. The cavalry had finally showed, and pushed through to the front of the protesting crowd forcefully, making the message clear that they weren't going to receive what they wished.

Orders weren't needed. The chief's officers grabbed each other and formed a barricade, blocking the crowd from inching closer to the building. The chain was strong and unbreakable, and Pattison stood there, leaning his elbow on the deputy. That grin wasn't fading anytime soon. This was the glorious mess made, and here were the Sunvalley Park residents proving his point as to why the townsfolk held so much disdain for them. The chief saw their true colours, the colours he always knew were in them, and because of this, there was all the more reason to keep Z locked up.

Catching, out of the corner of his eye, a number of residents trying to break the barrier of C.C.I.D officers made Pattison laugh out loud. Deputy Ton looked at him, expressionless. He shook his head and shrugged the chief's elbow off his shoulder.

Ton turned and walked back into the building.

The chief wanted to enjoy the moment for just a bit longer. He glanced over at one of the struggling officers and said, "Do what you must."

Then he, too, walked back into the building without a glance back at the mob.

4

Meanwhile, as Gemma walked into the sitting room of her house, she froze at the sight of her parents sitting in the exact same position as one another: their arms folded and their eyes full of care — and disappointment. It was the same look they would have given her back when she had unknowingly done something wrong, or come home later from a night out than promised.

"What's the matter?" she said, stepping forward.

"Sit down," said her mother. She spoke as if talking to an eleven-year-old Gemma.

Gemma sat in between her parents.

"Do you remember when you were Jason's age?"

Gemma shrugged, and mumbled, "Yeah." She wasn't certain, but she had a feeling where this was going. "And?"

"Your mother," Gemma's father butted in, "would be scared to death about you going out to town. The fake IDs, the booze, the late nights. Scared to the point she wouldn't leave the bus stop 'till you came back."

Gemma rolled her eyes. She was right in having an idea as to where this conversation was going.

"But we let you do it," added her father.

"You trust Jason, don't you?" asked her mother.

Gemma scoffed, "It's different."

Her father leaned in close and simply asked, "How?"

"Because... because," Gemma stammered.

Her parents kept their arms folded as they waited for an answer.

"Because writing isn't him. Writing doesn't have an annual salary. It doesn't have—"

"Let me just stop you there," spat her dad. "Have you *actually* read any of your son's work? I would, if I were you."

"He's not going to that fantasy school," argued Gemma stubbornly.

Her mother rested a hand on her daughter's lap and said quietly, "Just read his book."

There was a sudden look of surprise on Gemma's face. *He finished it?* Gemma thought. *Why didn't he tell me?*

"You didn't know that, did you?"

It was like her mother had just read her mind. A mother's instinct.

"You never condoned his publications in the paper, so why would he tell you he finished his first full book?"

Gemma fell silent, and her look of surprise turned into one of despondency. She always thought Jason could — and would — tell her everything. Clearly, that wasn't the case.

"Just read it, Gem," her father added, leaning back on the couch and waving his hand, as if swatting a fly away.

5

Jason's house felt like a sauna on Saturday. He sat waiting at the dining table, with a bag over his shoulder, for Clarke to arrive. Even though the group was on the verge of their prime teenage years, none of their parents allowed them to go to Jaxson Bay without a chaperone.

Jason kept checking his phone for the time, aware of the traffic that would grow if they didn't go soon. But then he remembered that Clarke had to pick up the other three first: Josh, Anna and Brandon.

Jason hadn't heard anything from Eli since he had stormed off the day before. It was unusual for them to talk every day, but this time felt different. Eli had looked almost hurt by the news of Jason's application to the Desmond School for Creative Arts. He thought it'd be best just to let Eli get on with it, let him sulk. *It's not like he's ever there, anyway*, he thought.

"HONK!"

"That's Clarke," announced Gemma.

Jason stood and forgot everything he had just been thinking about.

"You got everything?"

"Yeah," he said.

Jason walked across to the front door and began to open it.

Gemma's sudden touch on his shoulder stopped him from leaving. He turned and looked at her proud, tearful face.

"I'm so—" she started.

Jason butted in. "No, no." He shook his head and hugged her. "*Thank* you, Mam."

Jason released the embrace and turned to go outside.

On the road was a rusty, possibly second-hand vehicle that Clarke drove; Clarke waved embarrassingly. Anna sat in the passenger seat, with the boys in the back. They all looked summery, Anna with her beach hat, Josh with his sunglasses, and Brandon in a plain white vest.

Jason sat in the back with the other boys, in the middle, and Clarke drove off.

It was like everyone in the town had the same idea; the traffic on the motorway to Jaxson Bay was anger inducing for some, yet it still moved at a relatively regular pace. But the cars stopping once every few minutes wasn't such a bad thing, as it gave Josh and the others the opportunity to look out the car windows and examine the hills and countryside that surrounded Castlehead.

"What's that?" said Josh, gulping as he pointed at an eerie, abandoned building at the top of a hill on his side of the car.

There used to be great metal gates attached to the intimidating brick fence that stood at around fifteen feet; the bricks were mouldy with age, with moss growing. Wearing away after the many years it had sent shivers down people's spines. The large wooden cross with Christ nailed to it above the front entrance led all the kids to believe it had been built by Catholics. The windows to the outside world had been nailed shut, and if you squinted, you could make out the padlocked chains over the cracked double doors.

"They call it St. Jude's," answered Clarke, staring narrowly at the cars in front. His hands were still clenched around the wheel as he explained calmly, "Back in the 80s and 90s, it was a mental asylum. Since the government didn't — and still don't — acknowledge the town, the mayor at the time was able to get away with its construction after the impetus to close asylums for good in the 60s."

All the kids were intrigued by these facts, as if they were at a museum, and were still struck by the building that drifted off into the distance as the cars began to shift towards a near junction.

"The building shut at the turn of the millennium, but was said to be refurbished in 2009. There was a ceremony planned and everything. Think it was going to be a fancy hotel or something, I don't know. But what I do know is that once patients entered, they never left. Rumours of people hearing blood-curdling screams and the sounds of torture contraptions spread quicker than wildfire. But when the C.C.I.D went to investigate the noises at the end of '09, there was no sign of anyone. No doctors. No patients… Nothing. COME ON, YOU IDIOTS! DRIVE FORWARD!"

Time passed and they drove on down the rest of the motorway and turned off, continuing down the narrow stretch of road that led them to Jaxson Bay's seafront. But for the remainder of the journey, the kids couldn't help misconstruing the car engines around them for the screams that must've come from that mental institute. It was weird for them all, even Jason, the most observant investigator — no, *writer*, as he so desperately wanted to be — that none of them had been aware of St. Jude's existence until just now.

It was like doing laps around a racing track when trying to find a parking space. Clarke was becoming increasingly frustrated. When they thought they had found an opportune moment to strike by pulling into a tight parking space, another driver swooped in and took it.

"Is there anywhere else?" asked Jason.

"I can't park on the road, I'll get done," said Clarke. Then an idea came. He continued around the car park one last time, following the white arrows painted on the asphalt. Anna glanced out of the window and saw that they were heading towards the exit sign. Clarke turned onto the main road and did exactly what he said he couldn't. He pulled up to the curb, his car's tyres over the double yellow lines. Looking around, he said quickly, "Get out. Head down, and I'll try to find somewhere."

The kids grabbed their things and hopped out of the car. They all waited in a line on the path until Clarke readied the engine and drove further down the main road. Even on the pavement they could feel the grains of sand seeping into their flip-flops and shoes. Anna swung her beach bag onto her shoulder and led the way.

They kept in a line, looking like they were part of some strict school trip. Anna remained in front, guiding them safely through the car park to a series of stairs that gathered more and more sand with every descending step. The banisters on either side of the stairs weren't steady enough to keep a hold of. It felt like they would pop out of place with one tug.

Standing at the bottom of the stairs, the group scanned the beach for the perfect spot. The tide was out by a large margin, and Brandon and Anna caught sight of a group of children running towards the cool sea. Many couples and families sat on towels or plastic chairs, either under umbrellas to block the sunlight or within pastel-coloured windbreakers. Up by where the group was positioned, beach huts stood in rainbow formation.

Not here, Anna thought as Josh suggested, "Why not down by the rock pools?"

"Ya joking, aren't ye?" spat Jason. "We'll get soaked."

The rock pools lay by the two enormous pillars that were the cliffs. It was possible to hike up there, and the view was most definitely gorgeous, but getting soaked by the waves that collided with the foot of the cliffs wasn't on the group's agenda.

"How about down there, then?" Brandon pointed to an empty patch where the tide wouldn't hit them.

"Sorted," said Jason as he began to stumble towards the recommended spot.

The others followed. It wasn't easy trying to walk like a sober person on the bumpy beach, keeping an eye on their footing, trying not to trip over somebody else's belongings. The closer they got to the spot, the more the rippling waves relaxed them. Hypnotising. The tide wasn't in — that wouldn't happen for another couple of hours — but the North Sea still drew them all in.

As they finally plopped themselves down, laying out the towels each of them had brought, Josh and Jason saw Anna biting her lip, looking out to sea. They knew what she wanted, and she knew it also.

Jason scoffed and said, "God, just go."

Anna looked at them, smiled like a giddy ten-year-old. Brandon didn't have time to sit himself down, or even place his towel flat by his friends, for Anna grasped his wrist and dragged him with her out to the sea. He couldn't help it, almost collapsing over towels, buckets, and spades. *Come on, Anna,* he thought as he didn't want to be rude and ruin her fun, *if you keep this up, I'm not going to have an arm left to drag.* But he had to laugh... until his feet were in the water. He froze up, his fingers locked, and his back felt like it had been jabbed with a million pins and needles. And there Anna stood, splashing around, chucking water on him like she was in her natural habitat.

Back on the shore, Jason and Josh watched on. They couldn't help shaking their heads lightly and laughing.

Jason leaned back, planting his hands behind him into his towel. Josh sat with his arms wrapped around his legs. This was it, the escape they needed. Nothing was said for a long while and nothing *needed* to be said.

Not as the person, but as the writer, Jason continued to scan the beach and the people around him. With one book done, he wanted to get cracking on his second. A sequel? No. Original? Obviously. He had — or so he wanted to have — a talent for telling new, original tales. Knowing so much yet so little about a town was bound to brew up some ideas in that imagination of his, and he knew as he closely examined the many kinds of people around him (tall, thin, short, large, and of different races) that he had to up his game if he wanted to prove himself to the Desmond School for Creative Arts.

Not everyone can be inspired, he thought, *but anyone can be inspirational*. He just had to look.

"Jason?" said Josh suddenly. Jason saw that Josh wasn't looking at him or out to sea, but at a group of kids not too far from the rock pools. A group of nine or ten, perhaps, sat in a circle around a speaker, which was playing some modern twist on a classic hit. Josh continued to stare at them, and Jason grasped onto what was drawing him to the group. "Isn't that Kelsey and Eli?"

Josh wasn't wrong. The girl with the chocolate brown hair was using her boyfriend like a chair, his legs spread out on the towel, with her sitting in the middle. He had his arms wrapped around her and his chin resting on her shoulder.

"Cheeky get," blurted Jason.

"What?" asked Josh, looking at Jason.

Jason shook his head and said, "He said he couldn't make it today 'cause he had a *thing*."

Josh rose to his knees and began to suggest: "Why don't we call him—"

"NO! Just leave it."

"I don't get him, you know?" started Josh as he went back to his previous position. "The other day he stormed off when you said you got into that school, but apart from when he comes over to the table, I don't see you talk."

Jason didn't understand it either, if he had to be honest with himself. He looked at Josh then, around to where the couple sat. He shrugged, and that was where that conversation ended. But Jason saw the look Josh was giving him, tempting him to talk about the situation. Jason swayed away from his friend's look, focusing on the sea.

As Jason watched the North Sea twinkle, and made out Anna and Brandon collecting shells buried deep at the bottom, he still couldn't wrap his head around it all.

Josh didn't keep his eyes off him.

Seeing Josh's gaze in his peripheral vision, Jason turned fully towards him and huffed, "Okay." He bit his lip, angry at himself for caving in so easily. "We met in nursery. And we clicked—" as children do when they first meet "and we were best friends. Then we started Thomas Hill High, and it was what he *didn't* do that made me realise that not everyone you meet is your friend."

"What was that?" Immediately after asking the question, Josh wished he hadn't; he saw that Jason avoided eye contact now and focused on the sand. "Jason?"

"I… I was on the computer. Alone. The teacher let me use it, he knew I loved writing, and I thought nobody was going to bother me. And then, *them lot* over there…" Jason motioned to Kelsey's group with his head before he continued. "They… They pulled the chair from under me, grabbed me and sh-shoved me against the wall and wailed in on me."

"Christ," a flabbergasted Josh said.

"Eli was with them... and did absolutely nothing."

"That's shit." What else could Josh say to that? He couldn't, for Brandon and Anna, with their feet and ankles soggy and covered in wet sand, had returned. They both held cockles and sea shells.

"You okay?" Josh asked them.

Jason looked up and saw that their hair was dripping, too. He leaned back to where Anna and Brandon had placed their bags and dug around for their towels. Tossing them over, Anna caught both of them.

"I feel like I've been in the Antarctic," said Brandon as he wrapped his towel around his waist. As Anna wrapped hers around her torso, Brandon looked over at Josh and Jason, and said, "I've just thought... isn't that Kelsey and Eli? Thought you said they couldn't make it?"

All six eyes were on Jason.

"It's what Eli told me," he mumbled, shrugging.

All four glanced over at Kelsey and Eli, who were still in the same position as they had been when Josh first noticed them. They watched on. Eli kissed Kelsey on the cheek, then struggled to stand in the sand and walked past them like they were invisible.

"Oh... my God."

The group turned away instantly, all gulping and wondering what to do next. The moment was so awkward that none of them was able to get a word out about what they had just seen.

Anna ordered, "You have to tell Eli, Jason." She looked sharply at him.

Jason was avoiding eye contact again, for he knew he couldn't tell him. He knew Eli, and how much he cherished that girl, and if he said anything to him, he would be the one to get all the heat. Eli wouldn't believe him over Kelsey. That would have been a ludicrous fantasy.

Although Anna and Jason didn't necessarily agree on Jason being the one to tell Eli what they had seen that day, they did agree on one thing: He needed to find out somehow.

It was then, out of the blue, that Brandon said, as if everything had blindly gone over his head, "Clarke's taking a while."

6

With night came the moon, and with the moon came more warmth. But this warmth wasn't enjoyable. It was a warmth that told everyone they would be sleeping with a fan on and without the duvet.

"It's stuffy now," said Deputy Ton as he sat opposite the chief in his office.

Among the mess on the desk was a small working fan. Pattison had kept it focused on himself until Ton entered, dripping with sweat. The fan rotated now, gently blowing a refreshing breeze at the officers. Yet, over the noise the fan made, Pattison could make out the faint chants coming from outside the main entrance.

He glanced over at the window then back at Ton, and asked, "Are they still going at it?"

"Yep."

Pattison leaned back in his office chair, rubbing his mouth and thinking of a way to get the upper hand. It dawned on him — and the deputy — that the Sunvalley Park residents weren't going to give up easily. He also knew that they were adamant they would get what they wanted. Standing and chanting with signs for the simple benefit of being heard, for over a day, was nothing short of impressive, and Pattison couldn't deny giving them credit — even if he didn't want to admit it aloud.

"They won't quit," said the chief.

"So, what do we do?" asked Ton.

"We give them what they want."

That took the deputy by surprise, and for a moment he thought his chief was playing an unamusing joke on him. Then he saw Pattison's look. He was going to go through with it.

"Wait, hang on!" The deputy leaned forward and now rested his arms on the desk. "You know you're actually suggesting we give in to their demands?"

"Now…" Pattison's posture changed. He now sat up, complacent. "I didn't say that."

Outside, the officers barricading the mob weren't giving up, either. They continued to hold the protesters back. Chants of "FREE Z!" still echoed throughout the street, but some voices were less demanding than others. Noticing this, a few of the officers gave each other looks of hope. Sustaining this chaos was having an effect on the officers, also.

Then all of the officers snapped their heads towards the entrance. The chanting had faded at the sight of the chief standing there, with Deputy Ton by his side, and together they waited for him to say something. What the mass crowd wanted to hear varied between freeing Z and sending them away.

"Well?" said a voice. A face poked out from behind one of the officer's shoulders. The man — like most of the residents — looked like he had seen his fair share of fights. "Are you gonna let her go?"

The chief took a deep breath, like he was taking in the moment. He was enjoying this. To many, it seemed it was a joke to him and, as an extension, the whole department.

Ton nudged the chief warningly, to stop him from playing around by pausing for dramatic effect. This wasn't a movie. There were going to be real consequences for everyone involved in the events that had happened over the past couple of days.

"Yeah," said the chief with a shrug. "I'll let her go."

The crowd cheered, but a few members of Sunvalley Park noticed that the chief had flashed a virile grin at them as he agreed to their demands.

"On one condition…" *I win*, he thought. *I win*.

"What condition?" said someone from the back of the crowd.

"On the condition that all of you leave Sunvalley Park."

For everyone who lived in Sunvalley Park, there was a love for the place they called home.

But then there was the love they had for each other…

The love they had for Z.

CHAPTER ELEVEN

GCSE Option Day

1

After a week of celebrating the resurrection of Christ, the students of Thomas Hill High had returned, and it was truly time to put their heads down; more specifically, the Year 9s, for Friday 24th would be the day they chose their GCSEs. The teachers were unwavering in their efforts to persuade everyone to choose what they thought seemed right, as they — and Keeper — couldn't exaggerate enough how important it was; the next two years written out for them on one single form. But while teachers, parents, and (most) students were clamouring to get this day done and dusted, the news outlets in town were clamouring to get the latest intel on Z's premature release.

Only a select few knew the true sacrifices made by the Sunvalley Park residents in order to free Z. The now *ex*-Sunvalley Park residents.

As much as every single resident wanted to be there for Z's release, they knew it wasn't possible. But they couldn't have left her to walk out alone, so five went down to the station to meet her. The others had to stand in the park helplessly, watching C.C.I.D officers remove all of the furniture from the run-down trailers.

"It's like they think they're going to catch a virus off us," said one resident. The others noticed that some officers were wearing gloves, and some even went as far as to put on face coverings. "Typical."

A short lady resident waddled over and asked, "Where are they sending us?"

An officer carrying a nightstand walked past, not acknowledging their existence. But he had heard what she asked.

He stopped, his focus still on the large moving truck that blocked the entrance to the park, and said smugly, "The sewer sounds about right."

As the officer strode off towards the truck, the lady lunged for him, but was held back by a couple of the residents around her. She calmed down instantly and looked around. She noticed that those taking stuff out of Z's trailer were being very slow about it, yet causing a racket.

Then she heard, "Come on, old lady. Upsy-daisy."

Deputy Ton appeared in the trailer's doorway, his back towards the park. The residents saw that he was attempting — failing miserably, it looked like — to navigate a big crate, or a box. Or a bed. He stepped down carefully onto the rough ground, beginning to pull out Z's grandmother, who was lying there, oblivious, in her bed, being forced out of her home. The residents winced at her jolting in her bed as the deputy and a rookie officer (they assumed, judging by his teenage looks and paranoid expression) unprofessionally lowered her to the ground. But the wincing didn't match the level of frustration that elevated with each moment of watching the authorities take over.

"Be careful with her," a bushy-bearded resident warned.

The deputy and officer ignored the remark. The deputy pulled — as the officer pushed — the bed across the park by the truck. The residents couldn't sit there any longer; all of them walked towards the truck and waited for the deputy to turn around. He froze in mid-rotation, his eyebrows raising at the line of peasants.

"Yes?" he asked.

The bushy-bearded resident didn't hesitate to answer with, "Where are you taking her?" as he cocked his head towards the bedridden elder.

Ton looked around, leaned in secretly, and said, "We're going to take her to Oak Castle Hospital. She'll be in good hands there."

He turned back around, beginning to walk onwards.

Glancing at one another with the same unsatisfied expression, the residents knew that Ton just wanted get on with his duty. But enough was enough, and they weren't going to let him, until he justified the C.C.I.D's actions towards them.

"And… What about us?" asked the bearded resident.

The question caught Ton's attention. He sighed and turned back around.

"Huh? Where are we supposed to go?"

Deputy Ton sighed again and said, shaking his head lightly, "I can't help you there."

Then he continued on with his day like any other, and as he walked up towards the billboard that read **SUNVALLEY PARK**, he heard the crack in the woman's voice as she yelled, "You haven't helped us at all!"

Don't feel remorse for them, Deputy Ton thought.

2

Dear Parent/Guardian and Student

This is a reminder to all Year 9 students to attend school on Friday, April 24th, as this is the day you will decide what you want to do for the next two years. As a result of this, Year 9 students will be off timetable. However, that does not exclude all other years; they must attend and WILL BE on their normal timetables. To allow students to prepare and contemplate their choices, I have personally noted below all the available subjects. More information will be released on the day.

COMPULSORY SUBJECTS

- Mathematics
- English (Literature and Language)
- Science

OPTIONAL SUBJECTS

- Physical Education
- History
- Geography
- Further English
- Further Mathematics
- Further Science
- Drama and Theatre
- Music
- Dance
- Art
- Business Studies
- Design Technology
- Languages (French, Spanish, German or Italian)

I hope this is useful. I am looking forward to seeing you all on Friday and the choices you make for the benefit of the future.

Yours faithfully,
Principal Keeper

3

Walking out of the Castlehead Criminal Investigation Department building was as refreshing as it was annoying. The doors opened to the outside world, and for the first time, Z felt a wave of fresh air. She stood beside Chief Pattison, who had escorted her from her cell to this point. Z was unable to focus because of the flashes from the many cameras and the countless news reporters demanding answers to their questions, as Pattison stood with a wide, fake smile spread across his face.

"You're an arsehole for what you're doing to me and my family," whispered Z.

Luckily, the microphones were not close enough to catch the war of words between the two.

"Nothing personal," Pattison whispered back, looking out at the crowd. Now this was a crowd he liked to see around the building. He could get some good publicity from this, and he knew it would be beneficial; not just for the department, but for the town. "I'm just doing my job."

"Correction: What you're doing is bullshit."

"Hey," he snapped quietly, grasping Z's elbow in such a way that the cameras couldn't catch it. She hid the pain of what felt like a dog bite. "We negotiated, your family and I, and this was the result." He leaned in closer to her and added, "Your grandmother is being transferred to Oak Castle Hospital. You can go straight there or join the other residents at the housing shelter not too far from Central Church."

Z thought, *There is no housing shelter near Central Church*, and that's when she knew he was simply playing around with her.

"Either way, what you do now isn't our problem anymore."

It usually took a lot to surprise Z, but this was one of those times. She knew she couldn't stand there next to the chief any longer, unless she was willing to risk her life by swinging for him. All these heinous acts of framing someone for murder, evicting a group of misunderstood people that had been painted as dangerous years before Z was even born, were all for what, exactly? To purify the town? The satisfaction Z would've received in that moment if she had dragged the chief — and Madam Mayor, as an extension — down to earth in front of all those news channels, telling him that no town was pure, would've been well-deserved.

Then she had to dragged back into reality, as she knew she was getting ahead of herself. She knew she had to watch what she said from this point, because the chief could go back on his deal with her family straight away.

What was pure, she felt, was the sincere voice that started calling her name. Like a dog to a dog whistle, the yell of her name caught her attention. She stepped away from the chief, who kept a broad grin on his face for the crowd, and stumbled her way through them. The maze of people was easy, but just as irritating as the flashing lights of the camera. People who stood at the back tried to seek their opportunity to politely ask her what her next move was, or something as ridiculous as that. Frankly, she didn't see it as asking; she saw it as bothering. So she ignored it and kept to the sound of that one voice calling her name.

Making it through that maze had a reward, and it brightened her day, just like that.

Jason and the others stood there. *Eli, too?* Z thought. *Wow, they must've missed me.* Kelsey was nowhere to be seen, though. It didn't surprise her, nor did she acknowledge it.

Jason ran towards her into a quick embrace, which Z actually accepted. Very reluctantly. The group took turns to welcome her back, and Z's appreciation glowed on her face, like her smile when she had first seen them. The last to say hello was, to her surprise, Principal Keeper. As she made eye contact with him for the first time, she thought, looking at his serious expression, *I've pretty much been expelled since Abuela got sick, so you don't need to tell me I am.*

He stepped forward in his smart shirt, trousers, and polished shoes, and said "How are you?"

"I've... been better," she answered.

"Look," he added, "I know what you're going through is more important, and I don't mean to add to the stress..."

Here we go, Z thought, lowering her head shamefully. She didn't need this at that moment in time, but she understood the reasons behind Keeper's decision. She hadn't been at school a lot, prior to these recent unfortunate events, but there was something about Thomas Hill that made it different from any other school she could think of. She thought she would miss that the most.

Keeper continued, "But the offer to join us on Friday to choose your GCSEs is there, if you want to take it."

"Wait... Wait, what?" Z said. She had to make sure she heard that correctly. But from the smile appearing on the principal's face, Z *had* heard correctly. "You mean I'm not expelled?"

Keeper laughed, "Of course not. With everything I've seen you go through, you think I would give up on you now?"

Z had to laugh. The others joined in, and the group began to walk away from the building steadily.

Further down the road, Jason's phone pinged. He stopped, as did all the others, and they allowed him to check what the notification was.

"Who is it?" asked Anna.

"It's Maria," said Jason. "She's in Castlehead, and she wants to meet at Carl's sometime this week." Eli turned away, folding his arms, and impatiently waited as Jason continued.

Jason addressed, "Hey, perhaps you can meet her?"

"Maybe," said Anna.

Eli was the first to continue down the road, leaving the rest to struggle to catch up.

"You two are getting close, aren't you?" suggested Z.

4

Carl's Cafe was empty. Not an empty space that spread calmness, but empty to the point where Jason and Maria could hear Carl stirring sugar into the cups of coffee they had ordered up at the counter. The spoon made a ting*ing* sound on the cup as Carl stirred in a circular motion, but they couldn't let it distract them. They turned back to face one another at their table while Carl walked steadily over to hand them their coffees.

"Thanks, Carl," mumbled Jason.

Carl nodded in appreciation and walked back to the counter. He rested his elbows on the counter and stared at the entrance.

Jason, as he slowly sipped his coffee, saw guilt in Maria's eyes.

"So, what was it that you wanted to talk about?" he added, trying not to sound too serious. Just in case, he added quickly, "I mean, it's great that you've come up."

"Sorry, Jason," said Maria firmly, "but I didn't really come here to catch up." That flare of guilt was still in her eyes, but it had begun to fade. Just by the way she spoke, Jason knew she was a Desmond School student.

He leaned in to hear why she had really come to visit.

"You see, of course, the semester doesn't begin until September, but since you're technically going to be a transfer student, we need you there before the semester begins. It would also be beneficial for you, as it will give you the opportunity to get to know Valeland more and make yourself comfortable in a new school atmosphere."

"Okay…"

"And the thing is, we need you for the May half term."

Jason froze as suddenly as an old console game crashing. The May half term was mere weeks away, and he didn't want to get started on how fast the time would fly by. Assuming he would begin the school year in September, like all the other students, had allowed Jason to breathe and relax; he didn't have to worry about essentials or timetables, or have himself run madly around, overthinking about unnecessary stuff. But now, with this news, fear quickly rose within him.

All he could do was mumble, "Okay."

Maria couldn't gather his feelings by his blank expression, but Jason knew where she was coming from. It made sense to get a feel of a new town, where you would be spending the next few years of your life; he would've been stupid to go in blindly. All in all, he didn't know how to feel. That, Maria grasped.

He clutched the corners of his seat and leaned back. After a second of rubbing said corners, Jason tucked his hands underneath his armpits, like he had gone into a huff. He hoped he didn't come across as frustrated at the sudden decision. Again, he understood it. But being given such short notice, there was a bit of him that wanted to express said irritation.

I don't want her to feel guilty about it, he thought. Not looking at Maria made that thought seem more plausible by the silent minutes that followed.

Maria looked around the cafe awkwardly, as if waiting for a date, or for something to be said. Unbeknownst to Maria and her silent desire for conversation, Jason now slouched in his chair, kept his arms folded, and saw a speck; a drop of coffee he must've spilled on the table. *Just keep looking at it,* he thought. *If you look anywhere else...* He didn't want to tell himself what would happen if he looked anywhere else — though he knew it had something to do with his blended emotions of anguish and uncertainty being spilled for Maria to see.

Come on, Jason, she thought as she looked at him again. *You have to give me something.*

But that didn't happen; he kept himself slouched in his chair, and continued to focus on the speck of spilled coffee.

Maria sighed and said, "All right then." She started to rise as she added, "I'll let you think about it. But this is it." She started towards him. "You know your worth."

The compliment didn't work, either. Jason remained frozen.

"Goodbye, Jason."

With that, Maria left Jason in the empty cafe. The only sound he heard now was the stirring of a coffee. This time, the ting of the spoon was... soothing.

5

GCSE Options Day had arrived, and Keeper felt as anxious as all of his Year 9 students. As he stood by the reception desk, greeting the arriving students and parents, he saw that some of them couldn't be bothered and were only there for the sake of it. He wasn't surprised. Others, however, he could tell had jitters — whether they were nervous or excited was hard to make out.

Having been in the job for as long as he had, Principal Keeper had grown accustomed to this time of year. But this year was like no other. His students had been — and still were — grieving. Especially a select few. Being biased towards students was considered a violation against the whole teaching family, in Thomas Hill, but there was nothing stopping Keeper hoping that those particular students made it in today and would begin their journeys to becoming mature students and starting the rickety road that is life.

Knowing what they had gone through, not just as a group, but as individuals also, Keeper empathised with them. It had been a crazy year, and Aaron hadn't been just a friend; he had been a beloved student who brightened every room he walked in.

The principal smiled as more students and parents filed in, but the smile was because he was thinking of Aaron, and how he would feel about his closest friends starting their GCSEs. *He would be proud*, he thought.

Then he saw one of them walk in among the heaviest of the crowds that entered.

"Z," he announced, catching her attention quickly. "You came!"

She saw his face glow with glee, and she let loose and smiled back as she said, "Yes, I thought about your offer, and I'd be happy to come back."

That was the answer Keeper had clamoured for.

"I spend most nights at the hospital with my abuela, and the family are trying to make something of themselves to get out of that piss-take of a centre. So, I thought to make something of myself, too."

"So have you thought about what you might choose?"

Z stuffed her hands into her filthy tracksuit bottom pockets and answered with a grin, almost jokily, "Not a clue."

Her principal ushered her into the main hall after sharing a laugh. Keeper had shared similar conversations with the other *select* students, asking them, too, how they were, and if they had any idea which subjects they were going to choose. He remained still at the reception desk, like a promoter, until he knew all of his Year 9 students had entered...

And... Jason? And soon after, a postman, of all things, wielding a brown envelope.

After catching up with his former principal for a few minutes, Jason made his way into the main hall. For a brief moment, before talking to Keeper, Jason hadn't known what to call him. Sir? Mr Keeper? Or by his first name?

Walking into the main hall felt surreal to the former Thomas Hill student; it was the last time. He always thought his last time walking through the halls of Thomas Hill would be on the final day of Year 11, a day where the school would make a huge fuss over them leaving, forcing the students to wear graduation robes, and in the final assembly, to look back on the good times, the bad times, and — most of all — the embarrassing times. Jason, alongside Z, Brandon, Anna and Josh, would walk up the hall to reception and out of the gates, before looking back one last time, smiling, and going their separate ways.

But that wouldn't be happening. Jason had to accept it. He *had* to.

The regular, long dining tables had been folded up and shifted to one side to make space for the columns of small desks only big enough for two. The heads of each subject sat at a designated table, and a set of queues had formed in front of the columns; the firsts in line were ushered to a table, and the sequence had begun.

Jason watched on from the side lines, by the doors that led to the Musical Theatre department, as the teachers, for roughly five minutes, informed the interested students about the modules and possible opportunities said subjects could lead to.

It was like a game of *Where's Wally?* but it was easy to find his friends sitting there, choosing their subjects. He beamed as he noticed Z at one of the desks. She maintained a look of intrigue at each of the desks she shuffled over to.

After they had listened, the students were escorted to the side of the hall to make their final choices.

Kelsey and Eli did theirs together, as did Brandon and Anna. Z and Josh filled their forms in separately, but afterwards came over to Jason. Kelsey and Eli were stalling as they stood at the back of the group. He was overwhelmed, seeing them come over with figurative open arms.

"What subjects did you choose, then?" asked Jason, directing the question to those in front — not the two keeping their distance.

"Further English, History, and Art," answered Josh confidently.

"Business, Geography, and Further Science," said Anna.

Brandon grinned cheekily at Anna and echoed her answer.

"There's a surprise," chuckled Jason, and then he turned his attention to Z.

"Drama and Theatre, Dance, and Design Technology," she answered.

Never in a million years would Jason, or any of them, have thought Z was an aspiring musical theatre kid. Her choices didn't faze them. On the contrary, Jason, Anna, Brandon and Josh praised her for them.

"And what about you two?" Jason asked, trying to look over the others' heads and shoulders. Jason knew it would be rude if he didn't at least ask what his oldest friend was doing for GCSEs.

Eli and Kelsey stepped forward and glanced down at their forms.

"What'd you choose?"

Kelsey read aloud, "Design Technology, Dance… and Drama and Theatre."

She cringed at the subjects, fully aware that she would be — completely coincidentally, she would've told everyone — spend her GCSEs in the same classes as Z.

The two fellow subject buddies locked eyes and grunted at each other, but then a pair of light smiles appeared.

Mutual respect? They all knew that Kelsey and Z were far from best buds, but even they understood that if they were in the same classes for the next two years, they could at least try to get along.

"Go on, Eli, what about you?" asked Jason.

With everyone now in a misshapen semicircle in front of the pair of doors, it was only Jason that saw a concerned Principal Keeper walking towards them. There was a brown envelope in his hand.

"I chose P.E…" Eli started slowly.

He's either nervous or embarrassed to say, thought Jason, as Eli continued.

Keeper was gradually getting closer.

"Business."

Eli glanced up from the form and looked at Jason with a smile.

"And Further English."

Keeper was only a few steps away. The group started to feel the vibrations of someone's footsteps behind them.

Eli laughed, "That's your fault, that, Jason."

As a group, a full group, they laughed. But then stopped as Keeper stood over them, the brown envelope raised in his hand. Without a word, or a clue as to what it was, Keeper reached over Z and Brandon to hand Jason the envelope.

Then he walked back to reception.

It wasn't like Keeper to act so secretive and to look so worried.

Jason had caught on that the brown envelopes in Thomas Hill were only used to send forms to the higher-ups to see if the chosen subjects were eligible to participate in over the upcoming years.

"I thought I had told them I was moving," said Jason as he tore the envelope open carelessly.

Littering as he threw the torn envelope on the floor by his feet, Jason read, with the others reading over his shoulder:

yOu DidN'T sEE ClaRkE at Jaxson Bay, DID yOU? YOU DIDN'T SEE ME EITHER. HE'S WHERE THE DEAD PROPS LIVE.

"The dead props?" repeated Anna. "What does that mean?"

Z's eyes grew wide, and her face turned whiter than she already was. She bit her lip and hoped that the phrase didn't mean what she thought it meant.

"Hang on," said Brandon, snatching the sheet from Jason. "There's something on the back."

... AND SO AM I.

"Jesus Christ!" gasped Z. Yep, it was what she had dreaded.

"PRINCIPAL KEEPER!" she called, running towards reception.

The others quickly followed without hesitation, still with anxious looks on their faces.

Principal Keeper rushed towards the group and was all ears. *Has she chosen the wrong subject?* Keeper thought.

"WE NEED TO GET EVERYONE OUT OF HERE! NOW!!!"

There was no explanation, and Z then turned around and ran back towards the Musical Theatre department.

The principal stood there, startled and confused, as all the parents and other students turned away from what they were doing, wondering what on earth was going on.

"Why?" he asked.

"JUST CALL THE POLICE!" he heard from around the corner.

The rest of the group followed Z.

But none of them had any idea where the 'dead props' lived.

CHAPTER TWELVE

The Second Coming

1

Nobody, apart from Z and Principal Keeper, had known about the room under the theatre up until now. Jason couldn't help thinking that they were in a movie or a crime novel as they looked at the hostage with a bag over their head and the masked, gun-wielding psycho. The light flickered above them, but everyone could tell that the hostage had been forcibly tied to the wooden chair they sat on.

Kelsey huddled close to Eli, as if his comfort would protect her while Jason and Z raised their hands in front of them in an attempt to reason with this masked psycho.

"Kids, get behind me," whispered Principal Keeper. Without hesitation, they all did so as the psycho watched and the hostage screamed — despite the tape over their mouth — for help.

"The police have been informed," Keeper told the criminal. "Just, please, do not do anything."

The masked figure tilted their head sidewards ominously, forcing the cage of butterflies in all of the kids' stomachs to be released freely. With their principal shielding them, however, they still couldn't budge.

Then a sudden series of bangs filled the area and the door swung open off its hinges. Reinforcements had arrived, in the form of Deputy Ton and Chief Pattison. They ran in, stopped next to Principal Keeper, and had their guns mercilessly aimed at the figure — who mirrored their actions.

"You can't shoot your way out of this one," said the chief confidently.

The deputy pushed Keeper and the kids back as far away from the stalemate as possible, but Jason and Z still stood with intrigue.

"Just… put… the gun… down."

The figure looked down by their side; the hostage forced the chair to rattle. With one hand still wielding the gun, aiming it at the chief of the C.C.I.D, with their free hand, they ripped the bag off the hostage's head.

"Oh, my God," mumbled Jason.

Everything clicked.

"All will be okay," said the chief calmly as he diverted his eyes to the hostage.

To the C.C.I.D, it hadn't clicked yet. But Clarke sat in that chair against his will, tape over his mouth, with deep cuts all over his face.

The chief focused back on the figure. "Why are you doing this? He's innocent."

"*Ohhh* shit," muttered Anna. Both she and Jason broke free and stepped forward, next to the chief. The others followed them, but — like the chief and deputy — hadn't clicked as to why Clarke was being held hostage.

"Chief," she added calmly, "lower your gun."

"We need him to tell us why," Jason added. He quickly turned his head and looked at Kelsey. She didn't catch on, until Jason gave her a powerful look, as if to tell her to think back as hard as she could. Then images flashed rapidly through her head; images of the empty bed at Browning Medical Institute.

Jason stepped forward just a touch and whispered to the figure, "Why?"

The figure now aimed at Jason.

"Jason, what're you doin'?" asked Eli, suspicious.

"Just shush," ordered Jason. He stepped towards the figure again, a bigger step, and the figure's hand began to tremble. The gun began to rattle.

"Look, whatever it is you're thinking of doing, it won't solve anything." Jason was now at arm's length from the figure and Clarke; he could feel the trembling gun pressed against his chest. "Please, lower your gun."

There was a tear in Jason's eye. His face was red with fear… and unexplainable adrenaline.

The figure took a breath and slowly lowered the gun, once again mirroring the chief's actions.

"Jason, what is going on right now?" asked the principal.

Jason looked back at the group and said, "All he wanted was revenge."

"What are you getting at, Rayne?" said Pattison impatiently.

"Under the mask…"

Anna interrupted: "Is Aaron."

As Jason turned back around, the figure suddenly aimed his gun again at Jason, who leapt back. With his free hand, the figure grabbed the top of his mask and tossed it off and onto the floor. And there he was, Aaron Smith, in the flesh, still relatively taller than every kid (apart from Z), his hair still messy, but now with an unrecognisable, evil, villainous gaze. He was very much alive, yet looked as dead and intimidating as a ghost.

"But that's impossible," said the deputy. "We buried you."

Aaron grinned and corrected him, saying, "No, no, no. You buried a closed casket."

Z stepped forward and asked, "But what about the chief and deputy finding your body up by Michael Manor? I saw them dig you up."

"Oh," he started enthusiastically. "You mean the body bag filled with rubbish and shite that had been found by an anonymous caller? Maybe the chief can answer that one."

The guilt was written all over the chief's face.

"Well?"

"Were you in on this?" asked Z, her eyebrows narrowed, almost as if she was about to attack.

But before the chief, or the deputy, could answer, Aaron burst into hysterical, uncontrollable laughter.

"No, we weren't in on it. Not Aaron's plan, at least," said the chief finally, over the dying laughter. "Madam Mayor stopped at nothing to close the case, and so when we got the anonymous phone call, it was the best time. We would just say that it was Aaron, and there we go. Sorted."

"But why send me and Jason to Doctor Medica?" asked Kelsey suddenly, pushing away from Eli's cuddle.

"Only the two of us and the mayor knew of our plan. Medica was as clueless as you all were. He just assumed that someone — maybe a killer — had snatched the body before he could retrieve it from us. Then the funeral happened, so we explained that Clarke wanted the funeral ASAP."

"Same old corrupt Castlehead," mocked Aaron. "You just dug yourselves your own grave."

"But why go through all this trouble?" Everyone knew Jason wasn't talking about the lengths the Castlehead Criminal Investigation Department and the mayor had gone to just to cover up Aaron's disappearance. "Months of torment, for this?"

Aaron scoffed, and said, "Put your brains together. I'm sure you'll figure it out. If you can't, here are some clues...

Not long after my disappearance, my dad's work ends up in flames, then Central Church catches alight, with him in it. A masked figure breaks into his house, but is unsuccessful—"

Jason guessed, "So, you did all of this to kill your own father?"

"Ding-ding-ding, and the winning answer goes to…"

"But why all this trouble?"

Aaron felt a sudden tingling sensation in his hands. He was evidently fluctuating between emotions of frustration and guilt. But mostly frustration.

Jason warily took a step back.

"Yes," said Aaron collectively, "I could've done it the simple way, but I felt a desire to put my father through the same unimaginable torture he had put me and my mother through." He glanced over at the chief. "Where was justice then, huh?"

Neither Pattison nor Ton could respond. They were both trapped in the same web of corruption and regret.

This time, it was Z who stepped forward.

"What do you mean?" she asked.

"DON'T YOU IDIOTS GET IT!?" bellowed Aaron, tightening his grip on the gun again, impatiently. "My dad abused and eventually killed my mother by shoving her down the stairs… which, might I add, the C.C.I.D claimed to have been an unfortunate accident. Yet they most probably suspected it was murder, am I right?"

Pattison nodded.

"*And…* I'm also correct when I say that Madam Mayor wanted no more bad publicity for the town, so she told you to do nothing more. It tore me apart, losing the most important thing in my life. So, I pulled the *"I'm going to school, not really"* trick and decided to go missing for, say, I don't know, the summer."

"But you weren't," said Brandon suddenly. "You were the guy we bumped into during the church fire—"

Kelsey's eyes grew wide as she said, "And you were the hooded guy I walked past as I left the pharmacy."

"Clever Thomas Hill students," Aaron mocked, flailing his arms around as he spoke and walked around his trapped father. "It was after Central Church that I speculated you lot were wanting to investigate, and my-my you did a better job than the police ever could. It was also at this time I begin to grow a lust for these fires, so I decide to come into school one day, find youse sitting at the table, and overhear you talking about luring me out on Halloween Night."

"Wait! That was you? Not Z?" said Jason.

"What?" snapped Z.

Jason explained, keeping one eye on Aaron's gun hand and the other on Z, "When planning the Halloween debacle, we thought we saw you drop your bag by the doors, then leave after we set the date in motion."

"Then," interrupted Aaron, "the night comes and I see you, Z, starting the fire. And, hmmm, why not frame the fires on you?"

Z began to look back on her arrest; how the C.C.I.D didn't even question her as the chief aggressively shoved her into the cell. Frustrations began to build with the chief and Aaron. All this was his doing; it was common knowledge that the higher-ups didn't exactly like the Sunvalley Park folk, but the harassment they received wouldn't have happened if she hadn't been framed. Or did framing the White Shadow have anything to do with it? Did they just want someone to pin it on, so that, as with Aaron's mother, the investigation didn't have to happen?

"Ah," said Anna. "So, whoever is framed goes to prison, and you run away, home free?"

"Correct again. You see, when you put your minds to it, you aren't that stupid, are you?"

"What about the letters?" added Kelsey. "Were those you, too?" Her tone steadily rose in aggression. "Did you kill my dad?"

Jason thought, *How could she care about an abusive person like her father?*

Aaron chuckled as he stood by the chair again, and said, "Kelsey, love... I don't give enough of a shit about you to have done something like that." He raised a finger, adding, "Although, I did actually use the letters to my advantage and get youse all here... to kill."

Eli finally stepped forward and said idiotically, "You're just a psycho out for revenge. Is that it?" Aaron raised his gun again, as did the chief.

Eli sighed. "What happened to you, mate?"

"It's mad what a thirst for vengeance can do to someone," said Aaron flatly, determined to pull the trigger on anyone.

As each slow second passed, Aaron's temptation grew, aiming the gun at each person for a significant amount of time before grinning and moving on to the next.

The grin vanished. Everyone heard the gun click, and he looked down. A wave of gasps splashed over the room at the sight. Clarke screamed under the tape and wriggled in the seat, but he couldn't free himself. He closed his eyes tightly, at gunpoint.

"Aaron, hang on!" said Jason. "You're angry, and you're sad. But this isn't the way around this."

The group of kids slowly stepped forward. Aaron kept the gun on Clarke, but it became clear to the group that he had begun to grow increasingly nervous; his face turned red, and tears stung the sides of his eyes. He continued to look down, hiding the tears.

"STEP BACK!" he roared, jolting towards them, clearing space between him and the group again. He held his free hand up, in case they tried to step closer.

The chief and deputy looked at one another, agreeing — as if telepathically — not to draw their weapons. Too many young lives were at stake here.

"IT'S THE ONLY WAY AROUND THIS!"

Anna allowed the tears to stream down her face, while Jason and Brandon tried as hard as they could not to share theirs.

Now, Aaron was unhealthily shaking. The officers saw the boy's itchy trigger finger, and something had to be done. But they remained still as a pair of statues, for after the year the town had had due to Aaron's actions, they couldn't help agreeing with what Aaron claimed. These kids *were* more capable.

"Just come to us, put the gun down, and we can work this out together, okay?" cried Anna. Her heart felt like it was in her throat. This was a boy she had once considered a boyfriend... *Wait a second*, she thought. Everyone else nodded, agreeing to her suggestion. But then she added, keeping at a safe distance as the tears flowed down Aaron's face, "Do you remember Year 7?"

"Anna..." cautioned Brandon.

"*Shh.*" Anna turned her attention back to Aaron. "Do you remember Year 7? Skipping lessons? How my parents hated you for it?" She chuckled. "Nothing else mattered back then... when I was with Aaron Smith. But this isn't Aaron Smith."

The others glanced at one another, catching on quickly.

"Yeah, yeah," began Jason with a smile. "An-and, remember the first time we met? I was at a computer, writing, and you came up to me and asked what I was doing. I was expecting you to be sarcastic and just take the piss, but you didn't. And you were the *only* one who didn't."

"Or the time," added Brandon, "when — sorry, *times* — you allowed me to copy your homework when no one else did, because they thought I wouldn't have dared to not have completed it on time?"

"Honestly, mate," said Eli, with everyone beginning to smile lightly (apart from Aaron), "I was so, so thankful for all the times on the footy field when you helped us up. Everyone just laughed, but not you, pal."

Was it working?

Aaron couldn't feel the gun in his hand as he was trembling too much. Fallen tears dripped onto his shoes, feeling like he had stepped into a puddle.

The hostages looked at one another, wondering if it was safe to gently take the gun off him.

Anna shakily reached out, her hand trembling as much as Aaron was as a whole.

But then they caught Aaron say in the faintest of whispers, "I can't," as he sniffled. He shook his head lightly, the smiles on those who genuinely cared for him fading away.

The gun clicked once more, and with that click came a moment that felt like a nightmare.

It all happened in slow motion as Chief Pattison and Deputy Ton stormed forwards to pull the kids back.

Aaron dropped the gun instantly, crumpling to his knees. Tears swelled in everyone's eyes now as Keeper forcibly barricaded the kids from the officers taking Aaron away.

In that moment, however, Aaron felt free from everything: the trauma he had been through (and had severely caused), the town, the life he led. Everything.

He felt free from his father.

As the two officers dragged Aaron out of the room in cuffs — he didn't resist — the kids desperately wanted their principal to allow them to aid Clarke. But there was no saving him. The bullet had gone straight through his head.

Principal Keeper couldn't bear to look at the body, and saw the extremely concerned looks on his students' faces. That's when he let his arm down.

"We'll untie him," he said softly, although the kids had already begun doing so. "And we'll stay with him until they take him away."

Nothing was said until the scene had been taken care of and the group was allowed to leave the premises. Even then, nothing much was said, apart from saying goodbye to one another outside the gates.

A single thought came to Jason that night: *It could've been different.*

2

Nothing justifies the act of murder, but as the days turned into weeks, Jason and the rest started to understand Aaron's reasoning. Countless people seek revenge on those who have wronged them, and it doesn't always set you free. As much as you may feel like it will.

The next day, the Castlehead Criminal Investigation Department released information on the scene and claimed that Aaron would be moving to a heavily secured juvenile detention centre in the middle of nowhere. There was hope that he could mend his ways, if he were given time, but as Thomas Hill went into their annual May half-term holiday, exciting things were setting in motion; Jason begun packing for the Desmond School for Creative Arts, Chief Pattison and Madam Mayor tore up the Sunvalley Park eviction notice immediately after Clarke's death became public knowledge, and Z moved back into Sunvalley Park, full-time, along with the rest of the residents.

And if anyone involved in Clarke's murder had learned anything, it was that revenge can truly be a bitch.

CHAPTER THIRTEEN

New Beginnings

1

No one had reason to bring up what had ensued on GCSE Options Day. Before the students of Thomas Hill High knew it, it was the May holiday. And although they were edging closer to the ultimate summer holidays, the Year 9 students felt their stomachs churn knowing that, well, this was it for the next two years.

The relief of not having to get up never got old for Eli and Kelsey; they purposefully lay in bed, Kelsey's head resting gently on Eli's shoulder as they looked up at the ceiling. Kelsey, however, imagined that the ceiling wasn't there, so that she could drift off into a heavenly dream as she looked at the sky. Eli, on the other hand, was just happy. In the moment. Nothing to worry about.

"It's mad, isn't it," said Eli softly. "This time last month, we were being held hostage."

"Hm-hm."

Eli meant nothing by it, but that moment in the place the dead props lived didn't allow Kelsey to sleep. And now those memories were suddenly back.

Kelsey's stomach tickled, and she squirmed off Eli onto her own pillow. *You really had to say that*, she thought as they looked at one another. "Yeah… *mad*," she said.

Eli shifted onto his side, placing his elbow on the pillow and resting his chin on his hand. He grasped that something wasn't right. *Ruin the moment, Eli, you idiot*, he thought. They could've just remained silent and it would've been perfect.

"Sorry," he said. "I just meant that now we're here. Everything's sorted and all that, and we're all alive."

Kelsey looked up at him. She let out a giggle at the silly pout he made, as if he were a needy dog, and he knew he had redeemed himself straight away.

She mirrored his position.

"Kelsey?"

"Yeah?"

"I... I," he stammered. He breathed deeply and exhaled hard. "I... love you."

She couldn't believe he had actually said those three words, the words that cemented an honest, true relationship.

Eli heard the gulp of shock she made straight after. Had he said the wrong thing again? The prolonged silence made Eli wonder if he had. But it was true, he did love her. The crazy school year they had had proved to him that he didn't want to lose her.

Then a smile glimmered onto her face, and she whispered, "Yeah. Same."

With a kiss, both of them went back to lying down. This time, they spaced each other out. *Yes*, Eli thought, as he stared at the wall. *She feels the same.*

Kelsey stared blankly, wondering what was going through her boyfriend's head.

What have I done?

2

Sunvalley Park always got the best view of the town in the mornings. Z sat on the doorstep of her trailer, tossing a finished cigarette on the floor. She could tell nobody else was awake, as the trailers didn't stir or thump. There wasn't much to do, but Z liked it that way. It still wasn't easy, taking care of her abuela — whom she heard stirring as the trailer began to shake lightly — but now she wasn't going to hide.

She smiled instead, with her hood down.

The relaxing smell of air freshener filled Z's lungs as she entered the spruced up trailer. With a new and improved mindset came changes. No more cigarette cartons scattered around or smashed beer bottles or boarded up windows. No more dishes piling on top of one another; they were returned to their rightful place in the overhead cupboards. The tears in the couch had been stitched up, also. It felt homely.

She walked down the trailer into her grandmother's bedroom. It still felt like entering a room that would be seen in a care home, though this time, it had that homely feel to it.

Willow was sitting up, still white in the face and very weak, but Z thought: *She's very much alive.*

"Morning, *Abuela*," said Z, smiling.

"*Neita*, you're still here?" her grandmother said softly.

"I always will be."

Z leaned across the bed and pecked her abuela on the cheek. She steadied herself as she walked around to the wardrobe. "Time to take your medicine," she said, like a nurse happy to do her job. Opening the wardrobe doors, Z kneeled down. This routine hadn't changed. Picking up a tub of medication, Z steadied herself again and walked back to her abuela's side of the bed. "You know what to do."

"I need to take medicine."

Z chuckled and said, "Yes, you do."

"You're home every night, *Neita.*"

Z could easily tell between the wrinkles in Willow's face and the small crease she made with her lips that this was supposed to be a smile.

Z smiled back as she twisted the cap off and tipped two little white pills into her free hand. "You're still going to school?"

"Yes, I—"

"Very important," explained Willow, lifting a single finger.

"Come on, don't tire yourself. Take these." Z gently forced the pills into her grandmother's throat. It still hurt to swallow, but Z knew her abuela had managed it. She always did.

Z breathed deeply, adding with a chuckle, "I am actually starting my GCSEs in September."

"Very important."

"Yeah." Z twisted the cap back on the tub and put it by her side on the floor. She saw that her abuela was drifting off. "I... I will do my best," she whispered.

Z chuckled at her resting grandmother. She probably hadn't heard her, but Z knew deep down she would be proud. Whatever it took, Z would prove herself worthy of earning those results and go on to get her abuela the treatment she needed to keep pushing just that little bit more.

She just hoped that her abuela would be there to witness it.

She gently shut the bedroom door.

Walking back through the lounge, Z sat haphazardly on the stitched couch. Looking around, she had nothing to do. She sat there for a beat, and the sound of doors closing from outside ran through the trailer's walls and her ears. *Family's up*, she thought.

Then she rose and headed for the door. She closed it behind her quietly, returning to the doorstep. She smiled at the sight of the other residents gathering the used firewood in the centre of the park from the previous night. Walking from his trailer to the centre, the man with the shiny bowling ball head noticed her.

He waved and said, "Good morning, Z."

She waved back and said quietly, almost to herself, "Yes. Yes it is."

The man had reached the dead firewood as he asked, "Do you fancy going up the trail for more wood?"

Z remained seated, chuckling, and thought: *I'll help in a minute*. As the man continued on with his daily chores, all Z wanted to do for that minute was take in what she had. What she had was dearest to her heart: Sunvalley Park. Home.

3

Like Z, Jason had been up since the first ray of sunlight shone through his bedroom window. Instead of hanging up, the curtains had been placed on top of the pile of boxes that stood against the walls. Many of Jason's possessions were most likely going to go to the charity shop, Gemma told him, with those boxes being marked **FOR SHOPS**, whereas the boxes Jason would be taking with him to Valeland at the end of the week had been marked **VALELAND**.

Sitting on the edge of the wooden frame of his bed — the mattress had been taken off and was heading to the dump — Jason looked around his room. He soaked it in. His phone sat next to him, vibrating. Ignoring it, he continued to look around; it wasn't until now that he realised how big his room actually was. The chest of drawers, desk, and television made it seem less roomy. If he had to be honest with himself, while sitting there, he thought it had happened too fast. He hadn't been allowed to cherish, make the most of, these last few days. This was what he was leaving, for at least a few years. Home, friends, family… and even Castlehead.

But it had to be done…

Didn't it?

"Knock-knock."

Jason looked up. The sound of his mother embarrassingly knocking, as well as saying it, snapped him out of these thoughts and back to reality — at least, for a few moments.

"Hi, Mam," he said, sighing softly.

Gemma stood in the doorway, leaning against the frame.

Jason rose and saw the look on her face; she too let the sight of her son's empty room soak in.

"You look like you're all sorted," she said suddenly, breaking the silence. Jason stuffed his hands in his pockets and nodded. His phone continued to vibrate on the bed frame as Gemma added, "The room's bigger without your stuff in it."

They both chuckled, and Jason agreed. "Yeah, was just thinking that."

Together, they looked around the room one last time. But Jason heard his mother sniffling. Turning his head towards her, he watched as she wiped the tears away with her fingertips. He stepped forward. Nothing had to be said to break this silence. They embraced as mother and son, but this embrace, Gemma wished, wasn't with the mature fourteen-year-old that Jason had become. This was an embrace with her precious little boy; the boy who had needed her when he fell over in the park, or was being picked on.

Tightening her arms around Jason, like she didn't want to let him go, in between sniffs, she stammered, "I… I ju-just want to al-al-always be there for you."

Jason sniffled, "You will be. I love you."

His phone vibrated again.

Jason kissed his mother on the cheek and gently moved away from the hug.

Gemma wiped away the last of the tears as Jason picked up his phone and looked at it.

"Who is it, son?" asked Gemma, smiling.

Eli
Meeting at Carl's in ten, son. Gotta discuss something.

JASON
Okay. I'll be there.

Eli
Sound.

JASON
What's up like?

Eli
Nowt. Everyone just said to meet at Carl's.

"Just Eli," answered Jason, looking up from his phone. He stuffed it into his pocket. "I think everyone's meeting at Carl's Cafe in ten minutes."

Gemma kept a smile on her face. "Can I..?"

"Of course."

Gemma stepped aside and allowed him to head downstairs and leave. She heard the front door close, but stayed in the doorway. Looking at the empty room, then to where the boxes stood, she huffed and thought, *How the frigging hell am I going to get these downstairs?*

4

MARIA
You ready for Friday? X

JASON
Ready as I'll ever be. X

THE CORRUPT: A CASTLEHEAD NOVEL

MARIA
Good. We're booked on the last train. X

JASON
No problem.

"Jason said he's just around the corner," said Eli, sitting down at a round table with a cup of tea in one hand and his phone in the other.

With it being the May holiday, Carl's Cafe was as lively as it would be on a weekend.

Eli planted himself between Anna and Josh. Z and Brandon sat opposite them. Brandon's leg shook impatiently under the table. No other group was as quiet as they were.

"It's crazy that he's going," said Anna, her elbow leaning on the table, her head in her palm. "Thomas Hill will be very different."

"He needs to do it, though," argued Eli. "That school is where he should be."

Z looked over at Eli, glaring down at his phone as he spoke, and asked, "Where's your lass?"

Eli lifted his head. He saw all the looks he was getting from the rest of the group. He shrugged and focused on his phone again. It wasn't something he felt had any business to do with the group. Although he quietly accepted her response, it hadn't sat well afterwards. Kelsey had decided to leave, and they hadn't spoken since. Everyone knew something was wrong, they could see it in his face. *We'll work through it*, he kept telling himself. They were a unit, and he hoped to keep it that way.

The overhead bell above the entrance rang. The group glanced over.

"Here he is," announced Anna.

Jason searched the cafe, saw Carl catering to a married couple at the counter, then turned his head and saw his friends waving him across. He beamed at the sight of them all sitting there, but the limited time he had left with them slipped into mind again. Regardless, he kept a smile plastered on his face until he sat down next to Eli.

"Is everything okay?" he said.

Eli hid his phone from Jason's view as everyone else nodded.

"Ah, right." Jason raised an eyebrow, wondering why everyone was being mysterious. Then he caught Anna's grinning face. "What?"

Everyone then turned to Josh. Jason saw that they were all grinning now, and it was either making him worried or suspicious. Both? He couldn't decide. The silence for dramatic effect may have worked in the films and books Jason had, but it happening to him made him feel frustrated. That was it: the feeling he couldn't decide on.

"Well," began Josh, "what time are you leaving on Friday?"

"Umm... the last train," said Jason. "Why?" he asked sceptically.

The small smiles turned into undoubtable cheesy grins as Josh continued, "We were thinking about throwing you a farewell do before you go. Nothing too much, just us and family."

Eli nudged Jason and said, "It was Josh's idea, honestly, mate."

"Well, I-I just thought..." Josh started to get flustered. "I just thought, since you introduced me to this town... and the crraazzzyyy shit that goes on..." Everyone laughed. "I thought it'd be best to give you a good send-off."

Jason stammered, unsure of the idea. As he continued to struggle getting his words out, everyone gave him looks of disappointment. Like a group of begging dogs, they pouted pleadingly. He averted his eyes, clearly cracking under the pressure.

All of them leaned forward as Jason looked back at them.

Jason shrugged and said, "All right then."

Eli patted Jason on the back, Anna whooped, and Josh and Brandon pumped their fists in the air. *That's why Mam was so clear on letting me come*, Jason thought.

"Carl!" called Eli, raising his hand, grabbing the cafe owner's attention.

Carl strode over, twirling his pen in his hand, with a welcoming smile on his face. He saw the group's excitement. He took his small pad out of his apron, pen ready, and waited for their orders. The group looked at each other, grinning again — with Jason joining in this time round — and nodded.

"All of us will have… the Carl Deluxe," said Jason, looking up at Carl.

Carl nodded, impressed, as he noted the order down. This place was one of the main (only) things Jason was going to miss about Castlehead. The full English breakfasts (three sausages, two crispy bacon slices, two eggs, beans, toast, a hash brown, and the option of mushrooms or black pudding), the baked goods, the sandwiches, basically anything on the breakfast menu. How could he forget the American diner-style menu between 1pm and 8pm (juicy burgers, hotdogs, milkshakes, and fries)? The variety of coffees, teas, and soft drinks, too.

"Jason?" said Eli, nudging his arm. "You okay, mate?"

Jason shook his head, not realising he had just been sitting there, not blinking, as if staring into nothingness for a moment. He answered shakily, "Yeah, fine."

"You sure?"

"Absolutely."

5

A brightly-coloured 'Good Luck' banner hung on the wall in the dining room. Two stacks of red plastic cups sat on the table, alongside plates of party food: bite size sausage rolls, crisps, chicken wings, and small pizza slices. Music blasted throughout the house like a nightclub.

Gemma made sure to go all out for her son's final night in town.

The parents leaned against the kitchen counter, holding drinks of their choice, while Brandon, Anna, Josh and Eli sat on their chairs in a circle in the lounge, empty handed, like they were in a therapy group. With Jason nowhere to be seen.

He was sitting in his room, one final time, on the frame of his bed, like he had done earlier that week. The boxes were still stacked against the walls, and it began to hit him more and more. He looked down at his shoes, with his phone vibrating next to him. Hearing the many voices of the people he loved — and the people who loved him — forced him to wipe his eyes before the tears even came. That's all he — and everyone else needed — was for him to burst into tears, just hours from departing. He couldn't do that to them.

"Jason!" called his mother from the bottom of the stairs.

"Coming!" he answered.

Jason rose and picked up his phone. It was Maria messaging him, telling him she would be there in a while. Seeing the notification, and looking out the door to the landing, that uneasy feeling that made his stomach churn came back. *No*, he told himself, *not today*.

His stomach continued to churn as he walked out onto the landing and down the stairs, but the feeling eased as he saw Gemma standing there. She smiled at her son.

"Are you all right?" she asked.

"Never better," he lied confidently.

This time, Gemma couldn't see through her son, like a spotless window.

"Maria said she'll be here soon."

Gemma's stomach began to ache, but, like her son, she hid it well. They separated, with Gemma entering the kitchen and Jason stopping in the doorway of the lounge.

The group looked at him, smiling, but still very curious as to why Jason expressed that same blank look he had given at Carl's.

"All right Jason?" said Brandon, leaning over the back of his chair, matching Eli's position.

Jason said nothing.

"Jason?" said Eli. Seeing him standing there, looking back at them, was getting increasingly scary. "Jason?" repeated Eli, his tone heavy and louder than the music. After yet another blank response from Jason, Eli shook his head, slammed his hand hard on the back of the chair, and rose to go towards him. But as he did so, Jason stepped forward — still unresponsive.

"You okay?"

Jason slipped across to the empty chair, next to Anna. When he slid into the seat, Anna gently patted his knee. And that's when he looked around, like he had woken up from a coma.

"Yeah, I'm fine," he said, breathing hard.

Then the doorbell rang.

"Jason!" Gemma called. She poked her head into the lounge, all eyes staring back at her. "I think it's Maria."

"What? Oh… right," said Jason. Before doing anything, Jason gazed around the circle of friends. The last person he focused on was Eli. "Mam… is-is it okay if you get it?"

"Oh… Yeah," she said, a bit shaken by the unusual response.

She reversed out of the doorway, keeping the door ajar. Everyone shrugged secretly at each other. Jason continued to look at Eli, hesitant. The prolonged gaze made Eli uncomfortable.

"Can I talk to you for a second?" Jason finally asked, his voice breaking.

Eli looked surprised, and said unsurely, "Um... Yeah." They rose together. Jason directed them back to the bottom of the stairs.

Back in the room, the others shrugged again. But they decided to let them get on with it, understanding Jason's mixed emotions.

Jason and Eli sat on the bottom step. Jason looked down at his shoes while Eli looked at his friend, waiting for something to come from this.

"So? What's up?"

"I don't know if I can do this," whispered Jason, keeping his head down. He hoped to God nobody would interrupt him. "It's a lot."

"What is?"

"Just... this. Should I really be doing this? I mean, what if everything goes to shit?"

"Well," Eli started, rolling his eyes, thinking for a moment. "You're not gonna know 'till you do it. But I'll tell you this now, mate, *this* kid isn't the lad who in Year 7 done what he fucking wanted. Not caring what anyone thought, because he knew what he wanted."

The memories came flooding back, like a dam breaking. They both went back to a time before Year 7, a free time, a time where a playground could be a jungle, or an ocean, or even an obstacle course from *Super Mario Bros*. A time when nobody cared.

"Look, I'm not going to tell you what to do, mate, but I think you already know."

Out of the corner of his eye, Jason saw leggings under a knee-length skirt. He looked up, and there stood Maria, smiling at him; a beaming beauty, he thought, as always.

Jason looked back at Eli, who jerked his head towards her.

"You ready?" she yelled joyfully.

"Thank you," Jason mouthed.

Jason rose and walked towards Maria, his arms spread. He let his actions speak for him, nothing needed to be said, and there was only one word to describe the embrace between them: Magical. Everyone converged nor Maria cared about the crowd around them. Incoming tears stung the corners of Gemma's eyes.

Releasing the embrace, Jason jumped straight into another from his mother. He allowed her to whimper into his shoulder.

"The taxi's waiting," Maria said softly.

It was time to go.

EPILOGUE

All, even the juniors, of the Castlehead Criminal Investigation Department were set out on patrol to make sure the lively Friday nights didn't get out of control. From the chief's office window, Deputy Ton glanced down and saw groups of girls — all glammed up in heels and dresses — and boys — dressed in smart jeans, shoes, and shirts — heading to the back-alley nightclubs of Castlehead. He wheeled himself back to the chief's desk in his chair and got back to filling out a bunch of forms. Confidential, the chief had told him.

"Where did you say the chief was, again?" asked Madam Mayor, sitting opposite the deputy impatiently. The sound of her nails tapping on the arm of her seat was like listening to a ticking clock, its alarm ready to go off any second. "He knew I was coming, didn't he?"

Still looking at the forms, Ton said, "He knew, but as I said, he couldn't miss another patrol duty."

"And... is everything prepped for the residents to return?"

"Yes." Ton leaned down and pulled a yellow form out of a drawer on his side of the desk. He sat up and gave it to the mayor. "I just need you and Pattison to sign it. Oh, and anyone else who may need to sign it."

THE DEED TO SUNVALLEY PARK

Let it be known to all parties involved in the recent eviction of all members of Sunvalley Park (the Castlehead Criminal Investigation Department, the Mayor's Office, and the Sunvalley Park community)

that the ownership of the trailer park is hereby returned to said official members of the park.

Moreover, let it be made aware that anyone who wishes to testify against this decision will defend their case in a court of law. Should the Sunvalley Park community wish to expand on the park or disband from the community, this too will also be seen to in a court of law.

In conclusion, on behalf of one Chief Pattison and Madam Mayor, we formally apologise for the inconvenience that was caused due to prior events involving not just the eviction of the park but Sunvalley Park resident 'Z' and the recent homicide at Thomas Hill High.

SIGNED:
SIGNED: Chief Pattison and Deputy Ton of the C.C.I.D
SIGNED: The Sunvalley Park Community.

"That looks to be in order," said the mayor with a smile, folding the form and putting it in her handbag. "Now, we can put this mess behind us."

Ton said with a laugh, slowly rising from his chair, "If I had a drink, I would drink to that." They both laughed as the deputy opened the office door for the mayor. "I'll see you out, Madam Mayor."

The deputy led the way down the stairwell and onto the ground floor. It echoed as usual; Ton even wondered if the echo was getting louder with time. But believing in superstitions or ghosts wasn't what he was trained for, regardless of seeing Aaron Smith return from the dead.

"Talking about mess, is the kid still here?" asked the mayor as they continued towards reception.

The deputy had allowed the receptionist to leave early, and with that came silence as they entered reception. But they were met with a set of bulging headlights, glaring through the automatic glass doors. They heard a door slam, and it wasn't until the doors slid open and the headlights dimmed that Chief Pattison came into clear view.

"Evening, Madam Mayor," said the chief with a little bow of his head as he stepped into the building.

"I thought you were on patrol, Chief?" said Ton.

"I am. I ended up coming across the van to escort Aaron from here to the detention centre," explained the chief.

"Will we fetch him now?" suggested Ton.

Pattison gave the all clear with a little nod, and the three of them made their way deeper into the C.C.I.D building to where the cells were located. Only one was occupied. Ton shuffled around in his pockets as they reached the cell, and pulled out a set of keys.

The jingle of the keys and the click of the cell door as it was unlocked didn't faze a sleeping Aaron. The bedframes that the Castlehead Criminal Investigation Department used hadn't been constructed for comfort, but Aaron was sound asleep, far from reality. He slept on his side, facing the back wall.

Ton kicked one of the front legs of the frame, but he didn't stir.

"Come on, Aaron," ordered Ton. "Time to go."

No reply.

"Hey!"

No reply.

Ton had no choice, and he forced Aaron onto his back, but then jumped back. "No, no, no, no, no, no, no."

"What? What is it, Ton?" The chief rushed into the cell, with Madam Mayor entering slowly behind him. "Shit."

The pigment had faded from the kid's skin, his lips were covered in blood, and his throat had been slit from one side of his neck to the other. The veins in his hands looked like they were going to burst. The sight was sickening.

"What does this mean?" whispered the mayor.

Without hesitation, the chief said, "It means somebody is out to end the people of this town."

And above all this, it was Ton who noticed one thing...

The blood wasn't dry.

THE END...

.

By The Same Author

Have You Read…?

Isolation
The Story of Isabella Rose-Eccleby

Still to Come…

Det. Dom

And…

St. Jude's
A Castlehead Novel

Lightning Source UK Ltd.
Milton Keynes UK
UKHW011927100522
402775UK00001B/1